THE AUTHO

Roy Fuller's early life is recounted in his three quite recent volumes of memoirs, *Souvenirs*, *Vamp Till Ready* and *Home and Dry*. He was born in 1912 in Failsworth, Lancashire, but educated and articled to a solicitor in Blackpool. Soon after qualifying he moved south, eventually becoming a solicitor with the Woolwich Equitable Building Society, with whom he spent the rest of his professional life. In 1969 he retired as solicitor to join the Woolwich Board. He was Professor of Poetry at Oxford from 1968-73, and a Governor of the BBC from 1972-79.

During the war he served in the Royal Navy and became known as a poet through his two wartime books of verse, *The Middle of a War* and *A Lost Season*, both published by The Hogarth Press. He began as a writer of fiction after the war with a novel for children, and continued with three crime novels. Six 'straight' novels followed at fairly regular intervals, but he has not published a work of fiction since *The Carnal Island* of 1970. (This, along with *Image of a Society* and *My Child, My Sister*, is also appearing in Hogarth paperback.) However, he has gone on writing poetry. His monumental *New and Collected Poems 1934-84* came out in 1985, followed by *Subsequent to Summer* in the same year and *Consolations* (1987).

He married his wife Kate in 1936 and they have one son, the poet and author John Fuller. His brother, another John Fuller, is well known in the gastronomic world as a former head of the Scottish Hotel School, and the author and editor of many works on cooking and catering education.

THE
RUINED BOYS

Roy Fuller

New Introduction by
Jeremy Lewis

THE HOGARTH PRESS

LONDON

To
GRAHAM WATSON

Published in 1987 by
The Hogarth Press
Chatto and Windus Ltd
40 William IV Street, London WC2N 4DF

First published in Great Britain by André Deutsch Ltd 1959
Hogarth edition offset from original British edition
Copyright © Roy Fuller 1959
Introduction copyright © Jeremy Lewis 1987

British Library Cataloguing in Publication Data

Fuller, Roy
The ruined boys.
I. Title
823'.912[F]   PR6011.U55

ISBN 0 7012 0691 8

Printed in Great Britain by
Cox & Wyman Ltd
Reading, Berkshire

INTRODUCTION

As Isabel Quigly makes clear in her splendid survey of the subject, *The Heirs of Tom Brown*, the English public school has excited a rich if often eccentric crop of novels, from *Stalky and Co.* and *The Fifth Form at St Dominic's* to *Mr Perrin and Mr Traill* and P. G. Wodehouse's Psmith stories. First published in 1959, *The Ruined Boys* is, like many of the books Miss Quigly describes, much more than a one-dimensional 'genre' novel: viewed simply as a school story of an unusually sophisticated kind, it comes at the end of a once-confident tradition, and brings to its subject intimations of unease that might well have seemed shocking or subversive to earlier, more reverent practitioners.

There is a good deal to be said for school – and the boarding school in particular – as the setting for a novel. Each school is, or appears to be, a self-contained little universe, sealed off from the outside world, with strong rules and codes of conduct which, however pompous or absurd they may seem to the detached observer, have an absolute power and importance within; inside this claustrophobic, somewhat narcissistic community masters and matrons, swots and jokers, heroic sportsmen and beetle-browed bullies loom like Dickensian grotesques or figures in *grand guignol*, far larger and more forceful than they might by the light of day. Institutional life is all too easily seen in Manichean terms, providing the perfect platform for tales of good and evil, involving injustice, revenge, heroism and the eventual triumph of light over darkness, of the decent underdog over the bully and the brute. And, of course, the school story has the great advantages of universality – most of its readers must have undergone some form of education, however improbable that may seem – and of being able to evoke, and re-kindle, ancient, long-forgotten emotions. Far from the consolations of home, the child at school – and still more so at boarding school – seems exposed to extremes of fear and excitement, of tedium and expectation, and the clever chronicler can tap a great well of anxieties and grievances, as well as that unfathomable nostalgia that afflicts those curious souls for whom schooldays were indeed the happiest days of their lives. Not surprisingly, many school novels have a lurid, melodramatic quality, as though Eisenstein's shadowy, flickering film about Ivan the Terrible had been unexpectedly invaded by grim-featured Latin masters in gowns and mortar boards, small boys in Eton collars, and large-bosomed school matrons brandishing jars of radio malt. Whether the school story of the future – set, as it must be, in a milder, more strenuously benevolent world in which even public-school masters agree to being addressed by their Christian names, raffia work is more highly regarded than the rugger scrum, and the school cane has long been locked away – will have quite the same primordial appeal remains to be seen.

Indigent or imitation public schools, struggling to keep afloat and aping the customs and pretensions of their grander, more confident exemplars, have a melancholy, Pooterish pathos and fascination. Loosely based on Mr Fuller's own boarding school – which, he tells us in his autobiography, was 'on the downgrade' and 'traded on the gentility principle', offering a touch of class to boys who were unable to get into the grammar school, or whose parents considered their offspring to be a cut above the state sector – *The Ruined Boys* is set in a cut-price, very minor boys' public school in the 1930s. But although it has its fair share of school set pieces, from towel-flicking in the changing-rooms (the central figure is flicked with such vindictive precision that the weal comes up in a blister) to bed-wetting, feasts in the dorms and excited attempts to watch the school maid undressing in a window over the way, it could well seem a slightly low-key affair to those who want – and expect – any story set in a boarding school to include at least one scene in which a small boy is roast over a slow flame, a nerve-wracking climax to the Big Match against the rival school, and a rousing finale in which the school bully is punched sharply on the nose by the freckled, resolutely cheerful hero and retires sobbing from the scene to the derisive cheers of his erstwhile subjects. Far from such ripe absurdities, *The Ruined Boys* is a subtle, finely pointed novel, more concerned with a gradual, but radical, shifting of perspectives and realignment of loyalties than with the stark morality and gangster politics of the old-fashioned school story, and all the more impressive as a result.

These changes centre on the figure of Gerald Bracher, who is sent to Seafolde House after his parents have split up and his father has had to return home from South Africa. Most children are desperately anxious to conform – and none more so than Gerald, who comes to the school in mid-career (like Mr Fuller's own school, Seafolde House seems, unusually, to cater for boys between seven and seventeen) and finds himself adrift in a world in which 'everyone except himself seemed armed with singleness of purpose against the traps of existence'. Gerald's somewhat sycophantic eagerness for approval is particularly directed at the domineering figure of the headmaster, and at a dashing, irreverent older boy named Mountain. Like Roy Fuller's own headmaster, Mr Pemberton – a distinguished-looking clergyman who holds his head in a grave, impressive way, and is much given to sonorous sermonising about morality and the honour of the school – has a 'deep knowledge of the weakness of boys', and a ruthless readiness to induce, and trade upon, feelings of inadequacy and guilt. Lacking confidence in his own character, Gerald is wretchedly anxious to win the head's approval – in much the same way as, against his better self, he takes the lead in denouncing the weedy, spindle-shanked Slade for his miserable ineptitude on the football field or, sheltering under Mountain's wing, riskily joins in the baiting of less impressive senior boys, proving himself something of a wag and storing up trouble for the future, when his protector is no longer to hand.

'The overall plan of the novel,' Roy Fuller has written, 'is the young hero's gradual discovery during a school year of the moral truth of the school he newly joins (and, incidentally, of the outside world), a truth the reverse of what he first imagines'; and I don't think it gives too much away to say that, in the course of the novel, Gerald changes from being a nervous conformist to something of a rebel and an outsider – sceptical of the pretensions of those about him, agnostic in matters of religion and, thanks in part to the chance discovery of *Fabian Essays*, taken with a heady dose of H. G. Wells, leftwards-leaning in his politics. Mr Percy, a shy and outwardly unglamorous English master, awakens his interest in literature and music, mildly deflating his adolescent pretensions and lending him his copy of Shelley; the unsporting, sophisticated Slade reveals a far shrewder understanding of 'the truth behind life's immense façade of deceit' than any of his fellows, so much so that 'sometimes Gerald would think of the past and find it inconceivable that he had once, say, believed Slade's timidity at football to be morally reprehensible (for it was an axiom with them that games bred unwholesome passions, wasted time and stultified the intellect), or worried about Slade's untidiness and non-conformity with the rules of school'; and, above all, he comes to see that, for all his airs of moral rectitude, Mr Pemberton fails to match his deeds to his rhetoric, skimping on doctor's bills, extending favours to the son of an influential local dignitary and – despite subjecting Gerald to a reproachful lecture after he has forgotten to return 3*d* change – diverting the Chapel Funds in his anxiety to somehow keep the school solvent. So 'with the revelatory sense of shock that might accompany one's first sight of a piece of sculpture one has previously only seen in photographic repro- duction, lacking any comparative scale, he realised that the Headmaster was a small man' – a realisation that, one assumes, has more to do with morality than mere physical stature.

'Had I to write that book now I would not give it the confident ethics it possesses,' Roy Fuller tells us in his autobiography, ' . . . I would now be more indulgent of the school's deficiencies'; and certainly the jaded modern reader is more likely to extend a sympathetic hand to Mr Pemberton than the original blurb-writer, who saw him as a 'monstrous' figure. And were Gerald's new-found wisdom merely a matter of pointing out feet of clay and taking up an adolescent posture of rebellion, one might suspect him of lurching from a craven conformity to an equally unattractive, and equally conventional, priggishness and self-approval: but his moral education embraces as well a growing sense of charity, and a tolerance of the weaknesses and inadequacies of others. 'How often must one,' he comes to realise, 'ignorant of the prime motives in the lives of others, fail to understand or misinterpret what goes on? – thinking, for example, during an entire acquaintanceship, of a man as irascible who is merely shy'; or – while brooding on the dowdy, portly figure of Mr Percy, and his hesitant, circuitous affair with Mr Pemberton's niece – 'in a flash of understanding he saw that even the most austere master must be subject to human desires, suffer worldly cares: to talk with a girl might be a painful surmounting of shyness; a shabby jacket the mask not of eccentricity but of poverty.'

The Ruined Boys differs from many school stories not just in its sense of the complexity and the fragility of human affairs, but in its evocation of formal as well as moral education. Whereas the traditional school novel is – as befits the Arnoldian public school, perhaps – much more concerned with character than intellect, and either ignores the academic side of school life or treats it with a dismissive jocularity, Mr Fuller manages to capture the excitement, and not just the drudgery, of learning, of new vistas as opening up and worlds of which one has only heard rumours suddenly coming within one's ken. Above all, he evokes that innocent, touchingly optimistic belief of the young that – as happens to Gerald while reading *Fabian Essays* – 'perfect understanding of existence lay within his grasp': so that when Gerald moves up to Mr Percy's form, and learns what books he will be reading in the year ahead, 'he was seized by a vague but intense excitement, as though within his grasp was some key to happy existence, and he perceived that even in the most unlikely places there resided a mysterious fascination.'

Roy Fuller's novels are 'true to life' in the very best sense, in that they distil and reflect – often with uncomfortable accuracy – behaviour and states of mind that are familiar to us all; no doubt the verisimilitude of *The Ruined Boys* is enhanced by its being based, to some extent, on Mr Fuller's own schooldays. The Seafolde House of the autobiographies – to which Roy Fuller was sent in 1923, at the age of eleven – consisted of two linked suburban houses in Blackpool, whereas its fictional equivalent is set in the downs near a seaside town, taking its looks from a school in Hampshire, commandeered by the Navy, at which Mr Fuller spent some months during the war: but at least two of its masters seem to have resurfaced, some thirty years later, in fictional form. So the awestruck Gerald, within a short time of his arrival at Seafolde House, notices how 'the Headmaster walked rapidly away; his gown streaming behind him, his head carefully balanced, as though considering gravely every object, every situation in his path', while Roy Fuller remembers his own headmaster with 'the large head carried slightly at one side, as though perpetually considering some matter of grave consequence, his own virtue and right judgement being unquestionable'; and Mr Percy – so central and so sympathetic a figure, and so unlike his Head in every way – has much in common with a Mr Treganza, being short, stout, uncommunicative, liable to hold his hat on his head with the crook of his umbrella while walking a school crocodile in a sea wind, and able, like the best of teachers, to impart his own love and enthusiasm for music and literature to those, like Gerald Bracher and Roy Fuller, who were ready and eager to listen.

Jeremy Lewis, London 1986

Seekers after happiness, all who follow
The convolutions of your simple wish,
It is later than you think; nearer that day
Far other than that distant afternoon
Amid rustle of frocks and stamping feet
They gave the prizes to the ruined boys.

W. H. AUDEN

I

MR CHAPLIN glanced up from his exercise books. His round glasses and high bald head gleamed through the twilight. He looked like some powerfully cerebral denizen of the Moon. 'Switch the light on, Slade,' he commanded. What the window had been framing—the distant white blurs where the downs broke high into the sea and the single planet—suddenly vanished.

For the boys the light was like an injection of adrenalin. There was an excited murmur. One boy leaned his head far back, pulling a grotesque face: the boy behind lifted his desk-lid suddenly and gave the intruding occiput a brutal crack. A paper dart floated down one of the aisles. Mr Chaplin's sharp call for silence was obeyed: he was the Second Master and feared. He screwed the top on his bottle of green ink and wiped meticulously his pen nib on the blotting paper. He said: 'Are there any more letters?'

It was the first Sunday evening of the Spring term. The Anglicans had marched in crocodile to morning service: the few Dissenters had gone off to their chapel in anarchy. All had eaten mutton and cabbage and walked afterwards by the sea under Mr Chaplin's gold-rimmed eye. The period immediately after tea was set aside for letter writing.

Mr Chaplin was reading the last of the letters. 'Snape minor!' he called. A small boy stood up. 'What on earth does this mean, Snape? "I swolled a marpell." ' A balloon of laughter went up, as though Mr Chaplin had made an exquisite joke.

'I did, sir,' said Snape minor.

'Did what?' asked Mr Chaplin.

'Swallow a marble. On Friday.' The laughter broke out again, this time with horrible falsity.

'Good gracious!' said Mr Chaplin. 'Did you report to Miss Pemberton?'

'Yes, sir.'

'Hm,' said Mr Chaplin. 'Well, you can't put it in a letter home. Don't you see that, Snape? In any case the spelling is disgraceful. You'll have to write the letter again in the common room.' Mr Chaplin piled his ink, pen and blotting paper and the letters neatly on top of his exercise books. 'All right, boys. You can go over,' he said, and then added vehemently: 'Quietly,' as the noise began its Rossinian crescendo.

A playground, partly cobbled, partly cindered, lay in the L formed by the school buildings, where the letter writing had taken place, and the House, which contained the common room, the studies, the dining room and dormitories. The boys ran or drifted across it in twos and threes. 'Come and have a Jimmy Riddle, Bracher,' said a plump boy with two protruding front teeth to a tall dark boy standing hesitantly under the marble war memorial tablet in the lobby. Bracher assented, and the two went inside the urinals at the cobbled end of the playground. The urinals, smelling of a unique disinfectant, had been converted from the House's stabling and were surmounted by a now inappropriate cupola which had led them to be popularly known as the One Valve Receiver.

'What's up, Bracher?' said the plump boy, as they stood side by side. 'You look a bit putrid.'

'Nothing,' said Bracher. 'I've got toothache coming on.'

'You ought to go to Miss Pemberton.'

'She couldn't do anything,' said Bracher. For a moment he felt that life could never hold out pleasure again.

'Do you think there'll be dripping toast for supper?' said the plump boy. 'There used to be sometimes on Sunday last term.'

'Who is Miss Pemberton?' asked Bracher. 'She's not'—and he hesitated, feeling the title too formal for ordinary conversation, yet unable to sink to plain 'Mr'—'the Reverend Pemberton's daughter, is she?'

'No,' said the plump boy. 'She's the Grey Chap's niece.'

'Why do you call him the Grey Chap?' The Headmaster was ginger.

'Don't know.' The plump boy turned away from the wall and spied Snape minor standing against another wall. He kicked Snape minor in the bottom and said: 'Funny. I can't hear any rattle.'

'Chuck it, Haworth,' said Snape, in a whining voice.

' "Dear Mother," ' said Haworth, ' "I swolled a marpell. Your loving son, Snape minor." '

Haworth and Bracher strolled over to the House. Bracher's tooth had stopped throbbing: for a moment he, too, wondered about dripping toast. He said to Haworth: 'What happens now?'

'The Librarian opens the Library. Then we read in the common room until supper time.' The plump boy kicked an imaginary ball towards the door of the House. He said: 'Not a bad tart, Miss Pemberton.' The two boys passed through the lighted hall into the changing room where already some others were putting on their slippers. Howarth and Bracher got theirs out of their lockers. Mr Chaplin's tall emaciated figure tripped into the hall: he had prudently worn his hat for the journey across the playground. He said: 'Hurry up, boys,' and put his hat on one of the masters' hooks. It was the Sunday pearl-grey homburg.

The House Prefects were in their studies: the rest of the boys sat round the tables in the common room. The Librarian, an older boy called Cropper, unlocked the cupboard which contained the Library. From his register he then called the boys two at a time to come and take out a book. Bracher, as a new boy, was at the bottom of the list, despite his years. Many of the books on the four shelves were so battered that it was impossible to read their titles from the spines, and Bracher crouched before them helplessly, feeling the pain make one or two preliminary screws into his tooth before settling down again to a steady ache. He pulled out and rejected in succession *The Last of the Mohicans*, *Eothen* and *Dog Fiend*. He read a few lines of *The Gorilla Hunters*. His companion at the shelves changed and then disappeared, and he was left conspicuously alone, as agitated as though faced with some insoluble problem of conduct.

Cropper turned his head to look at him. 'What on earth are you doing—what's your name?' Cropper consulted the register. 'Bracher. I'm not going to stay here all night.' Cropper's hair was brushed to one side in a great fuzzy wedge: his nose was the long searching nose of a dog and in repose his small mouth assumed a pursed position as though he were silently whistling.

'Sorry,' said Bracher, in a panic. He immediately pulled out a book almost at random and took it to be entered. As he wrote, Cropper sniffed. He said: 'You want to buck your ideas up, Bracher. I know the best books go first but, after all, every book is new to you.'

'Yes, I see that.'

'Well, don't take so long next week.' Cropper shut his register.

There was some scuffling until Mr Chaplin appeared once more. A place had been kept for him at the head of one of the tables: he sat down and polished his glasses. His eyes, set in sockets that seemed curiously pale and naked, blinked round as though he had just emerged from the bottom of the sea. 'Snape minor,' he said.

'Yes, sir?'

'Have you written that letter yet?'

'No, sir.'

'Well, stop picking your nose and write it.' Mr Chaplin hooked the flexible gold side-pieces of his spectacles over his small white ears, and hushed the howl of derisive laughter.

The book Bracher had chosen was bound in purplish-blue, with end papers the colour of excrement. It was called *Letters from High Latitudes*. Bracher skipped over the dedication, contents, list of illustrations, epigraph, and a long invocatory poem which began 'Calm sculptured image of as sweet a face As ever lighted up an English home'. At last he came to the narrative. 'Our start has not been prosperous. Yesterday evening, on passing Carlisle, a telegraph was put into my hand, announcing the fact of the *Foam* having been obliged to put into Holyhead, in consequence of the sudden illness of my Master.'

The room was quiet except for an occasional cough

and the roaring of the gas fire. There was a curiously treacly atmosphere and a sensation as of time unable to plough through it—the tone of a Sunday evening at school. Bracher's tooth was now aching steadily and he longed for the moment to arrive when he could plunge into the privacy of his bedclothes and let his emotions loose out of the cage of his school personality. In front of him on the green baize table covering was a piece of blotting paper. He tore a corner off it surreptitiously, chewed it to pulp and wedged it in the cavity in his molar. For a moment the aching seemed to be dulled, the device brilliant—even a way of escaping the dentist. His body was in the sphere of his control after all, as he had never conceived otherwise. In one of the chairs near Mr Chaplin he could see Cropper sitting on his hands, his long nose near the book on the table before him. Cropper, he thought, was one of those persons unamenable to ordinary life, whom one fears—remembering seeing him earlier in the day in charge of the party for the Methodists' church, the sleeves of his marlborough jacket too long, his bowler hat with a peculiarly heavy and curveless brim.

Behind the plug of blotting paper Bracher's tooth began to ache as before. A difficult period of his life stretched before him when he would have to discover, through his pain, the unknown procedure for obtaining permission to leave the school premises, for finding the dentist's surgery: and then there was the apprehension, the agony of the actual operation. He bent down and pretended to read, in case the hopelessness and puerility of his thoughts should from his expression be detectable by others.

He looked up again when the entry of one of the maids

gave rise to a subdued hooting and barracking. Next to him Howarth leaned his chair back and said: 'Shure and begorrah, it's Lily of Ould Oireland.'

The maid, moustached and diminutive, whispered in Mr Chaplin's ear.

'Bracher,' said Mr Chaplin, 'you're to see the Headmaster at once in his study.'

There were a few long-drawn whistles of mock-terror. 'Whack, whack, whack,' said Howarth. Bracher followed the maid out of the room, his breast full of agitation.

When he saw the maid about to go through the door that he knew led to the kitchen quarters, he called out in terror: 'Lily! How do I get to the Headmaster's study?'

'Why, straight along the corridor,' she said, and disappeared.

He had never before been past the entrance to the dining room: beyond it the corridor ended in a door which he went through to find himself in a short passage lined on one side with windows. The moon threw shining oblongs on the concrete floor. Outside, the ground sloped down to a set of silvered goal posts; beyond was a dark hedge and the hidden sea: the sky above was barred with long unmoving clouds. It seemed to him that the landscape through the window was not a part of the world he inhabited—the world of his tooth, his hair unbrushed at the end of the long day, the sharp edge of his hard linen collar.

Opening yet another door at the end of the passage he came to the pictures and carpet of a normal hall, and realized that he had now passed into the real house—Mr Pemberton's dwelling—and that all that had previously been subsumed for him under the term was

15

mere makeshift and addition, concrete floors, plywood partitions, harsh brick. He stood for a moment, as awed as a savage at this sudden civilization, and then knocked at the nearest door. Miraculously the Headmaster's voice said: 'Come in.'

Bracher turned the handle: a heavy curtain hanging behind the door made his entry as sluggish as a movement in a nightmare.

'Sit down, Gerald,' said Mr Pemberton.

Hearing his Christian name, Bracher realized once more how strange the once calmly accepted trappings of ordinary life had become in the existence of boarding school. He sat at the side of the Headmaster's littered desk which was illuminated by a reading lamp. Through the gloom of the rest of the big, high room he could see over the fireplace the impressive engraving of the Death of Nelson which he had particularly observed when his father weeks ago had brought him to be interviewed by Mr Pemberton before his entry into the school.

'We have to consider the feelings of others in this life,' said Mr Pemberton, in a kindly voice. 'Don't you agree, Gerald?'

'Yes, sir,' Bracher said uncomprehendingly.

'And we ought to look at the person to whom we are speaking, you know,' added the Headmaster in the same tone.

Bracher nervously turned his eyes towards the Headmaster for the first time, and saw with amazement in Mr Pemberton's hand the letter he had written that evening to his father.

'Mr Chaplin thought I ought to see your letter home, Gerald,' said the Headmaster. 'He was quite right, as I'm sure you'll agree when you've thought about it. This is a very sad and depressed letter. It can't help but make your father sad and depressed. Haven't you enjoyed any part of your life since you came here, Gerald?'

'Oh yes, sir,' Bracher said, thinking of the unfamiliar appearance of bacon at the morning's breakfast.

'Isn't that what you should have told your father about?'

'Yes,' said Bracher, seeing that it was.

The Headmaster's tone became even more kindly. 'Your father has suffered a great loss. You know what I mean, Gerald?'

Bracher blushed and nodded. Once again he felt astonishment at the strange juxtaposition of emotion and milieu: a stranger, remote and awful, alluding to what he nursed in the deepest recess of his mind—his mother's cruel and inexplicable abandonment of him and of his father. He saw clearly that his father (perhaps at that first interview with the Headmaster, after he himself had left the study, having responded so foolishly to questions on the present participle of *avoir* and the authorship of *Guy Mannering*, questions which seemed specially for that occasion deeply ambiguous) had confided in the Headmaster the reason which had precipitated his leaving his home and employment in South Africa and thus seeking a boarding school for his son at this awkward point in the scholastic year.

'You have to be a support to him, not a burden,' the Headmaster was saying.

The moisture in Bracher's eyes refracted the light from the desk-lamp: he was moved not really by the bringing to consciousness of his and his father's loss but by the Headmaster's interest and concern.

The Headmaster looked down at the letter. ' "We only

have bread and jam for tea," ' he read. 'Now Gerald, your father doesn't want to hear of such things—trivialities, and trivialities which must give him a misleading picture of your life here. There are more important matters to write to him about. And you must show him, as I'm sure is going to be the case, that you've quickly become at home here and found a multitude of affairs to interest you.'

When Howarth had told him that envelopes must be handed in to Mr Chaplin unsealed, Gerald had thought of the direction as part of the often-inexplicable discipline of school life and had never conceived that his letter would be taken out and read—and by the Headmaster. And those few critical observations which had seemed to him so natural and proper for his father's eyes now appeared despicable and profoundly out of place. More, for as the Headmaster spoke Gerald saw that such things as the plain tea which he had imagined designed for his discomfort or rising from the school's parsimony had been arrived at thoughtfully for the boys' good. He was ashamed of his letter and, at the same time, he felt stir inside him the beginning of happiness rising out of the greater understanding of conduct which the Headmaster had given him—happiness because of the mildness of the Headmaster's reproof, of the possibility of behaving in the future (now that he knew the secret) so as to draw the Headmaster's admiration and, in some strange way, because of the existence of this quiet room where the open fire kept out the paralysing cold and the lamp illuminating the broad desk made possible the calm acquisition of knowledge and wisdom.

'When you have written another letter,' said the Headmaster, 'hand it in to Mr Chaplin.' He tore up the offending sheet and dropped the pieces into a waste paper basket at his side—further evidence of the convenience and luxury of the room. The envelope he gave to Gerald, saying: 'Go back to your reading now,' and for the first time—though his manner had never during the interview been severe—broke into a wide smile. Gerald dare not smile in return for that would have seemed to indicate that he had not taken to heart the Headmaster's reproof. But he slipped from the chair very quietly and almost imperceptibly closed the door behind him.

II

In the interval between morning school and lunch a football game played with a tennis ball and reserved for senior boys always monopolized the cindered part of the playground. This day a new figure appeared among the ranks of the players.

'Who's that?' Bracher asked Howarth.

'Who?' said Howarth, who was busy fixing in his shoes some little double-hooked metal bands, a patent substitute for laces.

'The chap with long hair.'

'Mountain.'

'Why wasn't he here at the beginning of term?'

'Sick.'

'He's pretty good at football, isn't he?'

'First eleven,' said Howarth, straightening up and looking down with satisfaction at his shoes.

'Where did you get those things from?' asked Bracher.

'Perkins,' said Howarth. 'He says his father invented them.'

'How much?'

'That Borneo stamp.'

'Good Lord!'

'They aren't being manufactured yet,' said Howarth defensively.

'Has he got any more?' The gadget suddenly seemed to Bracher infinitely desirable.

'Don't know,' said Howarth. 'He took these out of his own shoes and went home with them undone.'

Mountain went close by them, dribbling the tennis ball with great skill. His hair, brushed back without a parting, flapped up and down.

'He won't be allowed to keep that suit on, will he?' said Bracher.

'Of course not, you ass,' said Howarth. 'He'll change when he's unpacked his trunk.'

'Pretty daring of him to come back in it.' Bracher gazed admiringly, thinking what he could never confide to Howarth, that Mountain was extremely good-looking. The suit was plum-coloured and double-breasted and among the grey flannel made Mountain appear like another order of being. His name, too, seemed to Gerald extraordinarily distinguished. As Howarth was about to walk away Gerald said: 'I suppose you wouldn't sell those shoe-lace things, Howarth?'

'Not likely,' called Howarth over his shoulder.

The neatness and originality of the shoe clips were wasted on Howarth: on himself they would have helped to distinguish him from the ruck as clearly as the plum-coloured suit distinguished Mountain. He must get another set from Perkins at all costs. He felt himself emerging from the oppressed initial period of his existence at this school where his ignorance of routines and names had driven from his life almost everything except the struggle for survival. He saw that after all the school work was within his scope, that the boys of his age were friendly and approachable, and that he could now give names to the older boys and place them accurately in the hierarchy.

The Headmaster came out of the entrance to the school building. Gerald saw him at once and his heart gave a leap of awe and fear. He had been leaning his shoulders against the wall and immediately straightened himself, realizing instinctively how Mr Pemberton would disapprove of a slouching posture—as he himself in theory disapproved, knowing how much better it was to be active and athletic like Mountain, say, than to daydream the lunch hour away. Although the Headmaster's course lay diagonally away from him, he divined that he had not escaped being observed in an idle, lounging posture, and he longed to be able to join skilfully in the football game and for the Headmaster to halt for a moment, approvingly observing him. It seemed an enormous tragedy that he had presented himself to the Headmaster not in the character of keen courageous sportsman which was really his. The Headmaster walked rapidly away; his gown streaming behind him, his head carefully balanced, as though considering gravely every object, every situation in his path. Gerald watched him go through the private gate to the house. Even then the Headmaster did not pass completely from sight: his hat could be seen for a little while moving above the top of the garden wall like a strange target in a shooting gallery. Only when it had disappeared did Gerald feel free to respire and move normally—or, rather, not quite normally, for the Headmaster left behind him an atmosphere of endeavour and ardour in which Gerald for a while braced back his knees and breathed into his chest rather than his stomach.

III

A few wind-bent hedges stood between the playing fields and the sea. But not far away the town was extending a broken tentacle of red brick houses along the road that ran past the bottom of the school drive. The builders' workmen could be seen occasionally watching the games from scaffolding and ladders. Gerald Bracher was engaged in a pick-up match on the third pitch. Not very adroit at games, he was further handicapped by having played rugby at his previous school, and now found himself a giant among smaller boys. He was captain of the Whites, and playing at centre half. At first he had been embarrassed and disgusted at the size of the players and the aimlessness of the game, but had come to realize that it was right and important that he should take the match seriously and play his best, even though no one was watching it and it was refereed not by a master, as were the games on the two senior pitches, but by a boy with thick glasses called Matley, excused football and extremely ignorant of its rules. There was an almost unbroken shriek of conversation from the players.

'What's that for?' inquired the captain of the Colours after a blast of Matley's whistle.

'Offside,' said Matley.

'You ass,' said the captain of the Colours. 'You hopeless ass.'

'Less cheek, young Dover,' said Matley weakly. He

added: 'Only a second ago you said I never blew for offside.'

'It was obviously offside,' said Gerald.

'You can't be offside from a throw-in, you ass,' said the captain of the Colours.

'Can't you?' asked Gerald, feeling himself blush.

'Well, I'll give a bounce-up then,' said Matley, 'and those who come in it mind my shins.'

'Offside from a throw-in,' repeated the captain of the Colours pityingly.

'Come on, you chaps, play up!' shouted Gerald, to cover up his shame.

At left half in Gerald's team was a young boarder for whom he had already conceived a dislike—a thin pale boy who acting as monitor at lunch had once dropped a piece of ginger pudding on Gerald's shoulder and instead of apologizing had allowed tears to fill his great silly eyes. This boy—Slade—played football extremely badly and in such a manner that despite his covering a good deal of ground he rarely seemed able to get near the ball. The captain of the Colours, a lively centre forward, jumped up and deflected with his head towards the Whites' goal, employing a skill unusual on the third pitch, a high ball for which Gerald was waiting, with too much leisure, to come to his feet. The captain of the Colours dashed after it, leaving Gerald on the wrong foot, far behind. The backs were nowhere to be seen—no doubt engaged in some wrangle with Matley. Between the goalkeeper, a corpulent but indifferent performer called Brian Cole, and the onrushing centre forward there stood only Slade.

'Tackle him!' Gerald cried.

Slade executed a nervous shying movement which took him neatly out of the path of the centre forward—

who then shot. The ball glanced off Cole's stomach but with insufficient deflection to prevent it passing between the posts.

'Hopeless,' panted Gerald, 'absolutely hopeless.'

'It hit me full in the stomach,' complained Cole.

'You funked that tackle,' said Gerald to Slade.

The boy said: 'I'm sorry, Bracher.'

'There's nothing worse than a funk,' said Gerald, despising Slade and wishing that he could be hurt.

'A shot that hits you in the stomach is jolly painful,' said Cole.

'Go and get the ball,' Gerald ordered Slade. It was rolling gently towards the more serious game on the second pitch. Gerald walked back to take his position for the kick-off.

'That's seven–four,' said Matley as he cleaned his spectacles.

'Eight,' said the captain of the Colours. 'I like not ye man who cannot add up.'

'All right, eight,' said Matley.

An argument developed. Gerald's anger at captaining the losing side in this game of idiotic midgets inflamed his disgust with Slade. When play restarted he found himself watching the left half for further signs of cowardice. He saw the thin legs moving ineffectually in the voluminous shorts, and shouted: 'You there, Slade, mark your man! Wake up, Slade!' He himself performed prodigies of defensive running and kicking: his breathing became more laboured, his togs muddier, his glow of virtue intenser. We'll keep them down to eight goals, anyway, he said almost audibly to himself. The attacks on the Whites' goal became very persistent. Gerald remembered reading of a defender in a football match who, his goalkeeper out of position and to save a goal, had punched out a shot. Better the almost certainty of a penalty kick than a certain goal. Gerald wondered if the situation might ever arise for him. To handle the ball justifiably—how resourceful and dramatic! He began to look for the opportunity.

A topped corner kick against the Whites skidded over the grass to the Colours' inside right who had time to take deliberate aim. His shot came from an acute angle, breast high and rather soft. As it floated past him Gerald struck out what seemed to him a desperate arm and pushed the ball round the post.

'Penalty!' shrieked the captain of the Colours gleefully.

'What did you do that for, Bracher?' Brian Cole complained. 'I was just going to catch it.'

'You'd never have saved it,' said Gerald, feeling himself about to blush.

'Obvious penalty,' said the captain of the Colours. 'Even old Matley saw that.'

'I can't understand why you did it, Bracher,' said Cole, his fat face wearing a mournful and self-righteous expression. 'I could easily have caught it.'

'Oh, shut up, Cole,' said Gerald, his heart beating wildly as he realized perfectly that his imagination had led him into folly.

The captain of the Colours had already secured the ball and was pacing out the distance to the penalty spot. He said: 'Bracher thinks he's still at his old school playing rugby.'

There was derisive and exaggerated laughter. 'There's nothing certain about a penalty,' said Gerald. 'Cole could save it.' Cole, he thought, would save it, using unsus-

25

pected anticipation and daring, and his own action be justified after all. There was some argument about the position of the penalty spot, but at last the captain of the Colours swung his boot at the ball—nonchalantly almost—and it passed between the posts before Cole could move from the conventional crouching position he had quite uselessly assumed.

'Nine–four,' said the captain of the Colours.

Gerald wondered what it was that made him so often perform these romantic actions that left him always with the bitter taste of absurdity and regret. He found Slade at his side; the younger boy looked up and said: 'I don't think Cole would have saved it.'

'If you didn't funk so much,' Gerald said fiercely, 'it wouldn't be nine–four. For God's sake, play up.' Slade was the sort of chap who not only funked but funked and then tried to curry favour.

He was still thinking this as he walked from the field towards the pavilion after the final whistle. He felt a heart-warming physical exhaustion, knowing that he had battled honourably in a losing cause. With a rough gesture he wiped away a trace of moisture the cold air had brought to his nose, and then sniffed heartily, trudging on with faintly simulated effort, every now and again tossing back his tousled hair. His body was all-important, an instrument that responded to his demands, whose functions could not be shameful.

Then he saw the Headmaster, moving to the pavilion on a different diagonal. His hat cut a sky already tinged with the darkish pink of sunset. Gerald was so exalted that he kept on his own path with scarcely a slackening of pace even though this meant that he might very well actually encounter Mr Pemberton. A seagull screamed overhead. He passed a day boy tying his football boots to the handlebars of his bicycle and then discovered that a little way ahead the Headmaster had halted.

'A good game, Bracher?' asked Mr Pemberton.

'Yes, sir,' said Gerald, grinning and tossing back his locks.

The Headmaster's hat was large but not quite large enough to cover the thick, well-brushed hair over his temples. His regular white teeth were revealed by his smile. 'Were you on the winning side?' he pursued.

'No, sir, but it was a good game.'

To Gerald's astonishment Mr Pemberton stepped forward and put his hand in the v of Gerald's shirt. He said: 'It is a filthy habit to wear one's vest at sports. Don't let me catch you at it again, Bracher.'

The Headmaster went on his way leaving Gerald trembling and ashamed. What could he do to atone, to rehabilitate himself in the Headmaster's eyes? Mr Pemberton was utterly right. It was cowardly as well as unhygienic to put a football shirt over one's vest; and what was remarkable was that he had always known that, but until the Headmaster's words had never realized its importance, its role in the course of conduct that he must carry out not only to please Mr Pemberton but also to make his own life a happy and purposeful one.

IV

The boarders sat in a hierarchy of scholastic seniority at the tables in the dining room. Gerald's place was half-way down the main table. Opposite him was the long-nosed librarian, Cropper, and next to Cropper, higher up, was Mountain. At first it had seemed strange to be so near Mountain, still with an aura of glamour though he had changed into the regulation grey flannel suit and black tie, and Gerald had kept his eyes deferentially averted from him. Mountain usually conversed with the half-dozen people senior to him but sometimes—and the habit was becoming more frequent—passed some remarks with Cropper and with a moustached boy on Gerald's right, called Blakey. These remarks often concerned the home lives of Cropper and Blakey and, initially, were for Gerald swathed in obscurity. Gradually he came to understand that because of Blakey's dark skin and the fact that his parents lived in Jamaica, Blakey was in Mountain's fantasy a member of a primitive negro family. Mountain's conception of Cropper's private life was more esoteric.

'Has your father got a new car yet?' Mountain might ask Cropper.

'No,' Cropper would say solemnly.

'The Alsatians are still a bit cramped for room, then?' No reply.

'I can't understand why your father doesn't make the Alsatians *pull* the car. Eh, Cropper?' Mountain would be quietly amused at this for a few moments and then turn to his friends at the top of the table.

One morning the boys came in to find a plate containing three stewed figs at each place—an unprecedented overture to breakfast. There was a derisive hum of conversation.

'Blakey will enjoy them anyway,' said Gerald.

Mountain overheard the remark and laughed. 'Nice figgy-figgy?' he said to Blakey.

Emboldened by this response, Gerald said: 'They've probably been sent direct by Mr Blakey.'

'No doubt about it,' said Mountain.

'Personally trodden out by him,' added Gerald.

Mountain bent down and sniffed at his plate. 'They smell like Blakey's feet. The Blakey family smell. That's why they're such famous fig treaders—they add flavour to the crop.'

'Chuck it, Mountain,' said Blakey.

Some boy near the door hissed: 'The Grey Chap.' The talking died away, and a moment later the Headmaster entered, went to his place at the Masters' table, elevated on a dais at one end of the room, and said grace.

As everyone sat down, Mountain said: 'You can have my figs, Blakey,' and pushed his plate across the table.

'And mine,' said Gerald. Soon Blakey was surrounded by plates of figs.

'This is like being back on the plantation for Blakey,' said Mountain.

'I don't like figs,' said Blakey.

'Oh, Blakey,' said Mountain.

'Honestly.'

'Cropper will eat them,' said Gerald daringly. Attention was focused on Cropper's empty plate. Cropper gave Gerald an evil look.

'Cropper likes them,' said Mountain incredulously. 'Come on, Cropper. Another plateful.'

Flushed with his success at amusing Mountain, Gerald said: 'The Croppers never waste anything.'

'Of course not,' said Mountain. 'Think of the Cropper car. It stopped going five years ago.'

'Stopped going under its own power,' said Gerald, 'but they've fitted pedals to it now.'

29

'The Alsatians pedal it.'

'In winter they're harnessed to it, and Mr Cropper takes off the wheels and fits runners.'

Cropper was very pink but kept silent. Gerald had a moment of panic, knowing that he had gone too far ever to be on reasonable terms again with him, and fearing what might happen when he encountered him out of Mountain's presence. Then Gerald forgot his fear in the pleasure of Mountain's approval and the consciousness of his own power to amuse.

At the end of breakfast the Headmaster rose, followed by the masters at his table and then the boys. But instead of grace he said: 'I happen to know that Miss Pemberton was especially pleased to provide an unusual and refreshing start to breakfast this morning. It seems that you do not appreciate good food and, what is more serious, that you do not appreciate the thoughtfulness of others. Furthermore, you have caused food to be wasted, in a world where millions less fortunate than you are suffering from under-nourishment.'

Gerald stared at the tablecloth in an agony of shame. The joke now seemed pitifully feeble and he wished more than anything that he had had the insight and the courage to eat his plate of figs. As Cropper had. After all, despite his ridiculous nose and hair, his curious home life, it was Cropper who had proved himself truly virtuous.

'For what we have received may the Lord make us truly thankful,' said the Headmaster, bowing his head suddenly. For Gerald the familiar words were charged with embarrassing irony.

V

When the term was well under way an extraordinary rumour spread. During the blank half-hour between tea and prep Gerald said to Howarth: 'What's all this about a boxing tournament?'

'There's going to be a boxing tournament,' said Howarth. 'A compulsory one.'

'But we don't learn boxing.'

'That doesn't prevent there being a boxing tournament.'

'It's a mad idea.'

'It's Jacket's idea.' Howarth was referring to Mr Norfolk, a young master who was the form master of the lowest form.

'He's mad then.'

'Of course.'

'But some people will be murdered,' said Gerald, trying to keep the conversation on a general level but thinking with alarm of himself. Suppose he were drawn against Cropper?

'Possibly. But they'll be murdered fairly. Everyone is going to be classified according to weight and you won't have to box out of your weight.'

'How will they know our weights?' Gerald asked. It seemed to him that the more objections he could think of the less likely it was that the brutal affair would actually take place.

'They'll weigh us.'

'What with?'

'The weighing machine.'

'I didn't know there was one,' said Gerald despairingly.

'It's in the box-room. All the boarders are weighed at the end of term. It goes on your report. Last term on mine it said: "Weight five–two. Height eight–ten." Miss Pemberton had slipped.'

'It's a mad idea,' said Gerald again.

'Mad, but mad and of a madness.' Howarth had the lid of his desk open and on its inside upright face had made an elaborate descending runway of rulers held in position with compasses and dividers. He took a small marble from his pocket and put it at the start of the runway. It descended tortuously to finish in an inkwell in the corner of the desk. 'Ingenious, eh, Bracher?' Howarth said.

'And so intellectual.'

'You're jealous because you haven't made one yourself.'

'I could make a *really* ingenious one,' said Gerald. 'And I'd use a mint ball. Several mint balls following each other.'

'Brilliant. I'll get one of the day kids to get me some.'

Gerald sat in his desk, opened a book called Warner and Marten's *Groundwork of British History*, and hearing the repeated vicissitudes of Howarth's marble, wondered why suddenly he was not happy. This book, new to him and more adult, more scholarly, than any he had had to read before, held for him an imprecise but exciting promise. In History, as in most other subjects, he had found himself almost to his surprise more expert than the others in his form: in a way he looked forward to the period of preparation. And afterwards there was cocoa and perhaps biscuits. Even bedtime could be anticipated as an enjoyable opportunity for the exercise of wit, of playing to the characters of those in his dormitory, of reading under the bedclothes with a torch whose battery was still lively. But he was not happy. Howarth, for example, was always happy.

Already Gerald began to see that in some way and quite without his volition he was unlike the others. He had no definite character and so had never been given a nickname—as, say, Snape major was justly called Stink-Bomb Billy. Nor had he a predictable mind—as had Matley who was always religious or Blakey who was always slow on the uptake. Everyone except himself seemed armed with singleness of purpose against the traps of existence. But he was capable of misery because, for example, of the boxing tournament (he all at once remembered). He imagined the notice board used for sports announcements in the main vestibule: on a foolscap sheet headed 'Boxing Tournament' was a list of pairs above Mr Norfolk's authoritative 's.w.g.n.', and in the middle of it 'Cropper v. Bracher'. But perhaps on the fatal date he would be ill: he thought carefully about his body, swallowing for signs of an incipient sore throat; he imagined running up the steps of the House, falling, and breaking his ankle. In a few moments these projected events were so real that once again he forgot about the tournament and occupied his mind only with the unusual and therefore exciting train of events that could involve him were he by accident transported out of the dull routine of school.

During the ensuing days he had several more moments of terror when the fantastic notion of the tournament, as a man's death is announced by slight symptoms of a bad disease, began to clothe itself in recognizable and homely shapes. One evening when he was changing into his slippers he saw through the changing-room door Mr Norfolk emerge from the entrance to the cellar followed by Snape minor and Dover with their arms full of dusty boxing gloves, like some strange oriental fruit which has to be eaten dry and ancient. And then someone told him, circumstantially, that the venue of the tournament was to be the class-room of Mr Norfolk's own form—a dark and unfamiliar chamber with stunted desks and jam-jars filled with blanched tubers, the result of some experiment suitable to the infant mind, on the window sills.

But the next day at the time of the morning break Howarth came up to him wearing a studiedly nonchalant expression and said: 'You'll be sorry to hear that the boxing tournament is off.'

'How can it be off?'

'They can't find the weights.'

'The weights?'

'The weights for the weighing machine, fool,' said Howarth. 'You can't use a weighing machine without weights and you can't have a boxing tournament without a weighing machine.'

'Who told you?' asked Bracher, a delicious sense of joy creeping through his veins.

'Young Dover. He was among the first lot to be weighed. They all trooped into the House, Jacket at the head. A chap stepped on the machine and then Jacket discovered that the weights you put on it at the end of the arm thing were *non est*. They all had to search the big box-room. Then the little box-room. Then they were marched away, Jacket very displeased.'

'Typical,' said Bracher. 'Typical Jacket inefficiency.' It seemed to him that he had a right to complain at being

34

done out of the experience of participating in the boxing tournament. 'Why didn't he make sure the weights were there?'

'Well, he'd every reason to believe they were there,' said Howarth. 'I believe Miss Pemberton pinched them to put in those Cornish pasties we had yesterday.'

'Ha, ha,' said Bracher, ironically. Then he added, with elaborate casualness: 'Of course, you *could* have a boxing tournament without weights.'

'Never,' said Howarth, gleefully. 'Jacket must have things done properly. But they could find the weights.'

At prayers the following morning Mr Pemberton came to the front of the dais. His head was slightly bowed, his hands were clasped before him, and his look was severe. He said: 'On the initiative of Mr Norfolk, and with my full approval, arrangements were being made for a boxing tournament in which the whole school was to participate. This naturally involved the classifying of all boys according to their weights. For this purpose the weighing machine in the Boarders' House was to be used. But the weights for the machine cannot be found.' There was a mysterious sound of excitement, as though everyone was opening a box of chocolates. The Headmaster continued: 'I am satisfied, after the inquiries I have made, that the weights have not been lost or mislaid. Some wretched boy with a misguided sense of humour has stolen them.' The excitement crepitated again. The Headmaster's voice took on a tinge of sorrow. 'A parent of one of you boys here was generous enough to promise to award cups to the winners in the various classes of the tournament. With great regret I shall have to tell him that we cannot take advantage of his splendid gesture. What reason I shall give I do not know. I do not think

35

that I shall dare to admit that we have at Seafolde a clown with no thought of his fellows or for his school. Of course, it is possible that already or at this moment the culprit has repented. If so, there is still time for him to return the weights to their proper place and to do so surreptitiously will obviously be within his powers. Should the weights be returned within twenty-four hours I shall regard the ridiculous incident as closed. Should they not be so returned, the miscreant, when I discover who he is, will suffer my gravest displeasure. You may dismiss.'

It was only a false guilt that Gerald felt as he went to his first period, for he told himself that the notion of preventing the tournament by stealing the weights had never occurred to him. And when the guilt had passed off the revealed sensation of awe at a scandal not involving oneself and the prospective punishment of a crime for which one was not responsible were all the more delightful for the added sense of having had a phenomenally lucky escape.

'What would be the Grey Chap's gravest displeasure?' he asked Howarth as he opened his tattered Hall and Knight.

'Six of the best,' said Howarth. 'But of course you can always pad up—I'll lend you my big atlas.'

'Very funny.'

The same day, as Gerald was going back to the school block after lunch, a voice behind him called his name.

'Please, Bracher, can I speak to you?'

It was Slade. 'What do you want?' Gerald asked, feeling immediately the sense of power and contempt his dealings with this boy always gave him.

'It's about the weights.'

Gerald's heart gave a leap of cruelty. He had imagined, when trying to think of the culprit in the affair, some reckless character whose motive had been mischief and malice—he had even toyed with the idea of its being Mountain. But in this moment it came to him that some-one else besides himself had feared the tournament.

'You took them,' he said.

'No, Bracher, no I didn't.' Slade was alarmed. 'But you see, I know who did.'

'Who?'

Slade said quickly: 'Would it be too horribly sneaking if I told Mr Norfolk who took them? Do you think it would, Bracher? I feel we ought to have the tournament as a sort of test for us all. But it would be pretty horrible sneaking in a way to tell. Would *you* tell, Bracher?'

'You'll have to tell.' Quite remarkably Gerald felt him-self far above what was after all a petty affair: and yet, of course, he would have to see it played out to its dénouement. 'Too many people are involved for you not to tell. Think of those cups that were going to be presented.'

'Yes, I've thought of that.'

'Who was it?' inquired Gerald gently.

Slade looked round the playground. 'Cole.'

'Cole!' Gerald repeated. 'The fat——' He could find no word.

'I saw him carrying a cardboard box into the furnace house before breakfast. He didn't see me. I thought he was going to burn some mice or something awful. So I crept up and looked through the window and saw it was a box of round iron things. He put them under the coke. Then when the weights were missing I knew what they were. I went back to the furnace house but I couldn't find them. I daren't spend too much time messing about with the coke in case someone saw me. I was going to find the weights, put them back, and not say anything.'

Gerald said: 'You'll have to tell Jacket this right away.'

'Do you really think so, Bracher?'

'Well, isn't it better to get it off your chest than carry it round with you?'

'Yes, I think it is.'

'Go on, then.'

Slade took three steps away and then returned. 'Would you—would you consider'—he stuttered a little on the c—'coming with me, Bracher?'

'To Jacket?'

'Yes, please.'

'You are a specimen, aren't you, Slade? All right.'

As they walked back to the House Gerald suddenly thought, and his stomach descended sickeningly, that the result of all this would be that there would be a boxing tournament after all. Slade, his decision made and a champion found, was almost garrulous at his side. 'Where will Mr Norfolk be?' he asked.

'In the Masters' Common Room, of course,' said Gerald. This was a mere child, he thought. With an assurance he did not feel he marched up to the door he knew by repute but had never entered, and knocked. A voice bade them enter.

To Gerald's astonishment the room was full of tobacco smoke. In front of the fire a stout master called Percy lay back in an easy chair reading, a pipe in his mouth—as unfamiliar as if he had suddenly grown a beard. There were some cups and saucers on the table, an ashtray, and a novel in a bright jacket. Newspapers sprouted untidily from a rack on the wall next to a coloured reproduction of a painting of a French street. In this unanticipated atmosphere a pile of the exercise books used throughout the school looked as strange as if Gerald had come across them in his own home.

'Yes?' inquired Mr Percy without removing his pipe.

'Can I speak to Mr Norfolk, please, sir?' asked Gerald.

'You could no doubt if he were here.'

'Do you know where he is, sir?' Gerald felt both foolish and nervous.

'In his room, I expect,' said Mr Percy turning his eyes back to his book.

'Thank you, sir.' Gerald closed the door and looked venomously at Slade. 'Now what do you expect me to do?' he asked. But at that very moment there was a clattering on the linoleum of the stairs and Mr Norfolk was seen descending.

'What are you two still doing in the House?' he inquired aggressively. His eyebrows ran in a continuous line above a negligible nose.

'The weights, sir. Slade wants to tell you——' Gerald burst out. In a few moments the story was unfolded and Mr Norfolk stood thunderstruck.

'This is very serious,' he said and Gerald had a fresh awed sense of the enormity of Cole's action and the importance of his own role in the crisis that was now unfolding. Mr Norfolk considered the position for no more than a few seconds. 'Come along,' he said. 'Both of you.' And he set off with the long stride appropriate to one in charge of the school's games.

'Where are we going to, sir?' asked Gerald, knowing the dread answer but wanting the worst to be emphasized, as one waits for the mounting casualty list of some disaster.

'To the Headmaster, of course.'

And in a moment or two, an interval felt by Gerald to be disgracefully short—like the transition from the gossip outside a church door to the serious atmosphere within—for him to put himself into the proper state of mind, they were admitted to Mr Pemberton's study. He heard Mr Norfolk relate Slade's story. The Headmaster listened without comment, his face grave. Then he turned his eyes on Gerald who felt his legs lose their rigidity, fearing a question that would reveal some hidden deficiency of his own conduct in the affair. But Mr Pemberton only said, 'Bracher, go and see if Cole has returned to school after his luncheon.'

He sped out of the House and across the playground where he found Cole leaning against the battered mulberry tree by the tuck shop, stretching chewing gum from his teeth. Gerald said breathlessly: 'The Grey Chap wants to see you.' He tried to give his voice a neutral tone so that the dénouement would come for Cole with all the more crashing an effect, but the words, like some great Homeric line, were enough to create a sensation.

'What's up, Bracher?' inquired Cole. His habitual injured tone scarcely concealed a nervous agitation.

Gerald did not answer. As they went on their way his gait was sober and he refrained from running his hand as he usually did along the open fence of the vegetable garden.

'Did the Grey Chap look ratty?'

'I don't think I ought to say anything,' Gerald replied.

'You are a stinker, Bracher,' said Cole automatically. His mind was clearly indrawn and Gerald at last felt a pang of pity for hin, in spite of his corpulence and cowardice. But it was only a momentary pang: there was a profound justice in this particular end to the episode of the weights.

In the Headmaster's study no one seemed to have moved during Gerald's absence. He had knocked but let Cole in first, himself staying on the threshold, ready to leave if he could divine that that was Mr Pemberton's wish. But the Headmaster said: 'Come in, Bracher, and shut the door.' Mr Norfolk and Slade were in front of the desk: Cole sidled up to the side of it. 'Now, boy,' Mr Pemberton said to him: 'Can you guess why I have sent for you?'

'No, sir,' said Cole quickly.

'You can see that Mr Norfolk is here. Doesn't that give you a clue?'

'No, sir.'

The Headmaster turned to Slade. 'Are you sure you weren't mistaken, Slade?'

'I'm sure, sir,' said Slade, very nervous.

The Headmaster regarded Cole again. 'Come, boy,' he said in a terrible voice. 'I think you can guess what we are all here for.' Cole shook his head: Gerald's heart was beating heavily. 'The weights,' said Mr Pemberton in thrilling tones. 'The weights. The weights.'

By a supreme physical effort Cole uttered a few words: 'Oh, the weights.'

'What on earth were you doing with them in the furnace house?'

'Hiding them, sir.'

'Hiding them, boy?'

Suddenly Cole's power of human speech returned to him. 'Yes, sir. I wanted to stop the boxing tournament sir. I thought if I hid the weights there couldn't be one, sir. It was the only thing I could do, sir. You see I'm very heavy, sir, and so I should be in the heavy-weight class with Mountain and all those, sir, although I'm not really strong and I've never boxed before. It's all right for people who are the proper weight for their age, but it's rotten for me, sir. It's not really fair. I'd get knocked about by Mountain and all those, sir.'

The ensuing silence was broken only by a subdued sniff from Cole. Then the Headmaster said: ' "I'm very heavy, sir." ' Gerald saw that his body was shaken by rage and knew that he had sadly underestimated Cole's punishment. But in the same moment his apprehension was turned to astonishment. Mr Pemberton was shaking with laughter, a strange sound that he had never heard before and that he could not have imagined. He stole a glance at Mr Norfolk in case some reaction was demanded of him that he could not visualize from his own understanding of the situation—in case, say, the Headmaster had gone insane. But Mr Norfolk's countenance was still set in the severity of expression which a few moments ago had seemed infinitely appropriate, his bird's eyes half veiled.

'Mr Norfolk,' said the Headmaster, beaming, 'I think we must recognize that our friend here has reason on his side.'

'Of course, he wouldn't have fought with the heavy-weights, Headmaster.'

'But being indubitably a heavy-weight that was the impression he not unjustifiably formed. When I spoke to the school this morning I imagined that the weights had been taken by someone intending mischief. Now the complexion of things is altered. Naturally I cannot entirely excuse this action of Cole's: it was very wrong. Very wrong but very resourceful.' The Headmaster's

glance took in Gerald and Slade. 'I'm glad you two boys
are the witnesses of this little incident—you can learn
something from it. There is nothing wrong in protecting
oneself from injustice. Rebellion is often praiseworthy.
Our friend here went a little too far, that is all. Cole,
you will write a hundred times—let me see—the avoir-
dupois table. Now go and find the weights and return
them to the machine in the box-room. Bracher, you go
with him and see that it's done. Thank you, Mr Norfolk.'

They filed out of the study and Mr Norfolk strode off
without a word. 'You see, Bracher,' said Cole, shaken
but triumphant. Gerald was lost in meditation. He saw
how totally he had misjudged the situation: the Headmaster had not only extracted the true meaning from it
but put it in proper perspective. He regretted bitterly
not having had the resource himself to hide the weights:
in what a beautiful hand would he have written the
resulting imposition! And now he would have to suffer
injury in the tournament without the glory of having
rebelled against it.

But when they got to the furnace house the weights
were not to be found. The two largest were subsequently
raked out of the furnace but the others had obviously
fallen through and been thrown away with the ash. The
school handy-man had inadvertently taken up the weights
with a shovelful of coke and the boxing tournament was
postponed *sine die*.

VI

One night Gerald awoke with his stomach in a sad tur-
moil. He had suspected that something was amiss, for the

previous evening, after eating at tea-time the corned beef
of two boys who disliked it, his belches had tasted of
sulphuretted hydrogen. The dormitory was asleep: the
small lamp burned which always remained after the
duty master had switched out the main light. Could it
be that he was going to be sick? He visualized despairingly the far-off lavatories: the business of putting on
dressing-gown and slippers seemed beyond his powers.
Perhaps on the way he would meet someone in authority
who would challenge his right to be walking about at this
hour, his conduct even in being ill.

He needed someone to come to his bedside with a
suitable receptacle and to tell him to luxuriate in his
illness, not to worry about procedure (for what had one
to do if one were too ill to get up in the morning?). He
thought of his mother, remembering as though it were
something he had read in a book that once he had
accepted such attentions from her without question and
with tender love. Already he had forgotten quite what it
was like to have two parents, for he was changing so
rapidly that it seemed to him he had rightly outgrown
the mere infantile self which had accepted his mother
as a part of existence to which it was naturally entitled.
And it occurred to him, too, that many incidents which
at the time of their happening conferred pleasure upon
him were in the light of events already a warning of the
approaching end of the idyll of childhood. He remembered meeting with his mother a gentleman called Mr
Ayers. On the hotel terrace he had consumed his rasp-
berry drink and then Mr Ayers had given him a vast coin
to spend in the nearby slot-machine arcade. He had
looked back on his way there and seen, beneath the tall
building and the blue sky, the two figures wave to him.

44

Had there been even then, beneath the happiness, a premonition of loss? Certainly, he believed, a faint feeling of guilt—for he knew that on a mere weekday he should not in the order of things have a soft drink in a hotel in the middle of Durban and be given a sum exceeding his weekly pocket money. Thus and thus, through a succession of tiny wrongs, had come the final cataclysmic wrong —his mother's desertion of him. For though he had been involved in many of the meetings, pleasures, intense conversations, intense silences, the real meaning of them had evaded him, had been concealed from him, like one who connives at a crime but whose accomplices make off with the proceeds. And so it seemed to him that his relationship with his father which then should have been closer cemented was poisoned by his previous involvement with his mother, that he could have prevented the cataclysm by warning his father, persuading his mother, antagonizing Mr Ayers—though the precise role of these actors, or, rather, the motivation which caused them to behave so drastically, was by no means clear to him.

In the end bed Matley spoke in his sleep. Gerald's stomach continued in its awful courses. It had such a distinct and distasteful existence that he felt that if he could make some effort of will he could dissociate the rest of his body from it and so become well. But the effort, of course, was beyond him and his normal brain continued to receive from below the unwelcome signals of abnormality. At last he was convinced that he would have to vomit and laboriously made his way to the lavatories. The familiar act of walking, the brown and green walls, the terrible name 'Shark' on the lavatory pan, convinced him again that any serious mishap could be averted, and he bent indulgently over as though

45

merely to humour the notion that had got him out of bed. And then, surprisingly, involuntarily, painfully, he was sick.

He crept shivering back to bed. Now he would be all right. But instead of being gradually lapped in drowsiness he began to feel the nausea once more stealing from his stomach. Soon he was up again.

Before, finally, he fell asleep he thought of what the Headmaster had said to him on that first Sunday of term: that he had to be a support to his father. How fervently he agreed, but how difficult to translate the maxim into action! For he could not understand what, if anything, his father wanted from him, or how a son could replace anything taken away from a father by a mother.

In the morning he woke to find Matley at his bedside. 'The bell went long ago, Bracher,' Matley said, towelling his face which without glasses looked like the face of some dug-up underground creature. Everything about Matley was strange, Gerald thought—even his vests, which were made of a peculiarly dark coarse wool, no doubt clipped from a Tibetan beast of burden.

'I was sick in the night. I still feel sick.'

'Bracher's sick,' Matley announced.

Gerald sat up. There was a cold sweat on his forehead. 'I couldn't eat any breakfast.' He felt the deep embarrassment of one who does not know what behaviour is demanded of him and envied profoundly the health that was enabling the others to submit themselves to routine.

Howarth, who himself had not succeeded in rising to any greater extent than propping up his head on his bent arm, said: 'I'll tell Miss Pemberton.'

'You look yellow,' said Matley.

46

'Do I?' said Gerald. He sank back with more confidence.

Miss Pemberton took his temperature and made him move to the sickroom. While he was sliding between the cold sheets of the new bed she came in with a hot water bottle. The feel of it, the quiet situation of the room, the rain on the window, his abdication from responsibility, made him say confidentially: 'I think it's only a bilious attack.'

'Very like,' said Miss Pemberton. 'But you didn't want to stay in the dormitory, did you?'

'No, Miss Pemberton.'

She regarded the gas fire which she had just lit. 'Do you want something to read?'

'Is it all right to read?'

'Why not?' She went out of the room and returned a little later with two books which she put on the bedside locker. 'There's a chamber pot under the bed,' she said, 'if you want to be sick in a hurry.' Then she went out again.

Gerald closed his eyes, thinking that in a moment he would look at the books if his sickness did not return. But he fell asleep and was awakened by one of the maids putting a glass of warm milk on the locker. She winked and withdrew. A timeless air filled the sickroom: the milk could be in lieu of either breakfast or lunch. From the music room below came the sounds of someone intermittently playing the first movement of the 'Moonlight' Sonata; and once Gerald heard the distant animal cry of a very small boy at play. He thought of the life of the school going on without him, and—the idea gave him a momentary pang of panic—how he would miss this morning a vital part of the explanation of the business of

47

logarithms. Could he ever make up the period he was losing in his life of learning and responsibility?

It was after another glass of milk had been brought to him and which he had ascertained was his luncheon, that the maid re-entered with a hot water bottle. She proceeded to put it in another bed in the sickroom.

'Who's that for?' Gerald asked, but before she could reply Blakey entered carrying his pyjamas and a dressing gown of a chocolate colour which seemed peculiarly suited to his personality.

'Hello, Bracher,' said Blakey. His dark face looked as though a green spotlight were playing on it.

'What's up?' asked Gerald.

'Cold,' said Blakey. His teeth chattered as he undressed. When his legs were revealed they could be seen to be goose-fleshed like the skin of some large, predatory fish. Soon after he got to bed Miss Pemberton arrived to place a carafe of water at his side, to tuck in his bedclothes, and lay her hand on his forehead.

From behind the barrier of his half-closed, righteously bilious eyes, Gerald watched her movements. When she stooped her rather thin legs were revealed and he remembered in a puzzled way Howarth once remarking with some approval on her physical attractions. Swathed in a long heavy cardigan her bust could scarcely be remarked; round her straight brown hair she wore a childish and absurd ribbon, and a man's gunmetal watch made her wrist look disconcertingly white and fragile. It struck him, too, that her being related to the Headmaster precluded any possibility of regarding her as genuinely female.

She fussed over Blakey for an inordinately long time as though perversely fascinated by his aboriginal appearance and primitive mind. Only as an afterthought, it seemed, did she say to Gerald: 'Did you keep the milk down?'

'Yes, Miss Pemberton.' But despite his indifference to her as a person he was conscious that his respectful reply, neutral glance, the conventional attitude of a boy to school matron, hid an inchoate, potential, amazing commerce between them—as the bedclothes hid from her eyes the fact that his hand was touching his own naked flesh.

'Could you manage some bread and butter for tea?'

'Yes, please, Miss Pemberton.' Did her look conceal some secret knowledge of him, or was it merely that the crude relationships of school had made him unused to contact with anyone other than on a received and rigid basis?

An hour later she returned with a heavy hairy man who carried a small Gladstone bag. 'This is Blakey, Doctor,' she said, and Gerald was impressed at the hitherto unimagined importance of Blakey's illness.

'Unbutton your pyjama jacket, laddie,' said the doctor, diving into his capacious side pocket and then separating a stethoscope from a curved tobacco pipe. Blakey was auscultated and the doctor made some non-committal noises. He rose, stuffed the stethoscope back, turned to Gerald and said: 'What's the matter with you, laddie?'

Before Gerald could force his voice past a sudden hoarseness, Miss Pemberton said: 'An upset stomach.'

'Let's see your tongue.' The doctor lowered his head, the head of a very big walrus. 'Nasty,' he said.

Miss Pemberton followed him out of the room. 'How are you, really?' Gerald asked, almost timorously, as though Blakey's answer might reveal that he was dying.

'All right,' Blakey replied, down in the bedclothes again, his big nose resting on the folded sheet.

Dusk fell soon after tea: the notes from another practiser in the music room below ceased abruptly and the print blurred before Gerald's eyes. Imperceptibly he lost consciousness and a great epoch of time seemed to have elapsed when he was wakened by the sound of voices in the room and for a moment sensed the glare of electric light on his eyelids. He opened his eyes and closed them again quickly when they revealed that standing by his niece at the foot of Blakey's bed was Mr Pemberton.

'And what was Robertson's diagnosis?' asked the Headmaster.

'A feverish cold,' said Miss Pemberton.

A silence followed this exchange which Gerald, guiltless though he knew himself to be, felt oppressive and threatening.

'A feverish cold,' repeated the Headmaster, bringing out with the subtlety of a great actor the absurdity which previously one had not realized resided in the words. 'One is usually feverish in the first stages of a cold.'

'He had a temperature of a hundred and one,' said Miss Pemberton.

'Oh that thermometer!' exclaimed the Headmaster, with dreadful amusement.

'I think Dr. Robertson should be called when a boy has a temperature of a hundred and one.'

'Evie,' said the Headmaster gently, 'Robertson does not come here for nothing.'

'Of course not, Uncle.'

'Well, it rather suggests as much when he's called to hear the redoubtable Blakey sneeze,' said Mr Pemberton with warmth. 'Perhaps you haven't realized, Evie, that a casual visit such as this does not go on a boy's bill. It has to be borne by the school. And you must agree that it is unfair that the school should suffer the burden of unnecessary expense, especially in these days when the school requires so many things—the chapel, for example. If a boy should have a prolonged illness then of course Robertson would send in a bill wholly attributable to that boy and we could properly ask for it to be discharged by his parents. But a visit to a feverish cold—that represents an absolute loss to the School.'

'I think it's too risky to deal with a temperature of a hundred and one ourselves.'

'These are boys, Evie, healthy animals. Blakey will be roaring for his breakfast in the morning—and there will be a debit of half a guinea against the school.'

For Gerald this conversation, to which he listened excitedly, while with supreme histrionic ability he feigned the deep breathing and small abandoned movements of one in a heavy sleep, resolved beyond a doubt the ambivalent feelings he had had about Miss Pemberton. It was plain, and he had been blind to imagine otherwise, that she was quite a fool, capable of the most thoughtless and senseless acts, and giving proper consideration neither to the Headmaster nor to Seafolde House. Anyone with the slightest knowledge of illness and of Blakey would have known that comedy not tragedy lay in his shivers and pallor. With this realization of her silly and insignificant character came the proper evaluation of her physical person. She was dowdy, too thin, not even 'not a bad tart' but not a tart at all—a female, like Lily the Irish maid, beyond any romantic imaginings.

'Well, boy,' Gerald heard Mr Pemberton say with the

geniality that unlike the geniality of anyone else seemed to impose on the person on whom it was conferred a terribly difficult problem of moral conduct, 'how are you feeling this evening?'

Blakey had evidently been too stupid to feign sleep. 'Much better, thank you, sir.'

'Miss Pemberton will soon be sending round to Dr Robertson's for the medicine that you evidently need to make a complete recovery.'

'Thank you, sir,' said Blakey, the point of the situation completely escaping him. Through the open millimetre of his eyes, Gerald saw the Headmaster turn from Blakey's bed and felt a thrust of fear in case his own conduct in having a bilious attack could, as seemed possible from the Headmaster's healthy and thrifty standpoint, be called into question. But Mr Pemberton walked straight out of the room, switching off the electric light as he did so, leaving Gerald on reflection to agree that if one were ill enough for the sickroom one must be too ill to read.

VII

On Wednesdays and Saturdays after games the boarders were permitted to go into the nearby town. The hour appointed for their return was too early to allow them to visit a cinema and they used their time mostly in shopping—at sweetshops, at a shop which sold foreign stamps—or visiting cafés. On these expeditions Gerald often found himself with Howarth. This week, to save the fare, they had refrained from taking the bus, walking in the dark, a slight rain flicking their cheeks, down the long country road from the school drive that joined the road running along the sea wall, a road bare and unfinished that only gradually became the town's brief esplanade, railed and kerbed, with a garden, seats and a few iron and glass shelters.

'What about some fish and chips?' said Howarth.

'But the chip shop is out of bounds.'

'Of course it is.'

'Do you want to risk it?' asked Gerald, the world suddenly becoming perilous.

Howarth turned with assurance off the esplanade and brought them to the bright steamed windows of the fish and chip shop. Gerald said nervously: 'Hadn't we better take our caps off?'

'All right,' Howarth said, rolling his up and stowing it in his overcoat pocket. Gerald looked searchingly down the street and followed him into the shop. At a table in a corner of the tiled back room were sitting Mountain and Blakey: the intrepid explorers with a sinking of the heart saw the flag of another nation already planted at the Pole. Mountain smiled, as though recognizing that this action of Gerald and Howarth's brought them some little way up the height of *savoir faire* which he occupied. Howarth gave the order.

Gerald sat playing with the strange phallic vinegar bottle, looking in Mountain's direction. He found it hard to realize that since Mountain was equally guilty there could be no question of his reporting to those in authority the breaking of bounds. The woman of the shop passed them bearing a tray which she began to unload on Mountain and Blakey's table. Gerald stole a glance and saw that with his fish and chips Mountain had ordered a plate of peas. This enterprise and imagination marked

53

the extent of the gulf fixed between Mountain's character and his.

'I didn't know Mountain ever went about with Blakey,' said Gerald quietly.

'Pass the vinegar,' said Howarth. Their own order had arrived.

'Blakey's such an ass,' said Gerald.

'A chap in Blakey's dormitory told me that once Mountain appeared at the door and called Blakey out,' said Howarth.

At this remark, to which he did not reply, Gerald's ears grew hot and he applied himself with great elaboration to the eating of his fish and chips. The dormitories held six or more, but there was also a tiny room which Mountain occupied alone. When Gerald felt that he could speak without embarrassment, he said: 'Blakey's wolfed his already. Such a treat for him—no fish and chip shops in Jamaica.'

'They have fig and date shops,' said Howarth.

The relationship between Mountain and Blakey was too complicated to understand. Mountain's baiting of Blakey would seem to leave nothing for the relationship to subsist on: over the fish and chips, or in Mountain's dormitory, what could be passing between them except Mountain's idle and malicious fantasies and Blakey's monotonous and boring protests? Gerald had imagined that nothing was beyond Mountain's power—that, for example, though he was not a prefect the society of prefects was his for the asking. So, too, his occupation of the single dormitory had seemed not an accident of seniority, of Mountain's progress through the dormitories, but something to which his debonair looks and character had entitled him. But was there another Mountain behind the athlete, the dandy—a self like Gerald's, that was unsure of its power to draw affection, that was sometimes unhappy in its solitary moments? At the conception of this possibility Mountain's luxuriant hair and pale skin shed their glamour and took on an almost vulgar air as though Gerald had detected them giving off an odour of physical processes.

Going upstairs to bed, the House had for Gerald, following his fish and chip shop reverie, an air mysterious and even sinister, like a commonplace villa that has been the locale of a murder. The square landing, its linoleum dimly reflecting the low-powered electric lamp, held not only the familiar entrance to his own 'dormitory but also that to Mountain's solitary room which faced, he saw with new understanding, the dormitory in which Blakey slept. The latter he had seen occasionally—he had gone there for Blakey's stamp album while they had both been in the sick room and had noted as material for satire the peculiar travelling rug, as plain and coarse as a horse-cloth, which Cropper had supplied to cover his bed—and its strangeness was merely that of a place which one knows is to be one's own future habitat. But he had never been in Mountain's room and could not imagine it—nor the thoughts and actions which must go on in it. In a drawer Mountain's plum-coloured suit would be and on the bedside locker Mountain's wristwatch with the metal strap, and there Mountain would brilliantine and brush back his hair. But these were only the small material indications of a way of life that seemed to ignore the constrictions of school—as though, in fact, Mountain were, like a student of penal reform who deliberately gets himself imprisoned, not seriously or permanently bound by the disciplines that dictated to all his fellows. So that if one opened the door of Mountain's room one might without much surprise find it full of the aroma of cigars or furnished in oriental style or—and with excitement Gerald recognized this as the source of the mystery—the plain scene of emotions unenvisaged by the school's curriculum, architecture, sanctions, which the school in sheer ignorance had permitted to be available and enjoyed, as a father leaves abundant cigarettes in a box thinking his son too immature to be interested.

In his own dormitory the usual festive air of Saturday night showed itself in an extra bustle, an increase in conversation. It was forbidden to bring food into the dormitories but it was traditional to smuggle in the Wednesday or Saturday evening purchases of sweets and lately, in Bracher's dormitory, it was fashionable to add, as well, meat pies and packets of crisps to be consumed after lights out.

From under his armpits, beneath his jacket, Matley produced a packet of crisps and, with a flourish, a rather large white paper bag.

'That's a nice big meat pie you've got there, Matley,' said Howarth, equably.

'It's not a meat pie,' said Matley. 'It's a meat and potato pie.'

'Is it, now?' said Howarth. 'Where did you get that from?'

'Wouldn't you like to know?'

Howarth made as if to seize and carry off the unusual pie: Matley tenderly snatched it to his breast. 'That new shop opposite the station,' he said quickly. 'And keep your hands off my pie, Howarth.'

A boy returning from the bathroom, wearing, for some

56

esoteric reason, his towel like a turban, said: 'Percy's coming up the stairs.' Mr Percy was the duty master.

Matley hurriedly thrust his pie and crisps under his bedclothes. 'Look after these while I wash, Bracher,' he said, 'will you?'

'All right,' said Gerald.

'As though anyone wants his horrible pie,' said Howarth. 'That shop opposite the station used to be a pet shop. Still the same owners.'

Mr Percy's stout form appeared in the doorway.

'Matley,' he said indifferently.

'Yes, sir?'

'Get undressed and get to bed.'

'Yes, sir,' Matley said, with bogus enthusiasm.

Gerald tucked in his travelling rug so deeply along the sides of his bed that the mattress was bent into a bow. Then he put his dressing-gown on top of the rug and tucked the sleeves under the mattress. He insinuated himself between the sheets, their iciness delaying his lying down.

'I do believe Matley's going to bed without washing,' said Howarth.

'How can I wash with Percy on my tail?'

'Matley, Matley, you'll be the death of me.' Howarth tested his torch by aiming the beam at Matley as though firing a gun. Then he put the glass end in his mouth so that his cheeks were illuminated from within in a pink, ghastly way. Matley, now in his pyjamas and dressing-gown, knelt by his bed, clasped his hands and closed his eyes. No one took any ostensible notice of this action, which happened every night, but Gerald felt as usual an inward unease which made him attend conscientiously to the folding back of his sheet and search about in his mind for a remark to prevent the conversation from meaningfully lapsing. He had to admit that it was courageous of the otherwise foolish Matley to pray regularly and publicly, whereas he himself prayed merely when life became cruel and then in secret, under the bedclothes or in the lavatory.

Mr Percy returned, saw that everyone but Matley was in bed, said 'Good night', switched out the light and closed the door.

'I must say Percy is very inconsiderate,' Matley complained.

'Shut up, Matley,' a boy said automatically.

As his eyes got used to the dark Gerald saw Matley, faint in the moonlight coming through the uncurtained window, taking off his dressing-gown and climbing into bed. Matley fumbled about in his bedside locker and then said in alarm: 'What rotten beggar's pinched my meat and potato pie? Come on, Howarth, give it up.'

'I haven't got your pie,' said Howarth. 'As a matter of fact I've got a perfectly good pie of my own.'

'Liar. It's my pie.'

Gerald said: 'You put your pie in your bed.'

'Did I?' Matley questioned, but the horror of knowledge was already in his voice. 'Shine your torch over here, Howarth, quickly.'

The beam showed Matley on his knees among his rumpled bedclothes from which he soon produced a paper bag of obscene flatness. 'I sat on it,' said Matley.

'Matley's patent meat and potato pie mattress,' said Howarth, taking a large bite out of his own immaculate pie.

VIII

Before they marched to church on Sunday mornings, the Anglicans were inspected by the Headmaster who himself, with the duty master and the House Prefects, would walk on the pavement by the side of the crocodile. On the Sunday morning after his visit to the fish and chip shop, Gerald was struck afresh by Mr Pemberton's altered appearance for this occasion. The weekday hat, greying under its ceaseless impregnation with chalk, was replaced by a dead black headgear of less clerical cut—redolent, indeed, of diplomacy or high finance. The Headmaster had also put on spats, carried a rolled umbrella and—the most dramatic effect of all—wore glasses with a black ribbon, though on ordinary days he wore glasses only for reading and those quite ribbonless. This morning he had—with the impressive gesture peculiar to such an operation—to keep removing the pince-nez in order to wipe the cold-induced moisture from his eyes.

This was the day of the week and one of the seasons of the year for the boys to wear bowlers. On a few of the older boys the bowlers sat with some naturalism: Mountain, for example, wore his well to the front and it seemed the exotic but logical extension of his pale, ample face. But on most the hats seemed to have been designed only to hide some cranial excrescence, or alternatively came so close to both ears as to make the wearers the simulacra of stage Jews. Yet, Gerald felt, these intrinsically grotesque appendages actually reinforced—like kilts in a Scottish regiment or bandages in a hospital ward—the corporate spirit of those who wore them, and he wished, as the Headmaster moved down the line, that everyone would be found to have well-brushed shoes, clean ears and overcoats free from lint. They were about to represent Seafolde House to the outside world—to represent a mysterious, exclusive community which was not only smart and immaculate but also bound among itself with an ardour symbolized, perhaps, by the uncomfortable, inappropriate and disfiguring bowlers.

It was therefore with annoyance though with not much surprise that Gerald saw Mr Pemberton stop in front of Slade, pull the boy's overcoat collar to a respectable position above the jacket collar and adjust the bowler to a less oblique angle. Once again Gerald observed in Slade that spineless attitude to life which not only destroys its possessor but also shames and embarrasses his fellows.

The church bells began to ring in the distance and Mr Pemberton gave the signal to depart. Gerald's partner in the crocodile was Howarth, who said: 'Want a bet on how many times the Vicar says "in other words" during the sermon?' The wager was agreed. The road, its rurality soon extinguished by the spreading suburb, echoed under the thick-soled Sunday shoes and the sound of the bells came closer.

Once in the pew, Gerald, like all the others, knelt on his hassock and covered his eyes with one cupped hand, conscious as always of the lack of a formula for this opportunity and duty to pray. There was no time to say the Lord's Prayer. He thought of the phrase he used to use at night in his infancy: God bless Mother and Father, make me a good boy, for Jesus Christ's sake, Amen. One was still an infant when one prayed—wanting to be made good, knowing that one's parents were both blessed. As he sat back, Howarth said out of the side of his mouth: 'Big Conk's coming down the aisle.' Gerald injudiciously turned his head and saw the lady with the phenomenally large nose whose appearance each Sunday he and Howarth awaited with intense interest and all at once the familiar hysterical mood of being in church—the desire for solemnity, the fear of Mr Pemberton somewhere behind, the excruciatingly comic aspect of words and faces—descended on him. He tried to expunge from his mind and ears all knowledge of the plangent phrase 'Big Conk', but his body was convulsed by one silent and suppressed giggle. He hoped fervently that some calamity would prevent the Vicar from preaching.

In pews far away on the other side of the church sat the pupils from a nearby girls' school—equally with Big Conk and the Vicar's catch-phrase a fascinating feature of Sunday morning church. It was possible just to distinguish the features of individual girls, to sort the faces into the categories attractive and unattractive and from the former to select the two or three girls whose age and seeming character qualified them as objects of one's desire. No doubt Gerald had on a previous Sunday indicated one such girl to Howarth, for the latter, during the second hymn, asked: 'Where's your girl this morning?' But in the interim Gerald had settled on quite another girl as the most beautiful and sympathetic, for it was the characteristic of these one-sided and unfulfilled yearnings that they were fickle, always—like the manners and habits of a swiftly progressing *nouveau riche*—adjusting themselves to increasingly refined tastes and perceptions so that Gerald had to restrain himself from replying that she was there, at the end of the second pew, not the weakly blonde creature whom no doubt anaemia had prevented from attending today's service, but a slight, sallow, dark girl whom Gerald now saw as most capable of the vague but consuming relationship he demanded.

The sermon was preached not by the Vicar but by a strange clergyman on behalf of a missionary society. The twenty minutes were therefore merely boring. It was possible to read surreptitiously and once Gerald had found a Bible—in these constricted surroundings as exciting a book as an Edgar Rice Burroughs—with the Prayer Book and hymnal opposite his place, but now he was thrown back on the resources of those latter two tedious publications. He read the section called 'The Churching of Women' in the Book of Common Prayer—pages that he felt should be revelatory and exciting but which never got beyond the barbarous. Howarth rolled a mint ball over the foot of red detachable pew upholstery which separated them. Gerald ate it with a ventriloquist's face.

Sweet-eating—by those who had still not exhausted the Saturday evening supply—continued during the interval between the return from church to lunch. Consequently Gerald, at any rate, found the mutton and cabbage facing him like the ingredients of some medieval torture involving a preposterous power of assimilation on the part of the tortured. Perhaps, he thought, the food was not intrinsically disgusting but merely required a mental readjustment for him to find it readily eatable, and he stared at Cropper actually devouring forkfuls of cabbage alone, his canine nose bent low. But when he returned to his own plate the mess took on again its obdurate physical entity and he felt a clamminess on his brow. Between his teeth were particles of the liquorice allsorts he had lately been chewing and the teeth themselves were coated with the fur of the indulgent sweeteater. Next week, he swore, he would not during Sunday morning eat a single sweet.

Meanwhile the meat and vegetable, the dark unnatural grey and green of an amateur painter's cheap palette, confronted him. On one occasion already this term the Headmaster had observed a plate still loaded with much of its burden being passed to the end of the table between courses. Its owner, forced to confess his sin of waste and unconsideration, had been visited with Mr Pemberton's extreme displeasure. Gerald recalled, too, the episode of the stewed figs. And then an audacious idea occurred to him. He took the envelope containing his father's letter from his wallet, extracted the letter and restored it to the wallet. In the nest of his napkin on his knee he opened the throat of the envelope and looked down the room to the masters' table. He could see the Headmaster's great head, inclined a little in its deeper than weekday clerical collar, gravely munching, and even in this tense moment he had time to be impressed with the way Mr Pemberton kept his lips impeccably closed for this operation. Then Gerald slid the two slices of mutton off his plate into the envelope.

Next to him, Matley said: 'What do you think you're doing, Bracher?'

'Shut up, Matley,' he said amiably, stowing the envelope in his jacket pocket, and beginning almost with relish to make a reasonable demolition of his cabbage and potatoes. Next week, he thought, he would bring several envelopes in to lunch.

In the lavatory afterwards, he observed on the disgusting packet his father's handwriting, still recognizable under the grease, and quick tears came to his eyes. It was as though his father were dead and he had disgraced his memory. He was morbidly conscious, too, that in his wallet was a letter from his mother, with an equally stout envelope which he could have used, and he saw that even he, who had sided with his father—who had seen no other moral possibility—could nevertheless slight him, put on him, denigrate him behind his back.

The duty master took the Sunday afternoon walk. By tradition it extended either to the town's little pier or to the lighthouse the other way, though Mr Norfolk had been known to set off into the downs of the hinterland, a novelty at first found stimulating and then, as it prolonged itself beyond the allotted hour, greeted by many with wails of protest and lagging steps. Today the master was Mr Percy, who walked alone behind the long straggle of boys, his stout form boxed in a loud check overcoat, occasionally holding his hat on in the stiff sea breeze with the crook of his ashplant. Usually the House Prefects walked with the master, but Mr Percy's withdrawn personality acted on them like a leper in the Middle Ages. Gerald glanced back at his solitariness, feeling at first a pang of pity and guilt and then a little happy spurt of revenge as he remembered one or two exchanges in which the master had made him feel small. He was walking with Howarth and a boy called Thompson.

'Tell us some more about those servants your people had in Africa,' Thompson said to him.

Gerald picked up a stone and aimed it carefully at the middle of a lifebelt roped to the rail of the esplanade. 'I've told you all about them,' he said off-handedly.

'Don't be such a rotter, Bracher,' said Thompson. 'Out with it.'

'Honestly,' said Gerald.

Thompson stopped while Gerald searched for another pebble, and said that what he didn't understand was how Gerald managed to carry on a normal life with these women moving about the house. Gerald hid a blush with a show of exertion as he bowled a leg break at a seagull folded distantly on a breakwater. Why was he always being tempted to lie so outrageously he asked himself angrily. Carried away by a sense of power and companionship, one night in the dormitory he had under the cover of darkness told Thompson that the servants in his father's house when they had lived in Durban had been young girls, naked above the waist in the fashion of Africa.

The seagull revealed red feet and launched itself into the wind. 'Well, you fool,' Gerald said, 'they were black.'

'Wouldn't have made any difference to me,' said Thompson longingly.

It seemed to Gerald that Howarth had already seen through the ridiculous lie and that his silence was indicative of his contempt, but in a moment he, too, added his fantasy of desire to the conversation.

Gerald's own desire took more concrete and subtle form. The period from the return from the walk until tea time was a null and unsupervised time, with some boys in the House and a few others in the school. Gerald had discovered that a cupboard in a class-room senior to his own housed a collection of books known as the reference library. At this time on Sundays he would stroll nonchalantly but apprehensively into this class-room where he had really no right to be. Today its only occupant was Blakey, whose class-room it was.

'What do you want, Bracher?' asked Blakey, with feeble authority.

'Looking up something in the reference library.'

The most unlikely books sometimes proved to contain what he was seeking and the ardour of his quest seemed to give him a fine instinct not only for the right book but for the vital part of it. So that it was with scarcely any surprise that turning over the pages of a brown Victorian volume of small dull print whose title—*Hypatia*—had vaguely held out its only promise, he found: 'She shook herself free from her tormentors, and springing back, rose for one moment to her full height, naked, snow-white against the dusky mass around—shame and indignation in those wide clear eyes, but not a stain of fear.' His hand holding the book trembled as he read on a little way and then back through the events that led up to that astounding sentence. The silence round him was broken only by Blakey regularly lifting the lid of his desk and fumbling at a paper bag for a sweet. At last Gerald returned the book to the shelf, feeling that Blakey must divine, if he kept it longer, his ulterior and disgraceful purpose. He looked at another book at random, to keep up the fiction of his consultation of the library, and then, with a feeling of relief tinctured almost imperceptibly with regret—the emotion experienced perhaps by one who has returned to safety after an exposure to danger— strolled slowly towards the door.

'How do you manage to have any sweets still left over?' he said to Blakey, and the remark appeared to him as brilliantly resourceful and deceitful as the discovery of a neutral topic of conversation by a visitor to a doomed invalid.

'Because I'm not a hog like you,' replied Blakey with vulgar promptness.

IX

One morning there was some speculation in Gerald's form as to who would take the English period in the sudden absence of their English master with a carbuncle on the neck.

Gerald, lolling in his desk, said: 'They've obviously forgotten us.' He felt a pleasurable aura of anarchy and freedom tinging the dull, regimented weekday.

'Perhaps they'll rope in Miss Pemberton,' said a feeble boarder called Naylor, quite seriously. 'I've heard she's a B.A.'

'I've heard you're a b.f.,' said Howarth.

'She could give us a talk on the facts of life,' said Gerald, essaying a prurience which he realized immediately was of a cowardly feebleness.

'Down in a forest that nobody knows Stands Evie Pemberton without any clothes. Along came——' began Howarth, but his voice died as the Headmaster swept through the door. There was utter silence and Gerald unostentatiously assumed a straight back and an alert air. Mr Pemberton took the chair from behind the master's desk, which in this room stood on a dais, and brought it forward close to the front row of desks. As he sat down he said: 'What is Mr Marsh reading with you, boys?'

'*Modern English Lyrics*, sir,' said one or two voices.

'Take out your books.' The Headmaster crossed his legs. 'Thompson, what is your greatest ambition in life?'

Thompson looked alarmed, but after a moment said: 'To play for the first eleven, sir.' Gerald could not help admiring this foolish answer for he was forced to admit to himself that he could have given no kind of answer at all.

'*My* greatest ambition,' Mr Pemberton said and then tantalizingly paused. 'Can you guess, Bracher?'

'No, sir,' replied Gerald faintly.

'You know, boys,' said the Headmaster, 'the true aim of education is to make good men and women. Not clever men and women or men and women capable of earning a thousand a year or becoming Prime Minister. We all know what is good and what is bad, but we have to learn to choose what is good. You will hear some parents say: "I want my son to become a doctor" or "I want my son to go into the family business". But to train a boy for those things is not the primary concern of school. The primary concern of school is morals. When I see a boy go through the school quite clean in mind and deed, then I know that the school has done its job. To me it is only a secondary consideration that the boy may be brilliant or mediocre in class or on the sports field—though perhaps you wouldn't guess that when you read my comment on a boy's report, would you, Naylor?'

The joke got its laugh. But better than anyone present Gerald appreciated the seriousness of the Headmaster's words. More, he could not help feeling that in some occult way the Headmaster had seen into his mind, observed his most private actions, so that these remarks, almost casual though they were, bore like a code their

68

secret awful meaning for those to whom they were really addressed. At the same time he observed with fascination the details of the Headmaster's appearance, so close to the class, so unselfconscious, as appropriate for its purpose as the terrible mask worn by the leader of a tribal dance. The ears were long, set close to the shining skull with its fringe of abundant well-brushed locks, and hair grew out of them. Hair grew also in two patches high on the cheeks below the pouches under the eyes. And the backs of the hands were hairy, the nails ridged and horny but scrupulously scrubbed. The colour of this hair was not, as Gerald had once crudely imagined, ginger, but of various textures and tones curiously appropriate to the various places from which it grew—so that, for example, black hair mingled with the auburn on the cheeks, the hair of the head gleamed with the dark red lustre of copper, while the hands wore a fleece of an altogether more vivid and animal hue.

'I have felt that the school lacks a symbol,' Mr Pemberton was saying. 'What is a symbol, Snape?'

'A symbol, sir?' said Stink-Bomb Billy.

'Look it up, look it up in your dictionary. You boys must acquire the dictionary habit. The dictionary should always be by your side, whether you are doing English or History or Zulu. Well, boy, have you found it?'

'Yes, sir,' said Snape. ' "The sign or representation of any moral thing by the images or properties of natural things; an emblem or representation . . ." '

'That's enough,' said Mr Pemberton. Snape's reading was execrable. ' "The representation of any moral thing." ' The Headmaster seemed pleased with this phrase. 'My greatest ambition,' he went on solemnly, 'is to build a chapel for the school. We would assemble there in the mornings for prayers. The boarders—and any day boys and their parents who might wish to come —would attend service there on Sundays. There would be many occasions for special services—I can think of Speech Day and Ascension Day, and there must be many more, boys. The chapel would be built at the end of the class-room block, next to my garden. It would not be an ostentatious edifice. It would be quite small and plain. But it would be a symbol—a representation of a moral thing. Do you understand, Snape?' Snape said that he did. 'Have you any idea of the cost of such a place, boys?' continued Mr Pemberton. 'Of course you haven't. It is formidable. And yet the building of a school chapel is my greatest ambition, and we don't have ambitions unless there is some chance of our being capable of realizing them some day. Do we, Thompson?'

Thompson laughed with special emphasis to indicate that he understood the Headmaster's reference.

'*Modern English Lyrics*,' said Mr Pemberton, picking up a copy of the volume from the desk nearest to him. 'What is a lyric, Snape? Don't look at the dictionary, boy; you've been doing this book all year and if you don't know what its title means you've been wasting your time. Andrew?'

'I know, sir,' said Andrew, a plausible boy, 'but I just don't seem to be able to put it in words.'

'Hasn't Mr Marsh discussed the word with you?'

'No, sir,' said Andrew eagerly.

'I see,' said the Headmaster. What a remarkable faculty it was in Mr Pemberton, Gerald thought, to make one see with fresh eyes a thing about which one thought one had long since known everything! In two words the hitherto competent and unassailable Marshie stood revealed as inadequate and unthorough, unaware, it seemed, of the fundamentals of teaching English literature. And this from an amateur in the field, for Mr Pemberton's subject was classics. 'Then let us hear what the dictionary says, Snape.'

' "Pertaining to the lyre," sir.'

'Is that all it says, boy?'

'No, sir.'

'Well, read on, read on.'

' "Fit to be sung to the lyre; appropriate for singing. Lyric poetry . . ." '

'Ah,' murmured the Headmaster.

' "That kind of poetry in which the poet sympathetically sings of his own thoughts and emotions." '

'Good,' said Mr Pemberton. 'Now, Howarth, tell us what page we are on and start reading.'

'Page twenty-two, sir,' said Howarth. ' "I shall never love the snow again since Maurice died . . ." '

'Stop, boy.' The furrows grew between Mr Pemberton's eyebrows. 'The poet *sympathetically* sings. I don't find death a sympathetic subject. Death is a terrible subject. Let's hear no more of that poem, Howarth.' The Headmaster's voice had taken on a deep but tremulous tone. 'Turn over the page.'

Gerald, much affected by this speech, tried to imagine why death was a terrible subject, though he could see that it was scarcely suitable for lyric poetry. The life of the Headmaster that had brought him to the bald cranium, the coarse nails, the strong and slightly frightening emotions about morals and death, remained mysterious, unthinkable.

71

X

One morning, as the dormitory was dressing, the electric light was switched out. Everyone looked towards the door. Mr Pemberton stood there, fully clothed, neat, awful. 'There is no need for the light, boys,' he said, and disappeared. Sure enough, the dormitory was no darker than before: the lengthening days had arrived unknown to all except the Headmaster.

To Gerald the school had now become an utterly familiar place: its procedures and taboos were part of the habits of his life and anything out of the already unfolded routine was a matter on which he could ask for advice or enlightenment without embarrassment or the sense of being conspicuous—no more than it is remarked of a hardened criminal that he sometimes finds a little strange the different ways of a prison in which he has never before been incarcerated. And parallel with his discovery of the school's character was the school's discovery of his character, for it seemed almost as though during this first term a Gerald had been brought into being who previously had not existed, as a young girl who is given the trappings of womanhood—a husband, a kitchen, a shopping basket—immediately evolves an appropriate and quite different character. Just as when he had run in the company of his equals, to get back to school at the required time on Saturday evenings, for instance, he had found himself able easily to outdistance and outstay them, so his mind and tongue seemed to have greater penetration and sharpness than theirs—without his conscious volition, strange native qualities, like his height and colouring.

But though he had the power to make himself *persona grata* with such as Mountain, to put himself on the wrong side of Cropper, to be always with the extrovert and popular Howarth, it was recognized—he recognized himself—that he was virtuous. He worked, and he avoided the very last twist of conduct or speech that would bring him hard up against authority. To be virtuous was the only condition that could give him pleasure—to feel himself working with the machine of school, capable of being praised by its managers, conforming broadly with their desires—though he vaguely realized that by a curious paradox those conditions required from him the kind of distinction from the ruck that in a way could be achieved only by a measure of non-conformity.

And as the ways of school had gradually become a part of his essential being, so by a series of small encounters and rumours he had come to know more intimately and immediately than anyone else in his life the school's leading characters, whose attributes had thereby, without losing any distinction, become more logical and comprehensible. Mr Norfolk sometimes wore suede shoes; Mr Chaplin was contemplating emigration to New Zealand; Matley, despite his thinness, had white rudimentary breasts; Cropper's great friend Dyer wore a truss; Blakey was circumcised; Hamilton, the school handy-man, had lost two fingers in the War. Nevertheless not everyone in this space of time had shed their ambiguity: Miss Pemberton especially, still aroused in Gerald the conflicting feelings with which we regard one who we are not sure likes us.

Miss Pemberton dressed a boil with an impersonal but tender sympathy which sent the sensitive sufferer away with his opinion of her moderately exalted: she administered a rebuke—for a failure to put out one's laundry, say—with a disconcertingly sarcastic disinterest, as though one's affairs had the trivial crudity and disorder of those of a lower animal. She was not dowdy but her appearance often indicated a disregard of what could be properly regarded as becoming—as witness her practice of wearing coloured woollen stockings. And though she was surely not more than ten years older than oneself, she assumed without effort an air of maturity and wisdom that made one feel excessively masculine, as though masculinity was merely gaucheness. So that going into her room, for example, with whatever previously assumed air of contempt or *savoir faire*, one would usually find her capable of surprising one with a new facet of her personality—a pair of horn-rimmed reading glasses, say—that for some indefinable reason put one at a disadvantage.

Needless to say, though Gerald naturally came to know more about Mr Pemberton, the latter never took on any attributes that could be properly regarded as human, that could make him approachable or even less to be feared. Some of the older boys remembered when the Headmaster's wife was still alive, but to Gerald that was an unimaginable epoch, as impossible to conceive as living under a king other than George V or with a nationality other than British. Mr Pemberton's isolation and exemption from the weaknesses inseparable from personal relationships seemed axiomatic. Traits that in other men would be almost ludicrous were transformed by the force of Mr Pemberton's character into awesome, memorable, brilliantly original things. There was an unforgettable lesson during which he had demonstrated the polka and, with a divine change of mood, thrown a blackboard

cleaner at Naylor's head. Once he had sent over to the
House for a sheet to show how the Romans wore the
toga. Sometimes he conducted his Latin lessons entirely
in that tongue, giving the crudest names of boys the
dignity of sonorous suffixes. It was rarely that morning
prayers were not made extraordinary by his anger or
geniality, enlivened by some anecdote or precept or scrap
of knowledge poured from his abundant and uninhibited
mind, so that whatever disastrous consequence they
might engender one looked forward to them, as one looks
forward in the appropriate season to spectacularly bad
weather. He was obsessed with some topics, of which
posture was one. 'Sit up, boys, sit up,' he might cry, even
in the middle of his reading of the Lesson. 'Get your
posteriors as far into the backs of your desks as you can.
Sit up, sit *up*!' And though some farthest away from his
eye might exchange meaning glances, no one remained
unconvinced that Mr Pemberton was in the highest
degree correct and effective. Nor did it seem inappropriate that a clergyman should break off at this point to
call attention to what might superficially seem a less
serious matter, for the Headmaster's religion appeared
dominated not by some remote God and vague principles
but by the person and ethos of the Headmaster himself, as the emissary of an empire comes to act in a
remote province as though his power were without
derivation.

Once a week, after prayers, Mr Pemberton surveyed
the fruits of the school's premier system of rewards and
punishments. Every master had two books, both containing yellow paper, but one printed in white, the other
in black. The white-printed slips were popularly known
as 'whites', and were given for good work and conduct;

the others were 'blacks'. A black not only cancelled a white in the competition, rewarded in each form at Speech Day by a prize, but also qualified its possessor for a beating. The Headmaster alone had power to administer the cane, and no doubt this privilege contributed to the air of awe and dedication in which he was bathed—as the hangman, though perhaps in private a kindly and genial man, must through his unique and terrible function be to others a constant symbol of dread.

The distribution of whites, since they could be awarded for distinction in sport and conduct as well as in school work, was widespread, but for the most part the recipients of blacks formed, like every criminal class, a small, chronic section of the community. Gerald accepted whole-heartedly the ardours and pleasures of this system: more, he saw himself, immediately, as a competitor for its prizes. It became a serious part of his life that he should try to gain whites and be proud of his gains: it followed that to receive a black was unthinkable.

Nevertheless, the terrible moment arrived when he was forced, like a common criminal, to take from a master one of the fatal black-printed slips. His offence arose from the very quality that demanded he should collect only whites. During one of Mr Chaplin's periods he questioned aloud that master's accuracy of knowledge on some point of his dissertation, feeling as he did so not only a sense of personal virtue and distinction but also a conviction that he was helping the common good of the form. Mr Chaplin had taken the interruption ill, as well as denying Gerald's superior information, and a brief argument developed. As Gerald sat down, he muttered 'Ignoramus' in a voice that conviction and indignation made injudiciously loud. Mr. Chaplin had not failed to hear the word and had immediately taken out his black book.

The black-printed slip reposed in Gerald's wallet as a contraceptive might in that of a priest. Divorced from its circumstances, Mr Chaplin's abstract of his offence was to the highest degree alarming and disgraceful. Beneath Gerald's name as payee, as it were, the black characterized its occasion, in the appropriate space, as 'Gross impertinence'. At first, like one who has been told of a fatal medical diagnosis, he could scarcely realize that he was in truth the owner of this alien disaster, but as the weekly whites and blacks morning approached the full horror of his predicament grew upon him through countless enactments in his mind of the public revelation, the Headmaster's displeasure and the barbarous punishment. However, even up to the morning of waking to the day of the prospective dénouement he saw a possibility that he might even yet be spared the bitter cup: he imagined sometimes that Mr Chaplin, too, passed the affair constantly under review and that when the giving of the black had caused sufficient torture the master would cancel it, knowing that the final steps of the procedure were supererogatory in the case of a sensitive and intelligent boy who hitherto had borne an unblemished record.

This hope vanished at assembly when he saw Mr Chaplin sitting in front of the school in his place among the other masters, his pale face unagitated, his great brow shining with the morning's ablutions, a formidable pile of marked exercise books on the desk before him ready to take into his form. The familiar procedure assumed a nightmarish inexorability: the hymn, the prayer, the Headmaster's announcements. By Gerald's side Howarth fooled surreptitiously about, a being from another, and less responsible, order of existence. Out of his agony Gerald whispered at last: 'I've got to take a black up this morning.' It was inconceivable that Howarth had forgotten it.

'Lucky man,' said Howarth. 'Who was it from?'

'Charlie.'

'Well, ask him to take it back.'

After a moment Gerald saw that Howarth was quite serious and new and terrible emotions were immediately added to those he was racked with. He looked again at Mr Chaplin, who was patently busy with the superior thoughts of his own life, and knew that he dare not presume to make the approach.

The business of handing in the whites and blacks began, form by form, starting with the lowest. For Gerald the bustle went on like the noises heard in a fainting fit. Suddenly, before his form was reached, he found himself walking along the aisle of desks, like a robot. He went very close to Mr Chaplin and said in a low voice, his face hot with shame: 'Will you take back the black, please, sir?'

Immediately he divined from Mr Chaplin's expression that the master, far from being lost in a private world, appreciated every nuance of the position, and the discovery struck him as so touching that he felt the tears burn behind his eyelids. Mr Chaplin said simply: 'Yes, Bracher.'

'Thank you, sir.' As he turned to go he saw that behind the barricade of exercise books was Mr Chaplin's open black book and that a pearly finger marked a place among the counterfoils: Mr Chaplin was checking that all to whom he had given blacks since the last collection were surrendering them today. This, too, seemed to Gerald touching, that the power of so important a figure as the Second Master had in the end to rely on a primitive action that the stupidest of boys could have carried out. In this moment of happiness he swore to justify Mr Chaplin's faith in him.

XI

One Saturday night towards the end of term Gerald went into a stationer's shop with Howarth so that the latter might buy a bottle of purple ink which some quirk of aesthetic fancy demanded he should henceforth use in his fountain pen. At the back of the shop, in an alcove labelled 'Library', were some shelves of brightly-jacketed novels.

'That's the sort of library the boarders need,' Gerald remarked, dazzled by the promise of so much readable literature.

'Why don't you take a book out?' asked Howarth, with his enviable mastery of the mechanics of life.

'They wouldn't lend *me* one.'

'I'll ask them,' said Howarth.

It proved a simple and inexpensive matter. But in the face of such abundance the choice was not simple. Should one stick to an author one knew and take out, say, a new Edgar Wallace, or go for something adventurous—an author, for instance, that one had seen Mountain reading, E. Phillips Oppenheim?

'Buck up, Bracher,' said Howarth, who had already filled his pen with the new ink and was eager to get to the fish and chip shop.

Gerald quickly changed his mind twice and at last tore himself away from the shelves. By Sunday evening he had finished the book and it then occurred to him—the simple but profound discovery that changes the whole climate of thought—that he need not wait until Wednesday before borrowing another book but might slip into the town on Monday, during the convenient interim between the end of afternoon school and tea. That this action was illegal (the town was out of bounds to boarders except on Wednesday and Saturday evenings) struck him with little force for his imagination was almost wholly occupied with the purpose of his visit—as one of extreme covetousness fails really to conceive that the laws against fraud can apply to his cherished designs.

With the book in his overcoat pocket, he went down the drive among some knots of day boys. Most walked to the bus terminus but he took the sea road and had soon outdistanced the others who were going the same way, occupied as they were with cap snatching and stone throwing. He was struck by an aspect of the place that had never been presented to him before—its peculiar day-time face, a sense of life going on outside the insulated world of school—and he felt a stir of excitement, as though he were on his way to some long-anticipated entertainment. It might be that he would see coming towards him the girl from the girls' school, her face thin and mysterious under the black hat with its green cockade, and that she would be, not a stranger, but someone who had the right, the wish, to stop him and talk to him, having understood from the distant Sunday encounters exactly what he was like, as he had come to understand what she was like. Being alone, in fact, allowed him to assume a vast speculative identity quite ungoverned by the normal laws of existence, like some particle escaped from a self-contained system.

All went as he had planned it: among ladies carrying shopping baskets he changed his book, and he was on the road back to school with more than half his time unexpired. He saw that this expedition could be repeated, even that he was in some ill-defined way exempted by virtue of his identity from the restrictive rules that governed the rest of the boarders, as a man believes himself exempted from death. His breaking bounds struck him not only as innocent but even as praiseworthy—the ignoring of a No Bathing notice when one is rescuing the drowning.

It was therefore without the fullest sense of alarm that, as he was hanging up his overcoat, he received from Goff, one of the House Prefects, the intimation that the Headmaster wanted to see him. As a man with a suspected grave disease half imagines that a fresh attack of pain is the result of some common, fortuitous cause, like eating plums or catching cold, so Gerald was unwilling to believe that his expedition to the town had any connection with Mr Pemberton's summons. Even at the moment of knocking on the door his mind was still vainly searching for advantageous reasons for his presence there.

'Come in, boy,' said Mr Pemberton and at once a terrible dread filled Gerald's stomach. That the occasion was not one for surnames, let alone Christian names, meant the end of illusion.

Gerald stood in front of the desk. The light outside was failing but the Headmaster had not yet switched on his desk light. The time of day, the objects in the room, the moment in Gerald's life, all seemed to exude a chill cruelty, a future without happiness.

'Have you anything to tell me?' asked Mr Pemberton.

'I don't think so, sir.' It was not bravado or deceit but a desperate hanging on to the remnants of normal existence, the mattress borne away before the invading barbarians.

The Headmaster came simply to the point. 'Then it wasn't you who was seen half an hour ago in the town?'

For a moment the possibility of delaying longer the assumption of disgrace hovered in his mind—the moment when alone in a room one holds in one's hand a shattered ornament—and then he said: 'Yes, sir, it was.'

'Then why prevaricate, boy?'

'I only went to change a book, sir.'

'To change a book?'

Gerald, in awkward sentences, tried to dissipate the Headmaster's bafflement, but the more he said the more conscious he became of the preposterousness of his conduct.

'Have you read all your English set books, then, and the books in the Library?'

Gerald thought of *Quentin Durward* and *The Last of the Mohicans* and realized the utter futility of E. Phillips Oppenheim. But the Headmaster's thoughts had already taken another turn.

'I wonder,' he said, 'if you realize anything of the responsibility of looking after the Boarding House— sixty boys who have been entrusted to me in confidence by their parents. Those boys, even the senior boys, cannot be allowed to wander into the town at all hours so that nobody knows where they are. There is an adequate time twice a week for shopping. I am disappointed in you, Bracher, that you hadn't the thoughtfulness to understand this.'

Mr Pemberton's last sentence was spoken in a warmer tone: Gerald's heart leapt at the possibility that he was to be forgiven. 'I'm sorry, sir,' he said, and almost without the necessity of exaggeration the words came out vibrant with emotion.

'Bend over,' said the Headmaster.

In the moment before he complied he realized that the Headmaster had moved to the corner of the room where a cane stood against the wall—the cane which Gerald could not have failed to observe during this and his previous visits to the study but which, no doubt through some lack of psychic apprehension, as a child fails to register the fact of death, he could not remember seeing before. The command itself he received with fearful surprise, yet he complied with it promptly and familiarly, as a reader of historical romances might in real life respond to an order to 'stand and deliver'.

The Headmaster's hand lifted up the tail of Gerald's jacket and two swift strokes descended. The noise was far greater than Gerald could have imagined but it seemed to him that there was no pain at all. In a moment he had straightened up and the Headmaster was leaning the cane back in the corner and saying: 'You may go now, boy.' The whole operation, violent and radical as it was, had been compressed, like the extraction of a tooth, into a phenomenally and almost disappointingly short space of time.

But when he had fumbled through the curtain hanging in front of the door itself, he realized that he *was* hurt, and his throat and nose became liquid with emotion as

83

he thought how inadequately he had measured up to the Headmaster's estimate of him. Would Mr Pemberton ever understand the sincerity of his repentance, his resolve never again to offend against the school's morality? Remorse ate into his heart, the unfulfillable wish to return to the study to confess again, to explain, to promise. Though he could not help but be glad that his offence had been discovered, since otherwise he would never have known its heinousness, his gross punishment, like a girl's loss of virginity, seemed something that could be atoned for only by a life henceforth of extraordinary saintliness.

And later still, when the dormitory was quiet, going over the whole incident again and again as one probes, reckless of the pain, the sore places of one's body, he understood that even the excuse he had originally given himself for breaking bounds was tainted, for he now saw that his inordinate desire for books could not be separated from his desire for what he might find in them—the sometimes unrecognized but always present wish to turn page after innocent page and find at last the girl with her clothes torn savagely from her. Could he doubt that this was what the Headmaster's wisdom was trying to save him from?

XII

The charts which many boys had constructed during the dying weeks of term to show how many days—or even hours—there were before the holidays had, all at once it seemed, become black with ink. On the evening of the day when the day boys had gone for the last time, tea was taken at an unusually late hour and from the tables, unusually bright with bowls of jelly and plates of little cakes, rose the aromatic steam from sixty odd plates of sausages and mash. And at the Masters' table, instead of the solitary figure of the duty master as was normal at tea-time, were all the resident masters, rather crowded by the addition of Miss Pemberton and the assistant matron, Mrs Watt.

It seemed to Gerald that in this custom of a lavish and sociable last tea of term the school showed a noble and generous spirit. Since his beating he had felt a constraint in all the actions which the routine of school required him to carry out—the feeling with which a man walks down a street where once a chimney pot fell on his head. But now, seeing the Headmaster actually eating a piece of sausage and then speaking to Charlie with a twinkling smile, he knew that no one present could fail to be accepted as a member of the community of school, all his past faults forgiven, his intellectual and sporting attainments irrelevant.

'I don't see any chocolate biscuits,' said Snape major. 'We had them last year.'

'It's the economic blizzard,' said Howarth. 'Look at that sausage of Matley's.'

One of Matley's sausages was, indeed, of a curious foreshortened deformity

'Bad luck, Matley,' said Snape.

'I don't mind,' said Matley. 'I'm not very hungry.'

'It's well known,' said Gerald, 'the smaller the sausage the better Matley likes it.' He glanced across at Cropper and then higher up the table at Mountain. He longed for a chance to deride the former and amuse the latter, as though by establishing their characters and roles he was thereby more firmly establishing his own. For it was just as important for him to dig his roots in among the boys as display his fruits to Mr Pemberton and the masters. Life was a continual struggle to achieve security from terrible moments of insecurity.

The room got noisier and noisier, as though the boys were drinking not eating. But no word of reproach came from the Headmaster, nor did his smile grow less. The lights were switched on early: round the walls the photographs sprang to life of long-departed boys holding between their knees footballs painted with dates already historical, or posing in wrinkled tights and biblical beards, like so many apparitions, against various recognizable and solid parts of the dais end of the assembly hall. The tempo of eating on this day of abundant food had slowed down so that the meal appeared to be lasting an excitingly long time: it even seemed as though there would be some food of the coarser sort left on the table, though Gerald deemed it his duty, as a man will dance with plain girls, to eat a good deal of bread and butter with his jelly and choose from the plate of cakes one of the slices of madeira cake with which it was punctuated —the madeira cake which was familiar and despised from innumerable ordinary teas.

At last only one or two of the grosser appetites were still unsatisfied and the Headmaster rose against the dark green wall, brilliantly lit by one of the white-shaded lamps, not (Gerald realized with pleasurable surprise) to say grace but to make a little speech about the term's work, the imminent holidays and the work of Miss Pemberton and Mrs Watt in providing the handsome spread which they had just enjoyed. He sat down, still without saying grace, and immediately, Birnie, the senior House Pre-

86

fect, got up and called: 'Three cheers for Mr Pemberton. Hip, Hip——'

The hooray crashed out and Gerald felt an excited burning in his cheeks as though it were himself they were cheering. Without embarrassment, proprietorially proud, he gazed unwaveringly at the Headmaster as he responded with all the power of his lungs to Birnie's lead. In his turn, Mr Pemberton looked back at the boys, with no false modesty, a smile illuminating but not softening his powerful features, his great head gravely inclined, so that the bald cranium seemed to catch all the light in the room and send it back like the dazzling crown of some glorious monarch.

TWO

I

IT WAS still only twilight as they moved across the playground to supper in the House and through the rather warm air a yellow star fluttered on the hazed indigo sky.

'They say Snape minor was sick in the train,' said Howarth.

But Gerald could evince no interest. In the few hours since he had been back at school the excitement of the start of a new term had evaporated and he was left with a residue of sadness and depression. It had been almost miraculous to see again all the faces he had completely forgotten, and in the first minutes of establishing their familiarity they seemed to promise infinite sympathy and entertainment. And then, as one quickly recognizes the features of an indifferent repertory actor under the week's new wig, Gerald saw their real shallow and immature selves. Back into his mind came the thoughts of the holiday: the solitary walks, Communion on Easter Sunday, the rooms in which he and his father lived—rooms which before he had started school last term he had imagined were a mere expedient but which he now realized were their permanent way of life, those or rooms like them. It was as though his first term at Seafolde House had, like the period of a war, marked decisively, irrevocably, by its intervention two wholly different modes of existence—the first an age of promise, the second of decline. For now it was plain that there could be little hope that his father and mother would ever be together again: indeed, his father had long since ceased to speak of any subject that could even remotely have a bearing on the life that had ended when they had left South Africa.

A reprehensibly late trunk stood on its end outside the House door. Gerald turned its label to the light that streamed from the vestibule. 'J. P. S. Slade,' he read, disgustedly. At the same time, the three initials struck in him an envious and mysterious chord.

'There can't possibly be any dripping the first night of term,' said Howarth reflectively.

Gerald caught his first glimpse of Cropper and in that fresh vision saw that in fact he facially resembled one of the Alsatians which Mountain's satire had made appear so ludicrous a feature of the Cropper family life. On his part Cropper disguised his observation of Gerald and went on making some elaborate investigation into his attaché case and this minute dissembling seemed to Gerald frighteningly sinister, like the action of some perfect stranger who as one is drinking in a café late at night takes pains to hide from one the fact that he is carrying a pair of knuckle-dusters. His sense deepened that life could promise no pleasure.

'Homesick, Bracher, me old cock sparrer?' Howarth suddenly asked.

'Don't be bloody silly, Howarth,' he replied, concentrating with furious embarrassment on the business of changing into his house shoes. But he thought to himself: so this is what homesickness is.

Though how could he be homesick for those three rooms filled with someone else's furniture and the cross-eyed maid bringing in food that was really little better than the food at school? He imagined his father alone, sitting in the chair that seemed upholstered in carpet, gazing at the unplayed, the unplayable, gramophone, the polished shell-cases from the War on either side of the fire-place; and his heart yearned with pity. How could his mother have condemned them to this life?

II

But the following day Gerald discovered to his astonishment that he had been moved to the next higher form and all at once his existence was given purpose and excitement. Since it was not, of course, the end of the school year, his move was unique. As he gathered his things together with as modest a demeanour as he could muster, Mr Marsh said with heavy sarcasm, straddling the master's desk to the peril of his fly buttons in the manner a term with him had made so familiar: 'Well, good-bye, Bracher. It was very amiable of you to give us simpletons the benefit of your great brain so long. No doubt you'll find your intellectual level with Mr. Percy. And, of course, we all know you'll have a much pleasanter and easier time.'

Everyone laughed: from these lower slopes Mr Percy's form had always seemed a summit of impossible rarefaction and ardours. Gerald went with circumspection to the next class-room and found Mr Percy's bulk tucked neatly behind the master's desk and an atmosphere which showed that work this term had already begun. He was given a place just behind Matley, whose welcoming grin was tempered with the dignity of one who had long been initiated into the mysteries of Mr Percy's dispensation.

Gerald soon found out why Mr Percy was condemned on Sunday walks to walk alone. He was a man of cold temperament whose lessons were designed for the quick-witted and revealed nothing of his private life and thoughts on other subjects. He dispensed justice with uninterested impartiality, conferred no favours, and his periods were remarkable for absence of indiscipline. He accepted Gerald's arrival with the least possible fuss.

As Gerald accumulated his new form's textbooks in his desk and on the shelf by it, he was seized with a vague but intense excitement, as though within his grasp was some key to happy existence, and he perceived that even in the most unlikely places there resided a mysterious fascination. He saw, for example, that the last chapter of the algebra was on the Binomial Theorem, and the words struck him like the half-familiar words 'Gobi Desert' might strike a traveller who against all expectations is in fact about to start off on an expedition to Central Asia. One of the English books was *Twelfth Night* and in the pencil-scored pages of his copy he came with surprise on the phrase 'Excellent good, i' faith' which all last term he had heard used as a catch-word by more senior boys, and observed its precise spelling, punctuation and meaning (which had been obscured from him by its hitherto wholly oral tradition) with the ineffable pleasure of one who discovers the original setting of what has been corrupted to the song *Land of Hope and Glory*. In spite of the fears that had beset him as he made the change, he soon found that the work of the new form was not beyond his powers, and quite quickly he could look back on last term as the owner of an electric train remembers his clockwork mouse.

Although Mr Percy seemed incapable either of showing his own goodwill or receiving pleasure from the conduct of others, Gerald was at first constantly impelled to try to win his notice, even affection, not by behaving in his own proper person but by assuming the character which he divined the master would find most engaging. So it was on an occasion when Mr Percy was suggesting to the form that for extra-curricular study they should each order a volume in Harrap's Bilingual Series—pamphlets which contained a short work of fiction, the English on one page, the foreign version on the opposite page. The titles with the French text were what they were considering, and someone lit on a story by W. W. Jacobs.

Gerald had seen works by this author, in cheap modern bindings, in the Boarders' Library. 'Wouldn't the one by Joseph Conrad be better, sir—help our English at the same time?' he called out, conscious of Conrad's already classical status but without ever having read a word of him.

'Conrad was a foreigner,' said Mr Percy. 'I don't know why you should expect him to be able to write better English than W. W. Jacobs.'

Gerald, to whom this process of discussing and choosing new and unusual textbooks had been giving intense present and anticipatory pleasure, blushed scarlet at the indifferently administered rebuff and as he bent his head over his desk his mind formed over and over again the muttered words: 'You rotten sod.'

Even when he thought about the incident afterwards, Gerald could never, though shame at being pilloried made him curl his toes in impotent anguish, see any virtue in Mr Percy's view and he regarded his championship of Jacobs against Conrad as evidence of insensitivity, a second-class mind, and put it with the other evidence he had accumulated towards confirming that his own attitude to the master should be the conventional one—to ignore him whenever possible. Gerald wondered whether this isolation hurt Mr Percy but the speculation caused him only momentary concern, for the master's existence, like that of the insect kingdom, was really too remote for its sufferings to be of real importance.

But Gerald's nominally closer relationship this term with Mr Percy led him to greater cognizance of one of the master's habits which previously had been without significance. When the evening preparation period was over Mr Percy would often come over to the school block and play on the assembly hall piano. The distant reverberations had during the previous term impinged on Gerald's hearing with no more meaning than the regularities of a public clock, nor, indeed, could he have said that he had been conscious that Mr Percy was the author of them. But now, as he put his books away or chatted before going over to the House for supper, he began to appreciate the skill behind the arpeggios, the devotion represented by the long unwitnessed performance in the big, empty room, and even at last to recognize some of nightly or weekly recurring sequences of notes. So that what at first he would have characterized, had he thought about it, as classical music (a conception as irrelevant as the existence of the Americas to the European Middle Ages) became something as intimate and defined as a thought, sometimes appearing in his mind and struggling to his lips as soon as he woke in the morning and bringing with it the whole

94

atmosphere of evening—the boarders gradually deserting the school for the House, the dying light, one's eyes rather weary, one's fingers inkstained, from preparation, and the sound of the piano even from a distance betraying by its hollow tone the size and emptiness of the assembly hall.

It was without any motive of currying favour with Mr Percy or displaying his own intelligence by showing his interest in music (for by this time he had been forced to acknowledge that the master was like some far-advanced paranoic, beyond the influence of human motives) but simply because he was haunted and teased by the melodies he had imperfectly heard, that one night he gently opened one of the assembly hall's double doors and stood listening for a while with the new sense of tonal values a bather has who by some slight movement frees the channels of his ears from the water which he had not realized had been so muffling to his faculty of hearing. Another night he had plucked up courage actually to enter the room and close the door behind him, feigning an interest in, a legitimate business with, the series of prints of ethnological types which were hung along one wall. So it was that while the piano played one of the sequences which had touched his imagination he stared with embarrassment at the Blakey-like features of an Australian aboriginal, even trying to summon up the country of the creature's origin, its rainfall, crops and history, in an effort to justify his presence and to prepare his mind in case Mr Percy could, by some occult process, read it.

But if the master was conscious of Gerald's presence he did not betray it: the head remained on its thick neck orientated towards the music, the stream of notes continued to emerge. The immobility, like that of a cat for a bird, was both daunting and encouraging.

Thus, like the exploration of a continent, by stages which in retrospect are almost imperceptible though requiring for their execution enormous feats of courage, Gerald found himself one night sitting almost out of sight on one of the assembly hall benches at once excited and made embarrassed by this unequivocal acknowledgement of his relationship to the music—which was possessed at these close quarters by hitherto unsuspected human flaws and ardours that, like the similar discoveries one must make in becoming gradually intimate with a beautiful girl, only made it the more fascinating. And as though forced against his will to recognize that his performance was no longer solely for his own pleasure, Mr Percy at length took his hands from the keyboard, turned round on the bentwood chair and fixed Gerald with an ambiguous look.

It was Gerald who found himself obliged, able, to speak. 'Will you play the piece you played last week, sir?'

'What piece?' asked Mr Percy.

With dry lips Gerald whistled a few of the notes that haunted him.

'Oh, the Schubert Impromptu,' said Mr Percy. 'I've played that too much.'

All the same, he started to play it, and Gerald, since the performance was for him, felt obliged to move from his seat and hover somewhat nearer the piano. Not long before, Mr Percy had lit a cigarette and now he kept it in his mouth as he played, breathing the smoke away in time with his exertions. As the paper was consumed the ash remained in a drooping, corrugated tail, but crumbs of it fell nevertheless on Mr Percy's suit. This, and the music scattered over the piano top—some of it bearing the unfamiliar combination 'Edward Percy' in the owner's familiar hand—created for Gerald an atmosphere equally constrained and libertarian.

The Schubert Impromptu was not over when Gerald, hearing the door open behind him, turned and saw the Headmaster, who, since he was wearing his hat, had probably just come over to the school block from his house. The ill-defined alarm which immediately burst in Gerald's breast was stilled the moment after by the knowledge that the presence of Mr Percy not only guarded against the risk that he might be doing wrong but also ensured that he would not have to bear the brunt of the Headmaster's conversation.

But the alarm rose again when in fact he heard his name spoken, and sensed that the music had stopped. 'Yes, sir,' he said, braced, like a man at the first entry of a dentist's probe, for any shock or eventuality.

'Come with me, Bracher,' said Mr Pemberton. 'I want you to carry some books over to my study.'

Gerald's eager air was, if possible, intensified at the realization that the Headmaster had been seeking a beast of burden and had only fortuitously lighted on him. He stepped towards the door but was far from reaching it when he heard Mr Pemberton say: 'Mr Percy, I will not have my masters smoking in front of the boys.'

No reply came from Mr Percy, and a few seconds later Gerald was hurrying after the Headmaster, the incredible words echoing in his head. He could take no pleasure in the indubitable justice of the Headmaster's reproof (a reproof, moreover, applied to a person for whom he had no affection nor owed any gratitude) for

the guilt of the patient must in Mr Pemberton's eyes—
indeed, in verity—almost equal that of the agent: and
his presence with that obscene phallus, those smuts of
ash, was wholly voluntary.

But what was even more disturbing was the sense
that the Headmaster's condemnation extended beyond
the illicit communion of smoking to the real reason for
the presence together of master and boy, to what in
that light seemed shameful, enervating, unhealthy—
the music.

III

On the notice board appeared several elaborately-ruled
sheets, prepared by Mr Norfolk, inviting entries for the
Annual Sports Day, to be held in mid-term. All those
who showed any athletic promise began to be rounded
up by Birnie for half an hour's pre-breakfast training.
At that hour, the wind from the sea was still cold: jogging
round the playing field one's unwashed sleep-puffed
face and tousled hair seemed to be petrifying into some
uncomfortable gargoyle shape. But later, splashing
about righteously in the dormitory basins while less
athletic figures slowly roused themselves from sleep, one
seemed possessed with a vast potentiality for achievement and enjoyment, and even the knowledge that it was
herring morning could not take away one's keen anticipation of breakfast.

At the other end of the day the warmth and prolonged
twilight acted in the dormitories like caffeine. Gerald
acquired the habit, once the duty master had closed the
door, of taking his pillow to the salt-whitened window

and lying with his book held to the light so that he could read until the last possible moment. In the mild atmosphere Matley's religion flourished. He had come back this term with a new dressing-gown, long, hairy, dark brown, and fastened with a rather rope-like cord. Attired thus he evidently imagined—and quite rightly— that he had a monkish air, an effect contributed to by his walking about in bare feet and parting his hair nearer the middle so that it could hang over his temples in two locks. In this guise he now said his prayers, and disconcertingly for Gerald the action no longer represented courage and piety but a contribution to the evidence of Matley's general folly. On Sunday night Matley brought up to the dormitory a Bible and a prayer book and, quickly changing into the ecclesiastical dressing-gown, he reverently placed them on his bed and later, kneeling down, read several passages from them in a voice irritatingly hovering on the edge of audibility. Some pointedly ignored this ceremony, others watched it in a baffled way, as if waiting for Matley to make some error of sacerdotal procedure before being able derisively to unfrock him.

Gerald, still lolling by the window though it had become too dark to read, was startled by the sudden opening of the dormitory door. He sprang to his feet and feigned to be opening a window. But the intruder proved to be a boy from the dormitory across the landing who said: 'She's there.' The boy then disappeared.

Everyone knew the significance of this gnomic remark: from the other dormitory it was possible to see across to a short arm of the House where the maids slept. The occupants of this dormitory had alleged that a new maid called Helen sometimes came to one of the bedrooms before the others and undressed without drawing the curtains. Howarth had extracted a promise from them that his own dormitory should be given notice of the next occurrence of this unbelievable event.

Howarth now tipped down his throat the last of the bag of potato crisps he had been eating and leapt from his bed. 'Come on, Bracher,' he said, stopping by the door.

'I'm not being caught out of my dormitory,' said Gerald stiltedly.

'Oh, ballocks,' said Howarth and disappeared after the others.

Gerald found himself left with Matley, who said: 'Filthy pigs!'

'Shut up, Matley,' said Gerald, looking out at the far stars above the hump-back trees that fringed the playing fields. A terrible anxiety filled his stomach as though he had temporarily alighted from a train at a station to perform some necessary procrastinating errand. He strolled with deliberate leisureliness to his bed and fumbled under his pillow for a bag of sweets, as though these actions could in some way prevent time from passing—time that contained the revelation of astonishing and infinitely desirable events which for reasons he could not define he had shut out from his apprehension. But it was true that he was motivated in not following the others by his disinclination to break the rule which forbade visits to another dormitory, though he could see that this, like the refusal of a second helping by one who fears he will be embarrassed by the subsequent discovery that in actuality there is no food left, had been given undue strength by his conviction that it was impossible for him to see what was promised.

Nevertheless, he found himself slowly drawn out of the dormitory. He went to the door, opened it and looked out as though keeping *cave*. 'Filthy pigs,' Matley said again.

In the opposite dormitory pyjama-clad figures blocked the view out of the window. 'There,' Snape major was saying excitedly. 'Can't you see, you fool?'

Gerald thrust his head among the other heads: outside, all appeared to be pitch-dark. 'Where is she?' he asked, abandonedly. No one replied, and suddenly the group seemed to melt away. Gerald turned and saw quite clearly in the glow from the dormitory pilot light that Cropper was standing near him—an impossible state of affairs, since Cropper came neither from this nor Gerald's own dormitory.

'What are you doing here, Bracher?' Cropper asked.

Gerald was conscious of the listening ears of those who had sneaked back to bed, the younger members of this dormitory. 'Just going back,' said Gerald, making for the door.

'Don't give cheek, Bracher,' said Cropper, moving to cut him off. 'I want to know what's going on.'

'You're not a House Prefect,' said Gerald, in a voice he tried to keep from trembling.

'That doesn't matter,' said Cropper. 'I'm a good deal senior to you.'

'Buzz off, Cropper,' said Gerald and immediately after felt Cropper's open hand deal him an enormous blow across the cheek. He could see the nostrils of Cropper's long nose terribly dilated and knew what a harvest of hatred his long sarcasm had reaped. 'Thank you,' he said, marvelling that he could still speak out of his numb face. 'Thank you very much.' It did not strike him that the words were stupid: on the contrary they seemed precisely to express his contempt and uncrushed spirit.

He marched back to his own dormitory. Now his face began so to burn that he feared some frightful disfigurement.

'What did that shit Cropper say?' called Howarth from the safety and comfort of his bed. 'Didn't you notice him come in?'

'You're a nice lot,' said Gerald, and then stopped, feeling his voice thicken with self-pity.

'He'll not report you,' said Howarth, comfortingly.

'I saw her, you know,' said Stink-Bomb Billy.

'You saw her, my cock,' said Howarth. 'It was a wash-out, as I said it would be all along.'

Gerald curled up in bed, miserably conscious of a powerful enemy and his own lack of virtue.

IV

In the light of day Cropper dwindled back to his real stature: at mealtimes, Gerald, to Mountain's inexhaustible amusement, resumed his fantasies about Cropper's home life, his wit, it seemed to him, brilliantly sharpened by the memory of the blow Cropper had dealt him. And yet his whole school life was coloured by the knowledge that someone essentially stronger than himself detested and lay in wait for him. One day Blakey idly mentioned that this was Mountain's last term. To Gerald it was incredible: Mountain was quite far from the top level of the school. 'He's going in his father's business,' Blakey said. And of course it was true—it made rational Mountain's attitude to his life here, already half detached from it as he was. Gerald left Blakey with a feeling of sick apprehension, for he was convinced that only Mountain's presence kept Cropper as essentially a figure of fun and prevented him from assuming his true character, as the future mad, cruel and despotic monarch is indulgently regarded as a mere womanizer and idler while he is Crown Prince.

The landmarks of term took on for Gerald, therefore, an extra significance, as of time for an examination candidate. Sports Day arrived, welcome as a day of unusual happenings, of proving one's long nurtured ability to compete, and yet too soon slicing off an irretrievable part of term.

The strings and little flags marking out the track, the deck-chairs and marquee and tables of refreshments, were familiar to most from previous years but Gerald regarded them as sentimentally as one might creamy blossom on gnarled boughs or some energetic activity from an octogenarian—heart-warming evidence of the school's vivid hidden life, stemming, as Gerald recognized, from the inspiration, money, even, of the Headmaster. The masters, too, were transformed: by blazers, or white flannel trousers, and the badges that indicated their official roles.

The boarders were on the field early: some, noncombatants like Matley, to hand out programmes and show visitors to the deck-chairs, but all with the apprehension of seeing their parents against the background of school. Gerald took a programme from Matley. ' "Mrs Henry Cole has graciously consented to present the prizes," ' he read. 'Now who the heck is Mrs Henry Cole?'

'Cole's mother,' said Matley. 'And don't dirty that programme: I want it back.'

'Cole's mother,' Gerald repeated with astonishment. 'That fat slug.'

'Didn't you know that his father was an alderman?'

'I don't see that that gives his mother the privilege of presenting the prizes.'

'Wheels within wheels,' said Mountain, who was standing by looking strange and muscular in a roll-neck white sweater.

'What do you mean, Mountain?' asked Gerald.

But Mountain had suddenly seen that Cropper was within earshot. 'What I'm waiting for,' he said in a penetrating voice, 'is that team of dogs rushing up the drive dragging the famous Cropper automobile.'

'I see they've been thoughtful enough to put up a kennel in the car park,' said Gerald.

Mountain laughed and walked away. The first, the on the whole humbler, parents began to arrive—unsure, perhaps, of securing a seat near the finishing tape or at all. Gerald regarded them with outward contempt, but scrutinized them all as they came into view, willing them not to be his father. And then, as the groups began to thicken and the chairs to fill, the Headmaster could be seen moving slowly and purposefully about, and for Gerald he was like the protagonist in a newspaper photograph whose image alone among other images has not by some technical process been rendered pale. When Mr Pemberton made as though to come near—and then it could be seen clearly that he had marked the day by putting on a suit of a much lighter grey than the usual clerical shade which had no doubt given him his nick-name and by leaving off his hat, so that the breeze ruffled slightly the long hair above his ears—Gerald himself moved away, interposing between them a few knots of people, for he feared that his father might arrive and the Headmaster catch them together. In such circumstances it seemed inconceivable that Mr Pemberton would not bring up the beating he had given Gerald for breaking bounds last term, an event of which Gerald had allowed his father to remain ignorant.

It was on such an occasion as this that Gerald realized the extent of the gulf between his father's conception of him and the reality. The beating and the crime from which it had resulted were not perhaps in themselves utterly venal, but for the Headmaster to reveal them to his father would be an indication of the whole gross scale of behaviour on the part of the boys for which Mr Pemberton had evolved an appropriate penal code and against which he conducted his ceaseless battle. How much less a deceit was his relationship with the Headmaster than that with his father, though even from Mr. Pemberton he believed he was able to conceal the greater part of his affairs.

Blakey strolled up with the nonchalance of one whose parents were safely in the West Indies. 'Haven't your people come yet, Bracher?' he asked.

Gerald shook his head, too embarrassed to say that only his father would be coming since that would surely mean that he would not be able to withhold from Blakey the astounding fact of his parents' separation. He cast desperately round for a subject to divert Blakey's attention. 'My word,' he said, 'Percy looks pretty scruffy, doesn't he?'

The pavilion had been outlined with bunting: Mr Percy was leaning against the rail wearing a tweed jacket familiar from weeks of ordinary days, and grey flannel trousers whose shape was determined only by the bulk of the master's lower anatomy.

'They say he's getting a bit sweet on Evie,' remarked Blakey.

Gerald, whose attention had been attracted merely by Mr Percy's disgusting refusal to make any sartorial concession to the importance of the occasion, saw now that the master was talking to Miss Pemberton and was immediately envious to think of the possibility of the girl's affections being engaged, though in reality he had not the slightest regard for her. 'Balls,' he said.

'That's what they say,' Blakey affirmed.

Then Gerald saw his father coming through the crowd and felt a sharp, anxious pain in his solar plexus as though this were the start of one of the races in which he was to be, later in the afternoon, engaged. Mr Bracher was looking about him in a way that momentarily puzzled Gerald until he realized that it was he for whom his father was searching—that this place and these people were utterly strange and perhaps embarrassing to his father. And he foresaw in a flash how he would greet his father who immediately would wrongly see him as the centre of this world, wanting to know when he was running, what chances he had, whether or not he would be free to be taken out for tea. An immense burden of responsibility descended on Gerald, the responsibility of being the object of love, of cherished possession, and all he could feel in return was an unutterable and awkward pity.

V

One day in the vestibule of the House Gerald encountered Mr Percy and was about to pass him, as seemed natural, without acknowledgement, when the master said: 'Come in the Common Room a moment, Bracher.'

Gerald thought the boys' Common Room was meant and was astonished when Mr Percy walked the few steps to the masters' Common Room, opened the door and indicated that Gerald was to precede him. Once again, as at the time of the episode of the weights, this room cast on Gerald its alien spell. Mr Percy perched his bulk on the table on which was a pile of exercise books. 'Sit down, Bracher,' he said, indicating a basket chair. He took up the top exercise book. 'This was a good essay of yours.'

Gerald's apprehension turned to surprise and he mumbled something incoherent. He tried to remember what was in the essay (whose subject was 'Compare the characters of Edward I and Edward III') that it should have evoked such an unusual response.

'I liked your idea of opening with a quotation,' said Mr Percy. ' "Look here upon this picture, and on this, The counterfeit presentment of two brothers." When did you read *Hamlet*?'

Gerald, already at a disadvantage through being tilted back in the unaccustomed comfort of the chair, blushed scarlet. 'I've never read *Hamlet*, sir,' he was forced to confess. 'I got the quotation from the top of one of the chapters in *Quentin Durward*. We did it in my other form last term.' He felt guilty of an enormous and stupid deceit.

'Well,' said Mr Percy, 'it was still a bright idea. Though the quotation isn't really appropriate, you know. What Hamlet is doing is to remind his mother of the *contrast* in character between the late king and the brother she married after his murder. Whereas what *you* had to bring out was the similarity between Edwards One and Three. Eh?'

'Yes, I see, sir.'

'What *do* you read?'

Gerald had a vision of the blue cover of *The Mystery of Dr Fu-Manchu*, a work he had borrowed from Blakey when scrounging round the dormitories for something to exploit the light nights, and suddenly realized how preposterous it was. 'All sorts,' he said feebly, feeling that Mr Percy might be able to read his thoughts and see the cloudy hair of Kâramanèh and the malignant green eyes of the Doctor floating through his brain. And then, quite against his will, he added: 'At the moment I'm reading *Fu-Manchu.*'

'What do you think of it?'

'I suppose it's rubbish.'

'Yes, I suppose it is. I've one or two books in my room you might like. I'll look them out.'

This conversation, though conducted by Mr Percy in his normal manner of impenetrability and reserve, contained so many surprises that quite as a matter of course it was giving Gerald an impression of the master completely different from the one he had previously formed, as in a dream a person's name may reasonably be attached to someone who is simply not that person. And he remembered Sports Day, seeing Mr Percy talking to Miss Pemberton, and Blakey's piece of gossip, realizing that after all Mr Percy need not be merely a lifeless bundle of rather odd characteristics—a schoolmaster who carried a walking stick and held his hat on with it in a breeze—but a man susceptible to femininity, like Dr Petrie in the tergiversations of his pursuit of Fu-Manchu. In a flash of understanding he saw that even the most austere master must be subject to human desires, suffer worldly cares: to talk with a girl might be a painful surmounting of shyness; a shabby jacket the mask not of eccentricity but of poverty.

'All right, Bracher,' said Mr Percy, dismissively, and Gerald made for the door. Before he reached it Mr Percy added: 'Would you like a white for the essay, or are you above it?'

For a moment Gerald yearned covetously for the official reward. Then he said: 'I'm above it,' and went out of the room before he could observe Mr Percy's reaction. With those words he felt he had raised himself to a fresh intellectual level, and the vestibule with its hanging raincoats and caps and through the open door the far view of a knot of boys dragging the roller on to a cricket pitch seemed all at once subservient to his happy, masterful mind.

Since the beating, he had never visited the twopenny library in the town: when one evening Mr Percy, coming in to take prep, silently deposited two books on his desk he was seized with a twinge of the old guilt, and had immediately hidden them under a textbook as though Mr Percy had no authority but was equally with him a partner in some unofficial and therefore illicit act. And he waited for an utterly private moment to return the books after he had read them.

That was an occasion when he heard the piano in the assembly hall. He silently let himself into the room and stationed himself behind Mr Percy until the piece should end. A pianist's fingers, he would have thought, should have been long and tapering: Mr Percy's were pudgy and spatulate. And there was a strange discrepancy, too, between the delicate and sentimental melody, fascinating in its semi-familiarity, and the master's stout and impassive person. The music ended and Gerald asked:

'What was that called?'

'It was a prelude by Debussy,' said Mr Percy.

'I've brought the books back, sir. Thank you very much.'

'Which did you like the better?'

'Poe's *Tales of Mystery and Imagination*.'

'A bit nearer *Fu-Manchu*, eh?'

'Not really, sir.'

'No, not really. Would you like me to try to find you something else?'

'Please, sir.'

Then, to Gerald's horror, Mr Percy lit a cigarette: it must be that the Headmaster would now appear at the door. Smoke coiled into the virgin air, unconcealed, penetratingly fragrant. With an anguished sense that he was deserting the master who in his limited way had shown him interest and kindness, but with the certain knowledge that he could not let himself be party to this deliberate and nonchalant breach of Mr Pemberton's code, Gerald mumbled some phrase about getting over to the House, and made a swift exit. The haunting phrase of the Debussy prelude followed him as far as the doorway to the playground where, through the light coming from the school, rain could be seen softly falling in silver verticals.

VI

An extraordinary and for Gerald harrowingly memorable episode occurred on a Saturday afternoon later in the term during the progress of the games on the various cricket pitches. A car came up the sea road and parked on the verge behind the hedge that formed one of the boundaries of the playing fields. It disgorged three men and two girls who came through the hedge and sat in the uncut grass just beyond the actual playing area being used in the game in which Gerald was engaged.

'That lot have got a bloody cheek,' said Howarth, as Gerald passed him between overs.

'Trippers from the town,' said Gerald disgustedly. Later he saw that a man and a girl had detached themselves from the group and were wandering towards a broken-down and disused structure in the corner of the playing fields known as the Shed, in which Blakey had once been caught smoking. Despite the ambiguous shame he felt, Gerald yearned to watch every movement of this couple, who could be seen even at this distance to have their arms round each other as they walked. At last they reached the back of the Shed and there, though they were partially hidden by the building, it was evident that they were lying together in the grass.

By now all the participants in the match were aware of what was going on, but Gerald could not join in the sniggers. He asked himself incredulously if behind the

Shed could really be taking place the unimaginable happening which he had nevertheless so often attempted
to imagine and with results far other than the unrolling
of this casual and sordid incident. He wished himself in
the place of the man and at the same time wild thoughts
came to him of trying to preserve the girl's innocence.

'Wake up, Bracher,' someone shouted, and he saw as
in another existence that the ball had been clouted in his
direction.

It was not long before one of the two men near the
car also rose and walked over to the Shed. The remain-
ing man repeatedly and incoherently shouted after him.
The man making for the Shed was in his shirt sleeves:
the afternoon was very hot. A wicket had just fallen and
Howarth came up to Gerald. 'They're all absolutely
tight,' he said.

'Are they?' said Gerald. His fear for the girl increased.
'Somebody ought to clear them off.'

When Gerald's side had dismissed their opponents
and he was reclining among the cricket bags and the
blazers, the girl who had been behind the Shed came
towards the playing pitch. Now it could be seen that
her hair was dishevelled, her face puffed and pale.
Before she had got very far one of the two Shed men
came after her, caught her up and restrained her from
proceeding. Twice she broke away from him. Then
followed a long and earnest conversation, the man with
his arm round the girl's neck, his head bent very close
to hers.

What could be going on? What could be the relationships between this quintet? Gerald, his head propped
on his elbow, feigned somnolence while his half opened
eyes devoured every nuance of gesture of these aban-

doned creatures. At last it came his turn to bat and when his innings was over he saw that the group had gathered together round the car and that one of the men was offering a bottle to a girl. Soon afterwards they drove away.

During his visit to the town in the evening of the same Saturday Gerald bought, set the example by the enterprising Howarth, a pound of plums as well as the usual pie and potato crisps. They ate the fruit as they walked back to school. In the middle of the night Gerald woke with griping pains and hastened along the corridors to the lavatories. As he sat there he remembered in great detail the suggestive and disgraceful events of the afternoon.

He had never wholly conquered his childhood fear of the dark: when he had turned out the light in the lavatories he moved as quickly as he could to the comparative safety of the landing, lit as it was by a naked, low-powered, violet electric lamp. Before he reached it the dim sight of a moving white shape stabbed him to the heart. 'Who's that?' he quavered involuntarily.

'It's me,' said a small apologetic voice.

'Slade,' said Gerald, immediately recovering his official personality. 'What are you doing here?'

The boy came up to him and Gerald reached back and switched on the light in the lavatories. He was impressed to see that Slade was wearing completely white pyjamas of a superior material. 'I've got toothache,' replied Slade. 'I was just going to brush my teeth.'

'What good will brushing your teeth do, you ass?' said Gerald, but recalling his own hours of torture by toothache he could not help feeling pity for the sufferer whose face, he saw, was pale under the disarranged hair and whose eyes glittered with a suspicion of tears.

'Well, brushing your teeth is supposed to stop them going bad.'

'You *are* an ass.'

'I suppose it was a silly idea, but I couldn't think of anything else to do.'

'Is there a hole there?'

'Yes, Bracher.'

'Chew some blotting paper and make a plug for it.'

'The hole isn't big enough, I don't think.'

'Slade, Slade, you'll be the death of me.' It was a fashionable catch-phrase, picked up from the Assistant Matron.

'I'm sorry, Bracher.'

'Why be sorry? It's your toothache.'

'I wish I was you,' said Slade, 'with no toothache.'

Gerald considered the boy, surprised by the humour implicit in his last remark. The strange hour of the night and his infirmity seemed to have caused a blossoming of character in Slade. Gerald found it momentarily hard to attach to the slim white figure the usual reaction he had on the rare occasions when they met—the reaction compounded of Gerald's feeling that here was someone whom he could with impunity dominate, who ought to be dominated; of his knowledge of Slade's cowardice at football and timidity at the time of the weights episode, and that Slade was excessively likely to be guilty of leaving his slippers in the vestibule or a slice of mutton on his Sunday plate—a character, in fact, which almost completely failed to measure up to the school's arduous and elevated code. Perhaps, Gerald thought, he was being indulgent on this occasion because of the gnawing possibility that Slade had observed his momentary terror at encountering him in the dark.

'You wouldn't like to be me,' said Gerald. 'I've got the quirks.'

'Have you?' said Slade sympathetically. 'I wondered why you were up.'

'Well, now you know.' And seeing Slade yawn, Gerald added: 'Go off to bed. Sleep's the best cure for toothache.'

'All right, Bracher. Good night.'

'Good night.' How odd it was to be saying that to Slade! The white pyjamas vanished and as he went back to his dormitory Gerald began to think again of the afternoon's happenings on the playing field.

VII

At tea-time the following day the Headmaster made an appearance (unprecedented at this meal of the day) in the dining room. Everyone rose and those who were engaged in chewing swallowed hastily as though concealing an incriminating paper. 'Be seated, boys,' said Mr Pemberton, and it could be seen that he was in a serious but excellent humour. 'I thought this was an appropriate opportunity, when our thoughts must still be on the divine service we attended this morning, to tell you of the latest developments about the school chapel.' The Headmaster then announced that someone he referred to merely as 'a very good friend of the school' had with great generosity promised to subscribe out of his own pocket a sum equal to the total sum subscribed by all parents and old boys.

'I think you boys know,' Mr Pemberton continued, 'how dear this project is to my heart and what immeasurable good it would add to the school. I want you to think about the inspiration of having our own altar and pulpit, our own stained-glass windows, and no doubt in time our own plaques and other memorials to commemorate those who make their mark on our life here. All these things are within our grasp. And you boys can play your part in obtaining them. I would like you in your letters home next week to tell your parents quite simply in your own words something of what a school chapel would mean to us here at Seafolde House. Of course, I shall be making known what I have told you to the day boys as well at assembly next week. But I thought my boarders should have advance news, as it were, because in their lives the chapel will play a very special part indeed.' Mr Pemberton then turned forcefully to the duty master who was sitting at the masters' table and said: 'Thank you, Mr Marsh. I'm sorry to have interrupted your tea.'

Following this speech, Gerald became possessed of an excited concern about the chapel project analogous to the emotion with which we follow the progress of those fictions which tell of the slow but successful struggles of the hero to accumulate a fortune. He visualized the gradually increasing inflow of subscriptions and then the miraculous mathematical process which would double them, and he wished he could personally inject every potential subscriber with a sense of the importance of his effort, the sense of every little counting, of the beauty of the community of effort and the gradual achievement of a lofty and worthy end. As the Headmaster had suggested, he wrote about the appeal in his next letter to his father, which was consequently of unusual length, a fact which in itself gave him a rich sense of self-satisfaction. He had an impulse to mention the matter, too, in his letter to his mother, but realized on reflection that any contribution she might send would come, in fact, from the pocket of Mr Ayers—the impossible charity of a thief.

Gerald was a little disappointed to read in his father's reply that Mr Bracher had already received from the school a printed appeal for funds for the chapel. It was as though the Headmaster had decided that the boys could not be trusted to play their part nor, for that matter, without the boys' own approach the parents theirs. He was also disappointed that his father did not disclose the amount of his contribution so that Gerald could have the pleasure of imagining the Headmaster's pleasure at receiving it and of making the simple but satisfactory calculation of its ultimate double value. And then his disappointment turned to unease and guilt as the possibility occurred to him that his father had sent some totally inadequate sum because of the failure of Gerald's letter to characterize the importance of the chapel to the Headmaster and to the life of the school.

Soon after Mr Pemberton's disclosure of his plans for the chapel Gerald had to attend at the Matron's room with a septic heel, caused by the rubbing of a tight shoe. One of the minor worries of his life was the discomfort caused him by several articles of clothing which had become too small for him—or had always been so, for some perverse demon often seized him in a shop and made him assent to the fit of things which were patently not his size. And the discomfort was accompanied by a dogged parsimoniousness which forbade him giving up the offending garment, for he was excessively conscious of the burden of expense the replacement would put upon his father.

He waited while Mrs Watt applied hot compresses to a boil on Thompson's neck, leaning against the green distempered wall of the small room, observing from his height that the hair roots on the crown of Mrs Watt's glossy black head were pure white. Thompson groaned melodramatically.

'Stop it, Thompson,' said the Assistant Matron. 'I haven't touched you yet.'

'No, you're just burning my skin off, Mrs Watt.'

'Look at that, Bracher,' said Mrs Watt, removing the compress. 'I don't think I've ever seen a bigger boil.'

'It's a beauty,' agreed Gerald.

'And it's not come to a head yet.'

'Don't be so morbid, Mrs Watt,' said Thompson. 'Put the dressing on it and let me get out of here.'

While Mrs Watt snipped the lint and adhesive tape, Thompson, seeing the end of his torture, leaned back in the chair and said: 'What's the latest scandal, Mrs Watt? Is it true Percy's sweet on Miss Pemberton?'

'Thompson, Thompson, you'll be the death of me,' said the Assistant Matron.

'Come on, Mrs Watt, spill the beans.'

'Who wouldn't be sweet on Miss Pemberton,' said Mrs Watt. 'She's a very nice girl.'

'Then it's true?'

'I said nothing of the kind. Bend your head over.'

'Are they engaged?'

'Don't fool about, Thompson, or I shall get cross.'

Thompson submitted to the dressing, went out, and Gerald took his place in the chair of the Inquisition. He would have liked to continue the cross-examination of Mrs Watt about Mr Percy's affairs. She was, he saw, a sort of fault in the otherwise sealed-off world where the adults of the school lived their real lives, through which rumours and hints could sometimes escape. But he had only courage enough to ask her an innocent question.

'Do you think we shall get enough money to build the chapel, Mrs Watt?'

She raised her sharp nose. 'I don't know,' she said, 'and I don't care very much.'

'Really?' He was shocked.

'In my opinion there are better things to spend money on—if you can get any money. Only don't say I said so, Bracher.'

'Of course I shan't, Mrs Watt. Do you know who the friend of the school is who's going to double all the subscriptions?'

'There's no secret about that. Alderman Cole.'

'Cole's father?'

'Cole's father.'

'He's such a slug.'

'Alderman Cole?'

'Don't pull my leg, Mrs Watt. I mean Cole.'

'Slug or not, his father is a very good friend of the school's. You don't know how good.'

'You tell me, Mrs Watt.'

'I won't be pumped. Put your shoe and stocking on and get across to prep.' Mrs Watt felt in the pocket of her overall and took out a rather crumpled cigarette which she proceeded to break in half, as was her habit. One half she put back in her pocket, the other between her thin lips. She struck a match towards herself, like a man.

Gerald lingered at the door searching for a remark, feeling himself tantalizingly on the brink of some insight into the mysterious mechanics of school, of life itself. On a chintz-covered ottoman under the window, next to the sleeping Tomsky—a cat well known through its frequent appearance in the dining room—was a doll dressed as a French sailor.

'Whose is the doll?' asked Gerald, idly imagining a hitherto unrevealed offspring of the Assistant Matron.

'That's Marcel. He's Miss Pemberton's,' replied Mrs Watt, her half cigarette, kept in the mouth, wagging expertly with each syllable. 'Now, off you go.'

The taciturn Percy, the rather eccentrically clothed young woman who reacted so extremely to Blakey's temperature and possessed a doll—it was ludicrous to think there could possibly be any point of contact between them.

VIII

Like a frequent letter solved in a coded message, Gerald's reading of the books lent to him by Mr Percy opened up new areas of understanding and tantalizing half-understanding. A collection of absorbingly imaginative short stories led him to take out from the boarders' library a novel by the same author called *In the Days of the Comet*. But though this contained an exciting idea— the collision of a great comet and our world—it was embodied in what Gerald found a rather boring story of personal relationships and almost wholly unreadable chunks of philosophical harangue. The book was prefaced by some lines of poetry:

The World's Great Age begins anew,
  The Golden Years return,
The Earth doth like a Snake renew
  Her Winter Skin outworn :
Heaven smiles, and Faiths and Empires gleam
Like Wrecks of a Dissolving Dream.

Even though he had skipped through the book negligently he found afterwards that its theme—the Change—kept recurring to him in all sorts of contexts. The political map of the world, for example, whose phenomenally extensive areas of red denoting British rule had always caused him wonder and pleasure, now sometimes seemed to him almost purely of mere historical significance, as though the atlas which contained it were out of date. 'Empires gleam Like Wrecks of a Dissolving Dream.' And gradually he was led to the conclusion that such a book as *In the Days of the Comet*, though superficially boring, demanded to be carefully studied because of its power of bequeathing comprehension: that, in fact, perhaps the main function of reading was not to pass the time by giving entertainment but to confront the reader with a task—a task measured grossly by one's gradual and toilsome reduction of the number of unread pages but having also some correlative spiritual progress, just as the princess' task consisted of a roomful of straw to be tediously woven into gold but was the necessary prolegomenon to her happy and exalted fate.

In this light the reference library, which he still surreptitiously visited, took on a fresh dimension. Now it served him not merely with its lighter books and those passages, as in *Hypatia*, whose sensual imagination helped to satisfy his own: he also looked for titles and authors already prefigured in his more serious reading, and his explorations, striking almost blindly across barren and unknown country, would come accidentally across tracts whose reputation was already known to him, as famous lines will every now and then astonishingly leap out at the reader of a long poem.

It had recently occurred to him that without anyone being the wiser he might actually take books away from the reference library to ransack and read at his leisure, and this he did with a volume that had first attracted him by the drawing that formed its frontispiece: a sphinx faced the reader, her brows bent, her claws fixed on the world, and her naked bosom revealed, the nipples clearly marked; and on the other side of the globe was presented the back view of a kneeling female figure wearing a cap of liberty but otherwise nude and holding a banner on which was inscribed the title of the book—*Fabian Essays in Socialism*. Then he found that among the contributors was a name he knew.

How had this book come to be stealthily and secretly planted, like a grub in an apple, in the school's heart? It was too difficult, too boring, really to read, but Gerald divined its venality, as a young child instinctively evaluates the reprehensibility of a new act. Perhaps some dissident master or more intellectual Mountain had before his long-past departure slipped the thing into the library for it leisurely to gnaw at the school's foundations.

Gerald lay on his pillow at the dormitory window, holding the book in full view in reliance on the incuriosity and ignorance of his companions for the concealment of its nature, like Poe's hider of the purloined letter, yet feeling a worm of apprehension in his stomach knowing he could have no defence to a sudden challenge, and read: 'Since we were taught to revere proprietary respectability in our unfortunate childhood, and since we found our childish hearts so hard and unregenerate that they secretly hated and rebelled against respectability in spite of that teaching, it is impossible to express the relief with which we discover that our hearts were all along right, and that the current respectability of today is nothing but a huge inversion of righteous and scientific social order weltering in dishonesty, uselessness, selfishness, wanton misery, and idiotic waste of magnificent opportunities for noble and happy living.'

Raising his head and looking at the iron bedsteads, the sloping attic ceiling, the irrational occupations of the other boys, he had a momentary sense that perhaps these were not the realities of life, that in fact all that he had hitherto accepted as familiar he was imperceptibly casting off, leaving himself with a second skin which consisted of all those names and ideas which once he had thought alien, unspeakable, incomprehensible, but would, as he drew away from the old, be the utterly familiar and real ambience in which he moved.

He returned his second borrowing of books from Mr Percy as the master was going across the playground one evening after taking prep. Mr Percy acknowledged with a word Gerald's thanks and continued on his way as though there was no bond between them. Gerald kept pace with him, feeling as stupid as when he had urged the claims of Conrad against those of W. W. Jacobs. He yearned to be able to express the subtleties of his being, his discoveries in knowledge, feeling Mr Percy's potential sympathy moving away from him as, after the terribly brief visit, the desperately sick man parts with his doctor.

They were almost at the door of the House. 'Do you happen to know, sir,' Gerald said, breaking the silence, 'who wrote a poem with the first line "The World's Great Age begins anew?"'

Mr Percy did not slacken his steady stride. 'You must be careful, Bracher,' he said, 'not to become an intellectual snob.'

Gerald did not really understand the phrase, but it effectively cowed him. He told himself that it was time he came over to the House anyway and visualized how once he was in the hall he would sidle into the changing-room and ostentatiously busy himself looking for his slippers and leave Mr Percy to march on alone to the Masters' Common Room. But when they had passed through the doorway Mr Percy stopped and said: 'It isn't the first line of the poem. It's the first line of a chorus from it. By Shelley.'

Gerald, observing young Dover sitting near the changing-room door, picking his big toe through a hole in his stocking and listening to Mr Percy with open mouth, felt beneath his pleasure at the master's words a keen sense of the shame and sedition inherent in poetry and wished he had not been so anxious to prolong the commerce between himself and Mr Percy.

'Come up to my room,' Mr Percy went on, 'and I'll see if I can find a Shelley for you.'

The room was on the half-landing between the second and third floors: as though it were some foreign city, long known by its exotic name, but once visited discovered to contain tramcars and cloth caps, Gerald saw with surprise, when Mr Percy flung open the door, a room no bigger than Mountain's, with an iron bedstead like those used by the boys. There was a smell of stale tobacco, a pint mug with a rose in it on the bedside table, and Mr Percy's ashplant leaning in a corner. Gerald expected Mr Percy to make some comment on the unusual scene thus disclosed or the epoch-making occasion of a visit by a boy to a master's bedroom, but he was immediately fully engaged in looking along the rows of books that had overflowed from a hanging book-case to the small table in the window, and along the skirting board.

'I don't think I can have it here,' Mr Percy muttered at last. Gerald took a step over the threshold as though into the room of a dying man. 'But you wouldn't want to read *Hellas* anyway.'

'Wouldn't I, sir?' Gerald said, just beginning to feel, in the unusual setting, an anticipatory intellectual pleasure; the sensation brought by the sudden switching on of theatre footlights which at once illuminate and darken the folds of the proscenium curtain.

Mr Percy gave him the sharp look of a schoolmaster who must always suspect a concealed squirter in a prof-fered bouquet. 'Do you like reading poetry?'

'I don't really know, sir. I've never read it for pleasure.'

'It's just useful for quotations in history essays, eh?' Mr Percy sat on the bed as though suddenly tired of carrying his bulk and reached out for a book lying on the bedside table. 'What Shakespeare play are you doing in form? *Twelfth Night*?' Gerald nodded. 'What one doesn't always realize at school is that Shakespeare was only one of a lot of good poets who wrote at that time. And the things the others wrote are quite often more exciting than Shakespeare's—that's not quite the word: more morbid, violent, funny, filthy. More interesting to you—and to me, too, perhaps. Eh, Bracher?'

'They sound more interesting to me, sir.' And at once it seemed to Gerald that with a little practice he would know how to converse with Mr Percy, that he could evolve for him a rather superior brand of the facetiousness and outrageousness that so amused Mountain.

'There you are,' said Mr Percy. He held out the book. 'Borrow this if you like.'

'Thank you, sir.'

'Aren't you going to look and see what it is?'

'I think I can trust your taste, sir.'

' "The earth doth like a snake renew Her winter weeds outworn",' said Mr Percy.

'Shouldn't it be "winter skin", sir?'

'No, Bracher.'

'It says "winter skin" at the start of H. G. Wells's *In the Days of the Comet*.'

'Then H. G. Wells got it wrong,' said Mr Percy. 'But I was going to ask you what you thought the lines meant?'

Gerald thought. 'They mean that after the winter when spring comes everything on the earth starts to grow again,' he said. 'And that's all to do with the return of a Golden Age.'

'Do they, now?' said Mr Percy. 'Just go down and drink your cocoa and think them over.' The light on the curtain went out.

'Yes, sir,' said Gerald. He tried to think them over as he sat in the vestibule, putting on his slippers, but when he repeated them to himself all that struck him was the alliterative word 'weeds', for Mr Percy's emendation, far from having to be consciously recalled, had supplanted utterly the other word, as a superior arrangement of furniture in a room causes one to be unable to remember without a great effort what the room was like before. It was a few minutes before he realized that 'winter weeds' did not indicate those astonishing plantains and such that flourish so greenly and rather disgustingly when everything else in the garden is dead, but that 'weeds' here had its other, black, meaning. But could the two lines as a whole have any other interpretation than the one he had so baldly tried to give to Mr Percy?

When he got into the Common Room the younger boys had already gone to bed. He took a piece of the bread and butter laid out on the table and which he suspected had been left over from tea-time and sat down with his book. On the fly leaf was Mr Percy's name and underneath 'Queens' College, 1919'. Gerald looked at the title page and then opened the book at random: the pages fell open as at an accustomed place and he read:

> *Was this the face that launch'd a thousand ships,*
> *And burnt the topless towers of Ilium?—*
> *Sweet Helen, make me immortal with a kiss.*

A sharp sensation seized him compounded of the vision of ardent, unspecialized emotion and the memory of the gross words which Snape had used to describe what he alleged he had seen through the uncurtained window of the maid Helen's bedroom.

'Now if it were winter,' Howarth said, throwing himself in a chair at Gerald's side and tilting it far back,

127

'we could toast the dry side of this and make French toast.'

'Your flies are undone,' said Matley primly.

'So they are,' said Howarth, looking down. 'Are you interested?'

Thompson was sitting on the corner of the table. 'Charlie really is a swine,' he said vehemently. No one paid any attention.

Gerald closed his book. 'Have you chaps had cocoa?' he asked.

'We certainly haven't,' replied Howarth. 'Matley, go to the kitchen and see what they're doing.'

'Go yourself.'

Snape broke wind. Howarth said: ' "If music be the food of love, play on".'

'It's all right for you chaps,' said Thompson. 'Charlie hasn't got his knife into you.'

Gerald tucked the book under his arm. 'I'll go and see about the cocoa.'

'Good old Bracher.'

To get to the kitchen one had to cross the great, square vestibule. The open front door disclosed the deep blue dusk, the rising of a creamy moon and, at the foot of the steps, between the twin stone urns, an indistinguishable figure. 'Tommie, Tommie, Tommie,' this figure was calling, in a strange falsetto voice. Almost involuntarily Gerald took a few paces to investigate the curious phenomenon, but before he could reach the door the figure, as an aircraft banks and suddenly discloses to the puzzled watcher its alien and deadly silhouette, turned its head and Gerald recognized against the sky the inclination of the Headmaster's massive cranium. Simultaneously he saw the pallid form of the cat Tomsky move with nonchalant swiftness from the bushes on the far side of the drive to rub himself against Mr Pemberton's trouser legs.

The Headmaster's assumed voice and purpose—which was at once revealed by his picking Tomsky up in his arms and turning to come indoors—did not strike Gerald as a matter for amusement or derision: on the contrary they merely, like the Brides in the Bath murderer's playing of the organ, threw in greater relief the stronger and more fearful aspects of his character; and the action itself as performed by him seemed to differ wholly in quality from the action as it might have been performed by any other householder in the late evening, like a ceremony of marriage entered into by Henry VIII. So that Gerald felt as uneasy as though he had unwittingly watched some outwardly innocent happening—the purchase of a length of rope, say—which he knew in actuality to be a criminal preliminary. He pressed close against the hanging raincoats (which since it had been raining earlier in the day exuded their characteristic sickliness) and feigned to fumble in the pockets of one of them in the hope that the Headmaster would pass him by.

But Mr Pemberton did not fail to observe the lurking boy. He stopped, and seeing that nothing reprehensible was taking place, remarked: 'We have to make sure that our Tommie observes a proper bedtime just like everyone else. Don't we, Tommie?' The part of this speech that was addressed to Gerald was spoken in the Headmaster's normal tones, but for the questioning of the cat it made a rapid transition to the falsetto which had previously penetrated the garden. Gerald felt himself blushing with embarrassment, for though he himself could only too readily exculpate Mr Pemberton from any charge of puerility, he feared that someone might overhear who had a less nice sense of the Headmaster's inviolable power and dignity.

'Do you like cats, Gerald?' asked Mr Pemberton.

'Yes, I do, sir.'

'So do I. Of course, this is really Miss Pemberton's cat, not mine. He's rather a mean little thing, isn't he? My own cats have usually been larger. My last cat was a black Persian but I think she must have eaten some bait we laid down for the rats in the pavilion. And then Miss Pemberton produced this little creature and so I haven't been able to have another.'

During this speech Tomsky looked out quite complacently over the Headmaster's forearm: though without the true feline grandeur, even *his* head bore a resemblance to Mr Pemberton's—there was the same width at the cheeks, the same downward mouth that nevertheless eventually unamusedly smiled, the same broad nose. Gerald's hands began to sweat and ache holding Mr Percy's book behind his back in an immobile position.

'Mrs Pemberton was very fond of cats, Gerald,' the Headmaster went on. 'We always had a cat in the vicarage. Daughter succeeded mother and son daughter. The Salic Law applied not. Then when I came to Seafolde House I established a new dynasty. But this little fellow is an upstart pretender, like his namesake.'

What could be said in reply to these confidences? Gerald exercised his mind in vain. But Mr Pemberton appeared to be satisfied to be confronted with the primitive grinning mask into which Gerald's face had painfully set, and at last continued his way to the corridor that led to his own house. Then Gerald had to try to remember what he was doing among the damp raincoats.

IX

The great match of every season, whether at cricket or football, was that with Westport College, a school of similar size and standing some thirty miles along the coast. This year the cricket fixture was due to be played at Seafolde House. By tradition, no other games were played on the ground on the Saturday afternoon of the Westport College match, but the day boys were expected to turn up as spectators and for the boarders attendance was compulsory. After lunch Gerald, freed from the chore of changing into flannels, found himself with an hour of leisure before the start of the match, and wandered down the drive to a place behind the evergreens which, if not explicitly out of bounds, had the quiet air of being so.

He sprawled at full length and all at once was close to the jungle world of grass and ants, a world of painful effort and self-absorbed interest. And then it was only a few moments before he became aware of the noises of summer—of insects, larks, leaves—that provide the normally unidentified *ostinato* that nevertheless enriches the obvious themes of colour, sun and cloud. Into this harmonious buzz came suddenly some cacophonous and syncopated sounds. As was well known among the boarders, Mr Norfolk had recently bought a small, antique motor car. He now appeared in this round a bend in the drive pushed by three small boys from his form. When they had laboriously worked up speed he let in his clutch, a spurt of dark smoke came from the exhaust, and the car quickly petered to a standstill. At Mr Norfolk's bidding this process was several times repeated, and at length the car passed from Gerald's view down the drive.

Gerald opened his book, the Marlowe that Mr Percy had lent him, and turned over the pages, attracted by titles, names, lines, but too indolent, too daunted by his confrontation with so much of which he was ignorant, to start methodically reading. Between two pages of the last act of *Doctor Faustus* he came across a folded piece of grey writing paper. He opened it unthinkingly and read:

Dear Edward, When I got back to the smell of iodine I said to Marcel, that understanding Frog: 'No, he is *quite* wrong, quite *wrong*.' I am NOT a captive—at least, not a captive to any*body*. And I thought that even you must have a Grey streak, for what is romanticism but a kind of Greyness? I mean Heathcliff and Rochester are just the Brontës making the best of their Grey Chaps—invented Grey Chaps, but Grey Chaps all the same.

Our Grey Chap did *not* capture me. When I was left an orphing I was very thankful to be asked to live at Seafolde House. Aren't I better off as matron here than matron somewhere else? You don't know because no man can ever know, the squalor of female poverty: to escape from that women will put up with anything—only it is not 'putting up with', really: it is an inborn part of feminine character, a biological adaptation to a Grey Chap's world.

You say I am preparing myself to become the

Grey Chap's permanent appendage. Well, most women are destined to become *some* Grey Chap's appendage and surely a niece-like appendage is more detachable than a wife-like one. And besides, if you aren't going to be wagged you must show some signs of being able to wag, and that is what I've never been able to do. Will you please tell me how a tail gets on, all the time naïvely showing its two pathetic alternate moods of happiness or dejection, in a world where tails definitely come last?

Yes, you are romantic. Secretly, you would like your wife to be a fat lunatic hidden away in a tower so that you could be comforted by a demure little tail. And that in spite of the fact that you are the least grey chap I've ever met. Most people would call you white but I'm like one of those animals in psychologists' experiments that can respond to grey so pale it is quite invisible. You will not like to read this, but it is true. And I must write another thing, too, that perhaps I should be too shy to say to you. Wasn't it also the Brontës who suffered—no, that's not the word—stimulated, bathed in, toyed with, a succession of curates? I've no illusions about my anaemic charms, but in this isolated vicarage on the bleak moors they do probably have a spurious propinquitous appeal to the enforcedly celibate. So don't ever forget that terms don't last for ever.

Your sincere   Tail

Gerald read the first few lines of this letter as though it were part of the impersonal, remote text of the book in which he had found it, an illusion sustained by the half-baked impression that the initial 'Dear Edward' in some way referred to the play of *Edward the Second* he had noticed among the contents when he had been turning the pages over. And then in rapidly sequential but separate stages he realized that this was a letter to Mr Percy, used by him as a bookmark and left inadvertently there, and that it had been written by Miss Pemberton.

It was true, then, that Percy was keen on Evie. The certainty amazed him, for it was one thing to gossip idly about the school's remoter, authoritarian figures and quite another to have visual confirmation of the gossip, just as everyone delights to reiterate that a king is essentially no different from his subjects but would be profoundly disturbed to come across the monarch standing in a compartment of a public urinal. But when he had finished the letter he saw that the truth was not of this simple order, that it would be impossible for him when the subject was mentioned to smile knowingly to himself: he would still, in spite of his unique evidence, need to seize hungrily on every scrap of rumour and speculation in order to try to make rational the motives and actions of the protagonists of the affair, as a biographer with access to all the documents about his subject must yet out of his own head construct a theory in order to articulate them.

He stared at the unfamiliar handwriting, small, upright, feminine, and the urgent underlinings that gave the page an appearance at once meticulous and wild, like a memorial prepared by the inmate of an asylum; and he tried to apply to it his knowledge of what form the relations between man and woman could take—the pale dishevelled woman on the playing fields that hot afternoon pursued by, yielding to, the insistent louts;

his own imagined encounter on the deserted sea road with the dark sallow girl who sat far across the nave of the church; and Mr Ayers on the terrace of the hotel finding inexhaustible conversation with his mother. What, he had crudely to reduce it to, did Mr Percy and Miss Pemberton do? But the answer lay beyond him, a real but future point in his curriculum, like the Binomial Theorem.

Given the knowledge revealed by the letter, other small seemingly disparate phenomena that he would otherwise never have noticed or could never have explained, fell into place, as the orbit of a negligible planet is accounted for by a fundamental proposition about light. The growing infrequence of Mr Percy's piano playing in the assembly hall, even his lending books, was no doubt due to the unfolding of his relationship with Miss Pemberton, whose fresh hair style and occasional facetiousness with the boys sprang from the same root. How often must one, ignorant of the prime motives in the lives of others, fail to understand or misinterpret what goes on?—thinking, for example, during an entire acquaintanceship, of a man as irascible who is merely shy.

It was only at an advanced stage in these thoughts that the explicit nature of the letter's contents struck Gerald with any force. True, at the first sight of the words 'Grey Chap' he had felt an ambiguous vibration deep in his body at the force imparted, as in the case of certain phrases one may find scrawled on a lavatory wall, by words to an oral tradition. But these were as nothing to the eventual realization that in Mr Percy's and Miss Pemberton's conception the Headmaster played some repressive role, and that the symbolic use of his nickname by these adults signified that they held him in contempt. Such outrageous things confirmed the guilty nature of their association: after all, it is not very surprising to learn that a man charged with indecent exposure has a past record of petty thefts.

A sudden explosion broke into these absorbing thoughts, and Gerald looked up to see once again in the drive Mr Norfolk's car, this time facing the other way. From its stationary position it began slowly to move and soon Gerald could discern the bent figures of the boys at the back of it, trying against inertia and gradient to get up a reasonable speed. Mr Norfolk himself, head and shoulders fully revealed by the folded hood, sat motionless, hands on steering wheel, with a detached yet anxious expression, as of an artist showing his creations to an important critic. The machine eventually passed out of sight.

How ludicrous was this conduct of Mr Norfolk's! Could it be that Mr Percy's was just as ludicrous? And yet Gerald could see that only a hair's breadth divided Mr Norfolk's immobile car, and his enlistment of his pupils into the project of making it work, from the pathetic—and perhaps that was the word that had to be applied to this frail and seditious affair of Mr Percy and Miss Pemberton, that could blossom only in the Headmaster's ignorance or contempt, like a revolutionary party in an autocracy.

Gerald folded the letter at last and replaced it in the book, worried a little that he had not noted the precise leaves between which he had found it, for he realized that he must begin to lay the proofs of his innocence against Mr Percy's eventual discovery of it, as a cunning murderer in the very transaction of his crime plants a scrap of evidence to help establish his alibi. No longer capable of sufficient peace of mind to return to his reading, Gerald rose and stepped into the now deserted drive. When he had strolled a little way along it he saw the weedy figure of Dunstan, one of the school prefects, crossing towards the House. Dunstan stopped suddenly and shouted: 'You! You, there!'

'Me?' Gerald called, but too faintly for his voice to carry to the other, for his whole inner being had been seized with a spasm of fear that Mr Percy had remembered where he had left the letter and had set Dunstan to retrieve it and bring the thief, the pryer, before him.

'Yes, you,' cried Dunstan, waiting with fists on hips.

Gerald made a shambling pretence at haste and at length stationed himself apprehensively before the prefect.

'What do you think you're doing?' asked Dunstan.

'I've been for a walk, Dunstan. It's not out of bounds here, is it?'

' "I've been for a walk, Dunstan," ' repeated Dunstan derisively. 'Don't you know the Westport match has *started*?'

'Has it, Dunstan?' The Westport match: the phrase came from another, comfortingly less arduous order of existence. 'I'm afraid my watch must have stopped,' Gerald added in a cosy-making voice, feigning easily to have had the match constantly in mind.

'Well, get there at the double and don't be such a slacker in future.' Dunstan over-compensated for his lack of skill at games with a zealous interest in them.

Gerald came up to the First Pitch by the side of the pavilion in front of which, in honour of the match, had

137

been placed a few deck-chairs—not the sparkling uni-
form deck-chairs which had been hired for Sports Day
but a miscellaneous collection of rotting canvas, string-
spliced woodwork and projecting nails. In the least un-
safe sat Major Marriott, the headmaster of Westport
College, a little man with arched eyebrows and short
grey hair standing stiffly off his scalp, giving him the
look of one who has just suffered a terrible shock. When
Gerald had, by questioning the boy at his side, identified
this alien figure, he covertly watched it for several
minutes, marvelling that so undistinguished a man
could be a headmaster and at his own absence of fear.
Behind Major Marriott, at one of the pavilion's unglazed
windows, sat a boy wearing a cap quartered in unfamiliar
blue and yellow, the Westport scorer. Major Marriott,
who had been chewing a finger, turned round suddenly
and said to this boy: 'Ronnie, have you got a penknife?'

'Yes, sir,' said the scorer.

'Chuck it over, then,' said Major Marriott who, when
possessed of this instrument, began to pare one of his
nails.

This exchange staggered Gerald not only with its
revelation of the disgustingly casual and egalitarian conditions that must pertain at Westport College but also
because of Major Marriott's behaving in a manner that
made light of his position as a visitor in strange surroundings, and it was with the sense with which the
decent inhabitants of a rioting city welcome the arrival
of the military that a few moments later he observed
Mr Pemberton walking from the direction of the House
towards the pavilion. All the same, he saw no reason
why he should risk the unforeseeable hazards of an

encounter with the Headmaster, and so moved unobtrusively away round the boundary.

From a suitably distant vantage he watched Mr Pemberton greet Major Marriott and take the chair at the Westport headmaster's side, which had doubtless been kept specially vacant, so that the principals then sat side by side looking out over the field of friendly combat of their two forces, like two great potentates, for long deadly rivals, whom diplomacy or common interest has at last brought together in circumstances of ceremonial politeness and celebration which nevertheless cannot quite obliterate their past conflict or its possible future revival.

'Well, Bracher,' said a voice behind him, 'did you find out what it meant?'

Gerald turned round, startled, and saw Mr Percy leaning on his stick. 'What, sir?' he asked, with a flaming guilty face, knowing perfectly well that the master was referring to the letter which he must at last have remembered was in the Marlowe, but determined to try to maintain the fiction of ignorance.

'You have a very short memory, Bracher,' replied Mr Percy. 'The Shelley couplet.'

'Oh, that, sir,' said Gerald, with a rush of relief and love. 'No, sir.'

'You told me what the poet intended it to mean. But what he actually wrote means the exact opposite. Do you see?'

'Yes, sir.' Gerald pulled himself together. 'No, sir. I just can't remember the lines at the moment.'

'Ah, well,' said Mr Percy. 'You will. It's an interesting point. Not that I discovered it, I hasten to add, Bracher, because I don't want you with your increasingly extensive explorations into literature to catch me out in a plagiarism. Does it matter what poetry means? Was Shelley too careless to be a good poet? What's that book you've got there? *Fu-Manchu*?'

'The one you lent me, sir,' Gerald said, clasping it still tighter under his arm, for it seemed to him that it might have the special power of fragile things to leap from one's grasp in spite of all precautions, and he clearly visualized it spilling its secret contents at Mr Percy's feet.

'Very tactful of you, Bracher. I think I shall sit down on the grass. There's no obligation on you to stay.'

Nevertheless Gerald felt compelled to follow suit. Mr Percy lay on a plump elbow, his trilby hat resting on his nose. The silence was suddenly embarrassing and Gerald stared with bogus concentration at the field of play. The school, he saw, were batting first. Mr Marsh was standing as umpire at one end: at the other was an individual in a panama hat who Gerald assumed was a Westport College master. The bowler, a boy with flapping auburn locks, was walking back for his run.

Miss Pemberton dropped into the discreet gap Gerald had left between himself and Mr Percy. 'That's the famous Wilkes,' she announced.

Since Mr Percy made no response, Gerald said faintly: 'Who?'

'The bowler. He can bat, too. Thank goodness this is his last term. He's been a menace to the school for years.'

'Not as big a menace as some I know,' said Mr Percy.

Wilkes started on his enormous run up. 'How would you like to be on the receiving end of that, Bracher?'

inquired Miss Pemberton, plucking a stalk of grass and placing it in her mouth. Gerald grimaced suitably though he scarcely heard the question, being hard at work trying to evolve a scheme for getting decently away. It seemed to him that these idle and innocent remarks of Miss Pemberton and Mr Percy must soon give way to an excruciatingly embarrassing exchange that would reveal their true relationship and one which he felt powerless to keep at bay, as a visitor to a lunatic knows that talk of weather or food will be followed by the terrible obsessive theme which is the reason for his *vis-à-vis*'s incarceration.

Could it be that it was merely love—that euphemism, that vagueness—in which he feared to be implicated, as though it were not the desirable and elevated state sanctioned by cultural tradition but a conception which retained its merely verbal meaning while in practice it took on an entirely different connotation, like socialism? Or was it that he divined that love between these two must have a guilty quality—because, for example, it implied secrecy, flourishing among the celibate and adolescent, or the condemnation of the Headmaster? Perhaps, even, it was simply the emotion of others, emotion which he could neither share nor imagine, that, like an animal's moaning, so alarmed and sickened him. And he thought of tables in cafés where, for hours on end, his mother's hand had been covered by that of a stranger.

'Even a Wilkes must depart at last,' Mr Percy was saying. 'Nothing is really permanently oppressive, unless it is one's own nature.'

'All the same, some Wilkeses last longer than others,' said Miss Pemberton.

'Who's duty master tonight, Bracher?' Mr Percy asked.

'You are, sir, aren't you?'

'So I am,' said Mr Percy, without surprise. 'While you are gallivanting round the town I shall be mooching about the House, awaiting your plangent return. I shall turn the lights out sharply tonight, I promise you, Bracher.'

The pleasure in Mr Percy's voice, inexplicable as it was, was not lost to Gerald, and he stole a look at the master who, however, still presented the mask he had evolved for himself during his life—the absence of gestures, the slow movements, the clothes whose ordinariness was only relieved by their age.

'Major Marriott has brought his dog again,' observed Miss Pemberton. 'It seems to be different this term. Not so hairy.'

'It is quite hairy,' said Mr Percy.

'Quite, but not very,' said Miss Pemberton.

That they failed to use any name for each other in the exchanges only served, like a row of asterisks, to call attention to the prurient words that had to be supplied. At last Gerald brought himself to utter the sentence he had long tried over in his mind.

'I think I'll just walk round the boundary,' he said, rising quickly to his feet. Miss Pemberton smiled at him as he went and though he did not look back he strained his ears for some revelatory word, for he knew that it is our own presence in the world that, like a scientist's measuring instrument among electrons, prevents us from discovering exact truth. But all he heard was the general chatter of the watching groups and a lark's tireless but painful song.

By half past three the school XI had been dismissed for a fairly miserable 42. Gerald had joined a group not far from the pavilion. Across the field he could see Mr Percy and Miss Pemberton, no nearer to each other than when he had left them. Behind the fringe of spectators on the boundary numbers of smaller boys, long since bored with watching, wrestled with and pursued each other, like packs of indefatigably sportive dogs one is surprised to find all male. The Westport openers started well. They had made 20 before Mountain, coming on to bowl his slow leg-breaks, took a wicket with the last ball of the over.

'Wilkes is first wicket down,' remarked Thompson. 'He'll knock off the rest before you've time to fart.'

'I don't know,' said Gerald, feeling keenly the school's ignominious plight. 'Mountain might bowl them out.'

'It's as good as over,' said Thompson, lying back on the grass and closing his eyes.

The other opener's wicket fell in the next over: and Thompson struggled to an upright position. Wilkes had not yet had to play a ball: he stood leaning negligently on his bat, imperturbably watching the decay at the other end.

'Who said it was all over?' asked Gerald, a fragile worm of exaltation at his stomach.

'Wilkes hasn't had a chance yet,' said Thompson. 'Give him a couple of overs and he'll get the runs on his tod.'

It was still 20 for 2 when Wilkes at last faced Mountain and swept his first ball to the boundary. Thompson applauded with exaggerated enthusiasm. Wilkes hit the second ball of the over with the meat of the bat out of his block-hole towards square leg, where Blakey was fielding. As the ball was passing Blakey at shoulder height he thrust out his hand and the ball stuck. What followed had for Gerald all the confusion of a street accident or military engagement. Presumably there was an appeal and presumably the umpire at the bowler's end, the panama-hatted Westport master, shook his head. At Gerald's side Thompson was on his feet, crying: 'He's given him not out. What a sodding swiz!'

The ball had been thrown back to Mountain but instead of bowling his next ball he was tossing it up and down, one hand on hip. From a boy near Gerald came the familiar whisper: 'The Grey Chap!' and Gerald turned his eyes from the drama on the field of play to see that Mr Pemberton had indeed left his seat in front of the pavilion and was walking towards the Captain of the XI, who was fielding not ten yards from where Gerald was squatting.

The Headmaster's face was expressionless but very white. The Captain took a few uncertain steps towards him. In a firm voice, quite audible to Gerald, Mr Pemberton said: 'Lead your men off the field, Birnie.'

'Now, sir?' asked Birnie.

'Now,' said the Headmaster, and Gerald's heart warmed towards this prompt, effective and unparalleled action for justice and truth. The Headmaster turned and walked back towards his deck chair: Birnie falteringly moved in to the wicket and called in a strangled voice: 'Come on, you chaps. Back to the pavilion.' Slowly the command communicated itself to the team and it began to straggle off. For a few moments Wilkes and his fellow batsman and the two umpires were left in sole possession of the pitch and then they, too, drifted over to the pavilion where a crowd of people had gathered round some focal centre which Gerald divined must be the rival headmasters. Could Mr Pemberton and Major Marriott possibly be engaged in some form of physical combat? The idea had only to be formulated to be dismissed as absurd, but there was no doubt that some terrible conflict existed in front of the pavilion which he longed to but dared not witness.

'We'll never play Westport again, that's certain,' said Thompson. 'What an absolute swiz!'

Soon the knot in front of the pavilion loosened and though it was apparent that an amount of discussion was still in progress, the School XI began to wander back on the field. Howarth came up to Gerald and Thompson and said: 'They've given him out.' Sure enough, the two Westport batsmen could be seen making their way to the wickets and neither was Wilkes.

'What happened, Howarth?' asked Thompson. 'Were you there?'

'Front row,' said Howarth. 'The Westport umpire said it was a bump ball. Marshie said he hadn't seen properly and couldn't pass an opinion. The Grey Chap said he would call the match off if such a flagrantly and manifestly absurd decision were allowed to stand. The Westport Head caved in immediately and said Wilkes was to regard himself as out.'

'Good for the Grey Chap,' said Gerald joyfully.

'Of course,' said Thompson, 'it won't make any difference to the result.' Nor did it, for Westport got the necessary runs without further loss.

The day before Gerald had started at Seafolde House his father had taken him out specially to buy him a wristwatch. Every night at school Gerald took off the watch and strapped it to the thin iron wrist of his bed-head. Sometimes before going to sleep, or if he awoke in the night, he would tilt his eyes backward until he could see the writhing luminous numerals on the watch's dial and perhaps raise his head to hear the ticking, for him as distinctive as someone's voice. To the watch had become attached his affection for his father and the pathos of its purchase: it stood, too, for his separation from the easy, unworried, loved existence of the holidays. And because he knew its price—all the more significant in the changed circumstances of his father's life which, apart from complications beyond his understanding, he had more than once heard involved the exchange for the position in South Africa an altogether inferior and makeshift one here—it took on the fragility and preciousness of a last heirloom in an impoverished family. During the miserable periods of the early part of the previous term he had sometimes before going to sleep taken the watch from the bed rail and held it to his ear or even his lips for, though without intelligent comprehension, it seemed to have a life of its own and therefore, like a pet animal, the power to comfort.

It was touching to think of its sleepless vigil through the night looking out down the bed over his unconscious form. Occasionally a nightmare would wake him: he would stifle the cry on his lips, instantly aware of the need to hide it from the derision of his room-mates and yet scarcely out of the frightening world of the dream, not daring even to move his head to a safer place under the bedclothes. How familiar the nightmare was and how utterly indescribable! Its preliminaries would have been trivial had he not even in the dream had a sense of the coming terror. And the climax seemed to him, as he strove before going to sleep again to recapture and perhaps exorcise it by a calm dissection, merely an abstract affair of attenuation and swelling, taking place in a black void sprinkled liberally with stars. It was as difficult to accept this unknown drama as part of himself, his own creation, as to accept an X-ray photograph of one's abdomen which reveals an ulcer. What processes of gland or brain, what conscious conflicts or fears, transformed themselves into this involuntary and primitive moaning? With such thoughts he would sleepily move and see the glowing dial which would then seem the entrance to an ancestral life stretching through his father, and his father's dead parents, across the brief span of historical forefathers to the apish creatures which themselves had through time a continuous attachment to the slime of pools, the pools themselves, and the pulsing of single cells under the nebulae-filled night of original creation—he had read the beginning of H. G. Wells's *History of the World* during his sessions at the reference library, absorbed as a foundling discovering the secret of his parentage. The violent chemistry of the origin of the earth and of its life, seemed to him significant even beyond its actual function, to have some special poetic worth, and being set an essay into which this subject could be dragged, he had written all he could remember of Wells's description, embroidering it with colourful words of his own finding; and was astonished to have it returned to him with a mediocre mark, for he could not imagine that others were not as convinced as he was of the intrinsic value of the processes he had depicted.

It struck him eventually that the reason for his awe and pleasure at the gradual and wholly logical steps by which a cool planet and organic life came to exist was his new possession of a truth not only previously hidden but one for which his education had provided no need of discovery, as a nomadic tribe having no occasion to parcel out land fails to evolve the geometry whose demands alone will force their attention to the proper measurement of the movement of heavenly bodies. He realized, too, that though he could recognize truth he seemed incapable of initiating it. Had it been left to him the origin of life would have had to remain for ever mysterious, and even in simpler matters he was astonished by the perspectives revealed by other minds. On the evening following the Westport match, for example, Howarth had casually said to him: 'I hope I never have to meet a chap from Westport College.'

'Same here,' he had replied, mentally agreeing that everyone at that school must be tainted through having as a master one who could venally try to save the school from defeat.

'Think of being asked out to tea in the holidays and finding a Westport chap there,' Howarth went on. 'He'd be sure to let out that you came from a school where the headmaster had walked on the pitch in the middle of a game.'

'Sure to,' said Gerald, concealing without a tremor his vast amazement at the idea that someone could regard Mr Pemberton's action as improper, even disgraceful. He would have liked to question Howarth about it but dare not reveal what Howarth would certainly regard as the inadequacy of his moral code. He managed to get out: 'Was it a bump ball, really?'

'Who knows? And what does it matter, anyway?'

He could see, certainly, that facts were unimportant: conduct was the criterion. But how to judge conduct? His opinions and values were all in separate compartments, at different stages of evolution, like the specimens in some biological laboratory, or like the civilizations of the earth where the sophisticated citizen of a declining empire exists simultaneously with Stone Age man. And so were his emotions. One night as he was brushing his teeth before going to bed he thought of the episode at the Westport match when Miss Pemberton had come to sit between himself and Mr Percy. He remembered the pale blue cotton of her dress tightening as she tucked her legs under her and her initial remark. How easily, it seemed to him, he could, if Mr Percy had not been there, have replied! And more—have awakened in her a response to himself similar to that she aroused in him, so that in her eyes as he leant towards her would have disappeared the polite reflection of himself in the character of a schoolboy and shone instead the naked, physical being he desired to be.

Lost in this vision he returned to the dormitory and in hanging his watch on the bedrail, dropped it. He picked it up as though the swiftness of the action could somehow save it from damage, but saw that the glass had smashed against the linoleum. With false nonchalance he immediately strapped it to the rail since he felt he had to hide the disaster from his companions as though guilt or shame were attached to it, and through his outwardly normal actions until he fell asleep he thought of nothing else but his misfortune and what seemed to him the impossibility of ever retrieving it. For as our minds admit of no other possibility than parting when we detect in our beloved some cataclysmic amatory delinquency, never imagining that the love affair can be patched up and continue indefinitely, so it did not at first occur to Gerald that the watch could be repaired, still less that the mechanics of achieving that utopian end were, even for a boarder at Seafolde House, relatively simple. No doubt in the depth of his feelings was the sense that the pristine integrity of the watch represented his concerned but fragile relationship with his father, and that to treat it as though it were something capable of being, in the ignorance of his father, broken and patched up was subtly to deny its primary importance.

It was therefore only after much heart-ache that he was able to say to Howarth, as on the ensuing Wednesday evening they set out for the town, that he had broken his watch-glass and wanted to try to get it mended. Surprisingly enough the words slipped out easily, nor did Howarth appear to think them of much moment, for he merely remarked that a jeweller's existed just before one got to the fish and chip shop. Despite his long cogitation about it Gerald had never formulated the problem in such precise terms and had vaguely envisaged embarrassing calls at several establishments—an ironmonger's, say, and a glazier's—in order to try to have the repair effected. The proceedings at the jeweller's were, too, amazing in their concreteness and normality. The shopkeeper, on being presented with the watch, brought a box of watch-glasses out from under the counter and in a few seconds had clicked one into place: the cost, moreover, was negligible. Gerald came out of the shop, the watch once more back on his wrist, its hands again inviolate, with an infinitely sweet sense of relief and happiness.

Over their fish and chips, anxious to prolong his felicity, he speculated aloud on his chance of being moved up again at the beginning of next term which, of course, was the time of the school year for general promotion. Howarth was so unresponsive that Gerald imagined that since his friend had already become a form behind him the subject was distasteful. Immediately he dropped it, but Howarth, a moment after, pushing a burnt and inedible fragment of chip about his plate with his fork, said: 'I'm not coming back next term.'

'Not coming back?' Gerald quickly envisaged Howarth in terrible disgrace, the bankruptcy of Howarth's parents, Howarth's mortal illness.

'My father gave notice at half term. I'm going to Deighton.'

To Gerald the word, the school it signified, was meaningless, but he suffered a great pang of envy at what seemed, despite his loyalty to Seafolde House, Howarth's future translation to a more mature sphere, as a boy will envy another's assumption of long trousers though he knows that his own familiar short ones are far more comfortable. 'Are you?' he made his paralysed lips remark.

Howard steered the chip through a sea of vinegar. 'My father wanted me not to tell anyone until the end of term. So keep it under your hat. I haven't told anyone else.'

'I won't say a word.'

'Don't you want to know why I'm leaving?'

The utterance of the strange and pregnant syllables 'Deighton' had driven the question from Gerald's mind but he saw now that the reasons he had at first adumbrated were all untenable. 'Of course I do,' he replied.

'My father says that Seafolde House is going downhill.'

XI

One afternoon towards the end of term an annual ceremony took place, strange to Gerald but familiar to those who had been longer at the school. In front of a clump of trees on the border of the First Pitch a row of chairs was set out, and behind it a line of benches. Facing all this, while the whole school stood looking on, a smiling, bearded, old man set up a camera which was mounted, at the top of its tripod, on a cogged, brass semi-circle.

'We shall certainly miss first period,' remarked Thompson with satisfaction, 'and probably a good bit of second as well.'

'It's a very curious camera,' said Gerald.

'My dear fool, this is a *panoramic* photograph we're going to have taken.'

The masters came out in their gowns and sat in the middle of the row of chairs, the prefects occupying the rest of the row. Directed by Mr Norfolk, the taller among the rest of the boys stood behind the chairs. Small boys perched on the benches at the rear or squatted at the masters' and prefects' feet. The amiable photographer emerged from under his black cloth and requested Mr Norfolk to squeeze the group closer together. There was a good deal of horseplay in which boys were pushed off the benches. Miss Pemberton and Mrs Watt came over from the House and took two of the three vacant seats which had been left in the centre of the chairs. With a loud whirring sound the camera was set off by the photographer on a dummy run and Thompson, who was standing with Gerald at one end of the row immediately behind the chairs, said: 'After it starts I think I shall run round the back and stand at the other end of the row and be taken again as it comes round.'

But such remarks and the fooling about ceased as the Headmaster appeared. In his hand he carried a mortarboard which, in the same way as the ribbon on his Sunday pince-nez, was not only utterly appropriate for the occasion but revealed fresh depths in his *persona*, like the wearing, on a ceremonial occasion, by a long-known business acquaintance, of a decoration for some past military gallantry. Already there was on the Headmaster's face the smile necessary for the moment when the camera would swivel past him. He took the vacant chair between the two ladies.

There was something melancholy about this event that so unmistakably marked the approaching end of the school year, the slackening of tension, impending departures—despite the stainless blue skies and the sense that it was impossible for the breeze to strike chill. In the centre of the group the Headmaster seemed like a constant star in a cloud of planets that each over a few brief years moved in from its outer orbit to ever closer ones until, at last in its highest place near the source of light, it suddenly vanished.

As the photographer gave his final warning to be still and the sweeping camera eye started to make its irrevocable observation, Gerald thought how impossible was the conception that the school—so numerous, so brilliantly headmastered, capable of these unpredictable traditional occasions—was 'going downhill'. His astonishment and sense of doom at the revelation in the chip shop had become dulled with the passage of the days, just as the citizen of an empire threatened suddenly by barbarians or the strangulation of its grain supply reassuringly finds after the announcement of the catastrophe that he can still stroll on the city walls and sit down to his usual breakfast. Nevertheless Gerald continued to watch anxiously for signs that would confirm or deny Howarth's father's diagnosis, though he was at a loss to imagine precisely what would indicate any impending disaster, short of some obvious and Poesque symptom like a great fissure in the school walls. It had occurred to him that the phrase indicated some moral malady with which the school was riddled, evidenced by that strange nocturnal commerce between Mountain and Blakey he had heard of last term or even, indeed, his own occasional feverish searchings of dictionaries, old novels, books on art, for graphic information about the sensual life his body demanded with obvious depravity in this world which was designed to cater for its spiritual and hygienic welfare alone. But on reflection he realized that Mr Howarth could know nothing of this secret life at Seafolde House, since it was unthinkable that his son, involved in it as fully as anyone, would bring himself to reveal it.

154

'Going downhill' therefore, remained a mysterious term, ludicrously associated with such trivialities as the size of Matley's sausage at the end of term feast and the absence on Sports Day this year of the silver band of previous years—indications, like a giraffe's long neck, as much of accident as of design. It was a conception as far from the realities of school as that of 'economic crisis' from the realities of everyday existence. This latter phrase appeared to be, like a celebrated murder trial or a foreign war, an illusion created to fill certain pages of the newspapers, and not—as were the protagonists and scores of the cricket page—capable of verification in fact. For one could with confidence announce, say, one's intention of 'seeing' Hendren in the holidays, but this grave state of affairs in which the whole civilized world was alleged to have been plunged was incapable of discernment either in the streets or at home. One day Gerald had discovered that the art master, a small man with a red nose who visited the school twice a week, made his lunch on these occasions off sandwiches in one of the class-rooms, but on opening up the subject with Howarth he ascertained that this habit was of too long standing to be a symptom either of 'economic crisis' or of the school's 'going downhill' and was therefore to be regarded, as so many phenomena had to be regarded, as evidence merely of the essential eccentricity of human behaviour.

Indeed, there was no lack of signs that far from the school declining it bore within itself, and particularly in the character and activity of Mr Pemberton, potentials of expansion and new ambition. For instance, about this time there appeared on the main notice board a sheet of white cardboard to delineate, in the form of a

graph, the progress of the Chapel Fund and which week
by week showed a steeply ascending line. The explanation of the graph, at the foot of the notice, was written
in red ink in the Headmaster's admirably clear hand and
bore his signature, 'G. Howard Pemberton'. Gerald had
often pored over this signature (and, indeed, could
produce a passable imitation of it), never failing to be
impressed by the brilliant invention which continued
the G in an abruptly different direction to form the first
upright stroke of the H and had made the d a Greek d
which again could be continued and bent to make the
pillar of the P, whose pediment was an almost perfectly
drawn whorl. And how bold it was of the signature to
reveal one of its owner's Christian names in a world
where Christian names were slightly disgraceful! There
was, however, about 'Howard' a tantalizing and enviable ambiguity so that it revealed less than it promised,
for it seemed scarcely to be a Christian name at all but
an additional surname which gave to the Headmaster
additional masculinity and ferocity, like a fairy tale's
two-headed giant. Nor was this effect detracted from by
Gerald's knowing, in fact, Mr Pemberton's first
Christian name, for the Headmaster's practice of invariably representing it by its initial letter took away
from it almost every association—of weakness, say, or
vulgarity—it might have had in conjunction with another
person, rather as the letter W may be abstracted from
and seem to stand for something much politer and more
spiritual than the water-closet of its origin.

Other evidence of the school's continuing fertility
was also forthcoming by Mr Pemberton's purchase of a
rain-gauge, which he displayed and explained one morning at assembly. It was installed in a corner of the

vegetable garden, and for some weeks the Headmaster's hat could be observed from the playground appearing and disappearing as he took the reading before morning school, the result of which he subsequently entered in yet another graph on the notice board. But a boringly dry spell of weather persisting, Mr Pemberton eventually delegated the task appropriately to Matley, who he knew was reading Geography for the School Certificate and whose statistics were immediately thrown awry by Thompson one night urinating in the rain-gauge.

XII

It sometimes seemed to Gerald that the impedimenta of existence at school had a greater reality than those of the outside world. In one of the washrooms in the school block, for instance, there were several enamel mugs each of which soon acquired for him a distinct and immediately recognizable individuality, so that he would avoid drinking from one which had a permanent brown stain for a couple of inches up its interior, put up with another which although very chipped had sufficient of its rim unscathed to accommodate one's mouth, but would always, if he could, choose a mug ostensibly identical with the others but which in fact had a slightly larger and lighter handle. Occasionally, in the tranced condition in which he lay in bed after the morning rising bell, the images of all those mugs would rise up, for no reason, in his mind—or other images of trivial objects which had nevertheless through constant familiarity in a closed world acquired some obsessive, significant quality, as the very stones of an island beach might impress themselves on a shipwrecked sailor.

And yet this furniture of school—the chalk-eraser belonging peculiarly to each blackboard, the grain and carving of every desk at which he had ever sat, the shapes of scrubbed but indelible inkstains on the floorboards—was capable of being transformed in an instant into an unusual, even exotic setting by being called on to function for some purpose out of the school's everyday routine. So it was on Speech Day when the assembly hall had been arranged so that parents could sit in the body of it and boys along the side walls, while, on the dais, Mr Pemberton's desk, a Union Jack thrown over it and affixed neatly to the floor with drawing pins, bore several piles of new books and a carafe of water. This transformed milieu was all the more exciting to Gerald because of his father's absence: he gazed around with uncommitted interest, like a foreigner in the midst of a civil war.

Spilling over from the dais were the seated masters, those with degrees wearing not only gowns but also their hoods, whose varied fur and colours seemed not predetermined by the respective university authorities but to have been chosen at the whim of the wearer, so that, for instance, the primrose folds along Mr Chaplin's back were like some hitherto unrevealed prankishness of character, a determination to show at once that learning was important but could be lightly worn. When the Headmaster appeared it could be seen that his hood was not purple or dark red as one might have supposed, but pale blue, and this, too, by enlarging one's conception of Mr Pemberton, at once became his appropriate colour. With the Headmaster was a stout man in a morning coat whom Gerald knew to be Alderman Cole.

Mr Pemberton sat at the desk, Alderman Cole on his right. They both stared out for a few moments over the quietening audience in the manner of practised platform men and then, as though they were about to play a duet, they turned slightly to one another, the Headmaster indicating a barely perceptible question and Alderman Cole an almost invisible assent. Mr Pemberton rose and began to deliver his report on, as he put it, the school's year at work and play.

His fluent and confident public manner which Gerald, having heard it so often at morning assembly, took entirely for granted as though it were a natural attribute of headmasters, was suddenly felt by him under these circumstances to be a source of intense pleasure and pride, like the beauty of one's mother revealed at a party. And the slow and often tedious day-by-day surmounting of the obstacles, and assimilation of events, in one's life at school was similarly shown by Mr Pemberton's words to be a swift and progressive flight towards virtue, health and wisdom. The labours of the staff, scholastic routine, examination successes, matches played by the school XIs—even the matches lost—all these themes the Headmaster developed and gradually amalgamated until, as in a symphony of Sibelius, he was able to enunciate the grand and extended statement for which they had been the mere preliminaries, a statement no less impressive on this occasion for being familiar—that though the things he had been speaking of were of great importance yet they did not constitute the real work of the school which was, which must be or the school had failed utterly, the inculcation in the boys of a true moral sense, the ability to choose the good and reject the bad, to leave the school clean in mind and body, ready to serve as citizens of a still great nation.

Then Mr Pemberton introduced Alderman Cole, who was to present the prizes and who rose to make some remarks in a manner and tone which Gerald felt fell short of the standard set by the Headmaster. He could not help thinking, too, that Cole's parents were quite unjustifiably monopolizing these official occasions. Mrs Cole at Sports Day and now the Alderman: it was a bit much considering that their son was a mere junior. Remembering also Mr Pemberton's leniency over the matter of the weights, it flashed ludicrously through Gerald's mind that perhaps the Headmaster was being blackmailed by the Coles.

If it were not so Mr Pemberton was certainly guilty of a quite unjustifiable indulgence towards this corpulent family. Gerald hesitated at such a conception, refusing, unable, to formulate the fresh scale of values that its acceptance implied, as one who feels that his rejection of a life-long belief in the artistic supremacy of *Omar Khayyam* will force him to admit the validity of the extreme and obscure poets he has always scorned. For despite his admiration of the Headmaster's address it had struck him that during the review of the year's sport no mention had been made of the irregular events of the Westport match, a dubious page in an otherwise honourable history, nor had Mr Pemberton from his Olympian viewpoint indicated how delicately poised was the struggle between good and evil.

Alderman Cole ended his speech and began to distribute the prizes as Mr Chaplin, standing by his side, called out the names of the winners. The fortunate boys threaded their way to the dais through the applauding be-hatted mothers, groomed fathers and the occasional attractive sister, under the smiling gaze of the Headmaster whose legs and lower torso being cut off from view by the beflagged desk appeared like a commemorative bust of himself.

THREE

I

As GERALD, after unpacking, lugged his empty trunk to the box-room, he passed on the landing a small boy he had never seen before in his life and whose appearance in these familiar surroundings was as strange and exotic as a foreign coin in a handful of change. When he got back to the dormitory, Gerald said to Matley: 'I see there's a new boarder.'

'There are two,' said Matley, who had moved to the next bed to Gerald, once occupied by Howarth. Matley's old bed, which was in an inferior, exposed position by the door, now belonged to Dover who last term had been in the next lower dormitory and had seemed a very junior boy indeed. Another junior now slept in Snape major's place, for Stink-Bomb Billy had not inappropriately been translated to the single room which had formerly seemed Mountain's own peculiar milieu.

At first blush this dilution of society had seemed to Gerald proof positive that the school was in a decline. Matley was a quite inadequate substitute for Howarth; Dover and the other junior had brought with them the immature habits of an inferior civilization; and Gerald felt the despair of an officer at the quality of his reinforcements. But the knowledge that the scale was being extended at the other end reconciled him somewhat to these sad changes, and he cherished the idea of these two new boys as fondly as the leader of a splinter party his new recruits, even strolling with a casual air to the most junior dormitory of all, where they were housed, and verifying their existence and appearance. And as he did so it seemed to him that they in their turn must look on him as a member of a totally superior species, and when he had gone would timidly inquire about his name and reputation, as he himself as a new boy had inquired about such giants as Mountain.

But it was not until breakfast the next morning, the first meal of the new term, that the startling changes brought about by the ending of the school year were fully revealed. At the head of the main table, in place of Birnie, sat Goff and at his right hand was the negligible Blakey. Opposite Blakey was Cropper and then Cropper's friend Dyce. Thompson came next to Blakey and then Gerald himself, feeling as he walked to his chair the places where he might have sat falling past him like defeated runners in a race. He sat with a false air of nonchalance, as a frequenter of the pit might sit with complimentary tickets in the stalls, convinced that he was now *too* near and that his neighbours were phoneys.

Could it be that the great ones who had occupied these places last term had been great only in the minds of their beholders, that they, too, had been in reality weak like Goff, stupid like Blakey, as undistinguished as Gerald felt himself to be? Or had the school suffered the blow that Howarth's father had predicted and must now be governed by usurpers, boys not tall enough and of insufficient individuality of character? Gerald was sure at least that among Birnie and his fellows there could have been no apprehensive relationships such as existed between himself and Cropper. The latter, in a new suit and with an attitude permanently orientated towards Goff, had effortlessly cast from himself all the ludicrous associations of the previous term. In his new place and with the absence of Mountain, he could not be conceived as coming from a family which bred Alsatians and owned a bull-nosed Morris, and it was almost impossible to imagine that his serious questing profile and abundant hair could be associated with anything comic. He looked heavier, older, dangerous.

When Gerald turned to inspect the Masters' table, he saw a change less dramatic but scarcely less disturbing. The chair at the Headmaster's right was occupied not by Mr Chaplin but by Mr Marsh and there was no new master to fill up the gap left by the re-shuffling of places. In his exalted position Mr Marsh's character stood truly revealed and plainly condemned itself as inadequate. As the shortcomings of a reserve summon up the ghost of the player he has replaced, so Mr Marsh's barbarous black curls and leather-bound sports jacket poignantly reminded Gerald of Mr Chaplin's neat baldness and dark suit, their utter appropriateness taken so heartlessly for granted. And on Mr Pemberton's other side, like the unreliable future deviationist of a revolutionary government, was Mr Percy. So ill-supported by his staff as he was and with such inferior material among the boys, Gerald felt for the Headmaster the pang of pity one feels for the only good member of a ghastly provincial repertory company.

But Mr Pemberton seemed utterly unconscious of these changes and, as an old inhabitant of a mountain village will go about his trivial business in the face of the most frightful volcanic rumblings, having already undergone every possible shade of cataclysm, he calmly popped fragment after fragment of butter- and marmalade-loaded toast into his mouth and masticated them with impeccably closed mouth.

It had never struck Gerald that the triangles of toast in their silver rack which, like a problem in three dimensional geometry, confronted the Headmaster every morning at a meal where everyone else ate bread, were other than Mr Pemberton's unquestionable right; but now they seemed like all privileges in a time of crisis— its precipitating cause and their abolition its *raison d'être*. But in the manner of the most moderate wing of a movement for reform, Gerald believed only in the evil of the privilege, not of its enjoyer, and thought also of the fillip it would give the school if the provision of toast could be universal.

Many boys had brought back with them pots of preserve or tins of syrup and these now stood before them on the table to be resorted to when the always inadequate supplies provided by the school at breakfast were exhausted. That Cropper had never subscribed to this custom had often in previous terms been remarked on by Mountain and put down to his parents' poverty or parsimony. His place this morning was innocent of pot or tin, but the austerity seemed a sign of strength. And when Thompson had opened and helped himself to his strawberry jam it appeared a diplomatic and respectful gesture that he should push the jar across the table and say: 'Have some jam, Cropper?'

Cropper accepted it with the lack of embarrassment, even the faint disdain, of a conqueror seeing put before him the tribute of a pile of valuable but smelly pelts. Gerald formed the phrase: 'Cropper's forgotten to unpack his jam,' but it stuck in his throat. Not only was there no audience to appreciate and enlarge on it, but he was, he suddenly realized, frightened of Cropper. The unwritten treaties, the buffer states, which formerly had protected him, had all been swept away. The balance of power was disastrously changed.

The deformed Dyce leaned and whispered in Cropper's ear and Cropper nodded and smiled one of his rare smiles: Gerald's cheeks began to burn, for he was sure something derogatory had been said about him. For the first time at Seafolde House he felt that he was despised, disliked, thought ridiculous, and since he was the same as he had always been the foundations of his life were for a few terrible moments threatened with complete destruction.

When the day boys had arrived and prayers were over, the same profound shift in status could be observed in the school block as in the House. Although Gerald found himself in a different class-room, Mr Percy had moved up with him into the gap left by Mr Chaplin, while lower down in the school some Procrustean arrangement had made Mr Norfolk a more important master without relieving him of his most junior status. And here could be still more clearly seen the ambiguous nature of the changes the new term had brought. Was it decay or time alone that had placed Cropper and even Blakey in the form that was traditionally under Mr Pemberton's care, that occupied a room different in kind from the other class-rooms, that had formerly seemed mysterious and remote? Gerald himself, now sitting as of right next to the reference library where he had so often nervously and illegally stood, felt that he had not by his own growth become entitled to his new place, but that the school had moved back, fitting a quite inappropriate frame round his immaturity.

Perhaps Mr Percy was seized with not dissimilar emotions for when he came into the class-room he opened the lid of the master's desk and gazed inside it for a moment, as though he had expected it still to contain Mr Chaplin's possessions—a bottle of green ink, a pen with a clean nib, a guide to New Zealand, a spectacle case. Then he closed the lid, put his books and papers on top of it, and tucked his corpulence on to the chair. He looked round the class and said: 'It takes all the running you can do, to keep in the same place. Eh, Bracher?'

Gerald wanted to reply that he was glad that Mr Percy had moved up with him, but of course that was impossible. He contented himself with saying very promptly: '*Through the Looking-Glass*, sir.' The words had come almost automatically to his lips and with them the memory rose of the remote days before they had gone to Durban. He saw a picture of himself reading aloud to his mother as she lay in bed and then of his climbing into her arms and looking beyond her to the baby in the cot, the brother who had not survived his infancy. And he sensed vividly the atmosphere of books, of warmth and softness, of uninhibited kissing, that had surrounded those days. Since then he had been a quite different being, in whom until recently the sap of sensuality and intellectualism had slept, so that he could marvel at the child of long ago who had laid his cheek against other soft cheeks and who had read without thought of any particular books being boring or difficult, recognizing him with delighted surprise as his true self who now perhaps was in the process of being reborn.

II

Despite his recognition of the changes the new term had brought, it was nevertheless a shock to Gerald to find on the House notice board a day or two later an announcement, above the Headmaster's initials, that Cropper had been appointed a House Prefect. Blakey's was the other name on the list but its effect was wholly absorbed by that emanating from the word 'Cropper', as the farce of, say, Otway's *Venice Preserv'd* is subordinated in the memory to its tragic tone. Gerald tried to discover in the appointment the excellent motive which Mr Pemberton must have had, but without success. At lunch-time he kept up a continuous conversation with Thompson, occasionally casting a cautious look at Cropper, who, however, betrayed no outward sign of the honour that had been done him, and as the day wore on he became, like those who have voted against an extremist party which has nevertheless come into power, half reassured by the unexpected continuance of ordinary existence. And at tea-time, when once more the private pots and tins appeared on the table, he was so far convinced by the absence of unusual events that Cropper's House Prefectship was a mere title, without plenipotentiary significance—as it were an honorary Air Commodoreship bestowed on a Bank Manager—that he remarked so that Cropper could hear him: 'Your jam's gone down rather quickly, Thompson. Have the dogs been at it?'

Cropper said nothing. Gerald inwardly exulted at the power of the word, of intellect, the power he possessed as of right, like the absence of glasses and pimples, and which gave him natural superiority even over those on whom titular distinctions had been conferred. During the evening he forgot completely about the threat of Cropper's power and physique, as between pangs of pain even the most frightful disease can be forgotten, and the alarm that seized him was therefore all the more acute when, as he was snatching a few minutes at a book before Lights Out, Dyce appeared at the door and said: 'Bracher, Cropper wants to see you in our dormitory.'

'What?'

'Never mind what for.'

'You aren't a House Prefect, Dyce, so don't give yourself airs.'

'Cropper is,' said Dyce. 'And he wants to see you.'

'He's no right to get me out of bed. Jacket'll be round soon for Lights Out.' The taint of illegality in the summons was all the more sinister because Dyce (and no doubt Cropper) was fully dressed while he was in vulnerable pyjamas, like some ill patient confronted by a surgeon or a liberal by secret police.

'Are you coming or not, Bracher?'

Gerald felt a desire at once to get Dyce out of his sight and to prolong the conversation, both courses seeming to offer the chance of averting the vague but terrible encounter that threatened him. 'I think it could wait until morning.'

'He said he wanted to see you now,' said Dyce. 'Have I to tell him you refuse to come?'

Though the exchanges with Dyce were of vital interest and importance, Gerald's eyes were directed all the time towards his book and he even contrived to take in a few words, though without in the least understanding their relation to the narrative he had previously been reading. At last he looked up, as though reluctant to tear himself away from an absorbingly interesting occupation. 'Tell him what you like,' he said with trembling lips.

When Dyce had gone out, Matley, who was still messing about in his monkish dressing-gown, said: 'You were quite right not to go.'

'I'm very glad you approve,' said Gerald, trying to siphon off his accumulated bitterness on an object incapable of aggression, feeling the future as a sickening weight in his stomach.

Mr Norfolk came and turned out the light. Not very long after it was put on again and Gerald, blinking through the glare, saw Cropper, with Dyce, the shark's attendant sucker fish, close by his side. Both were now in pyjamas and dressing-gowns.

'Get out of bed, Bracher,' said Cropper.

'Why?' asked Gerald, out of the dozen questions that flooded his mind.

'Because I tell you to.'

'Being a House Prefect doesn't entitle you to wake me up in the middle of the night.'

'Don't be a fool, Bracher.'

A huge wish to hurt Cropper, to pick up some cruel missile and crash it into his face, to utter some outrageous words about his family, seized Gerald and made him shake almost with pleasure, for the thought was so vivid and urgent that the mere formulation of it seemed to translate it into reality.

'Are you going to get out or have we to get you out?' asked Cropper.

Cropper and Dyce, though they had now advanced close to the bed, were not the sole, nor the most actual, objects in Gerald's vision. For he still had time to look round (at his fellow members of the dormitory, propped interestedly on their elbows, at the white bulge of the chamber, like some piece of sculpture glimpsed in a gloomy grove, under Matley's bed) even to think for a moment that tomorrow he must glue down the broken spine of his book—as a condemned man may, on the very scaffold, retain sufficient interest in life to consider the convenience of the executioner. In the same way he was tempted to answer Cropper's question not with the brevity and point it demanded but with some general and totally unconnected observation.

But this strange, alert detachment was dispersed in an instant as Cropper grasped him under the arms and began to pull him out of bed. He felt, too, Dyce's moist hands round his neck pulling with gratuitous force— gratuitous because up to this moment Gerald had neglected to form any intention of resisting physically. But now he did resist, holding on to the cold iron of the bed-head—even in that instant carefully avoiding his watch—and, as he was drawn out of the bed clothes, bending his legs so that his feet could get a leverage against the bodies that leaned over him. It soon became apparent that Cropper and Dyce were trying to turn him over on his stomach across the bed but they made little progress. From one of the other beds in the dormitory a dissident voice called out: 'Keep it up, Bracher!"

In the very moment, however, when he was most conscious of the reserve of power that would enable him to hold out indefinitely against the assault, his body relented as though taking pity on the strenuous attempts by Cropper and Dyce to attain their desire, or perhaps because secretly it wished to suffer martyrdom; but its capitulation was accompanied with such a convincing show of struggle that he could half believe that it was in truth by the opposition of superior physical and mental force that he was bound to lie face downward under the pressing hands of his tormentors. His gasping for breath, too, he found that he could simulate with complete realism and lack of effort.

And so, his complete degradation brought about less by the action of Cropper and Dyce than his own volition, he heard the former say: 'This is for being too cheeky, Bracher.' He had time to criticize in his own mind this piffling, ill-expressed remark before his whole concentration was absorbed by the pain of a hair-brush, no doubt transported by Cropper in his dressing-gown pocket, falling repeatedly on his ill-protected buttocks.

When Cropper and Dyce had gone, turning out the light as they left and thus mercifully leaving him without the almost impossible task of assuming a face that would hide his shame and hurt, it came to him that though Cropper had exercised his authority in a most ludicrous manner, that did not subtract any terror from him. On the contrary, Gerald saw clearly an indefinitely long future haunted not only by the threat of Cropper's power to inflict corporal punishment but also by his mere presence in the school that could, like the serious illness of someone one loves, impregnate with its evil effluence occasions and anticipations of happiness, the otherwise noble and pleasurable books and music, the very seasons of the year.

Howarth's defection had left Gerald without a companion for the twice-weekly excursions to the town. On the first Saturday of the new term he had (Thompson having paired off with Blakey) gone in with Matley who, however, had refused to enter the fish and chip shop and had, under the stimulus of this sudden intimacy with Gerald, related embarrassing stories about his mother's numerous surgical operations. The following Wednesday Gerald had made the expedition alone and, after the first uneasiness of walking down the drive solitary among the talking groups, he had found in the evening a rather melancholy but stimulating air and now, on this third Saturday of term, he set out unaccompanied almost out of habit and with the vague anticipation of experiences beyond the scope of the conventional twos and threes.

The remains of summer persisted: the darkening sky was calm over the sea, to which the low land lay open: one of the eastern invasion routes (of which he remembered Mr Percy speaking) for the Anglo-Saxons against the original darker men—as the fair, barbarous Cropper was warring against him.

Ahead of him and walking in the same direction, he saw a girl's slim figure, and he quickened his steps so that he should eventually pass her, for always lively within him was the instinct to display himself and—an almost instantaneous process consisting of the evaluation of a series of deductions from such minute particulars as an ankle, an arrangement of hair, a style of dress—to explore, an instinct of animal simplicity but upon which was built a structure complicated beyond analysis by his shyness, ignorance, yearning and remembrance of the details of paintings and of literature. He set his course to come up rather wide of her so that he would be able to send glances in her direction with less chance of detection. He was still some distance away when, conscious probably of his purposeful steps, she turned her head and he saw what he might have known long before had his senses not been deranged by his excited imaginings about the encounter—that it was Miss Pemberton. No doubt because she recognized the colours of his cap she waited for him to come up to her.

'Oh, it's you, Bracher,' she said in her small but clear and penetrating voice.

'Yes, Miss Pemberton.' He stood at a loss for the correct behaviour but in a moment he saw that she expected him to fall in at her side as she set off again towards the beginnings of the concrete esplanade.

'Are you going in to town by yourself?' she asked.

'Yes, Miss Pemberton.'

'Why?'

Because Howarth left at the end of last term; because I like being alone on these evenings out: either would have been a true and sensible reply, but all he said was: 'I don't know, Miss Pemberton.'

He found that he could not keep step with her because her stride was shorter than his, but before he could discover the precise nature of the sensation that this gave him she said: 'Where did you go for your holidays?'

'Cornwall,' he said. 'Near Falmouth.' And the memory came to him of waiting in a tobacconist's while his father walked across the shop floor trying out an ashplant before buying it. He wondered why this recollection should send a pang to his heart.

'Did you do any sailing?'

'No, Miss Pemberton.'

At first he thought that she must know how far the notion of sailing was from his father's character and habits and that her question had been ironic, but she went on: 'Very wise. It's a horrible pastime. That was just a trap question. I know a sailor—a nominal sailor—who simply refuses to go to sea any more. But of course he's a Frenchman.'

Almost immediately he realized to what she was referring and the idea that she should trouble to make the fanciful allusion before someone who she could not anticipate would understand it struck him as so extraordinary that involuntarily he laughed aloud.

'What are you laughing at, Bracher?' she inquired sharply.

'Nothing, Miss Pemberton.'

'What did you find amusing in my remarks?'

Then it was as though some obstruction, which for a long time had been poked at without result, suddenly flew out, and there poured from him easily word after word, arranged in that slightly facetious manner which came to him in his best moments and which perhaps even communicated his true self: 'I happen to know that nautical friend of yours.'

'What nautical friend?' Her voice squeaked incredulously on the absurd adjective.

'Marcel.'

'How could you possibly know Marcel?'

A knife plunged itself in Gerald's guts as for a second

he failed to disentangle his knowledge of the doll's existence from the letter he had guiltily read on the afternoon of the Westport match. All his mind could form was the phrase: 'Marcel, that understanding Frog', which came to him in the very shape of her hand-writing. Then, with the special fluency of the dissembler, he said: 'I've seen him on the sofa in your room at the House. Watching boils squeezed and cascaras handed out.'

'Yes,' said Miss Pemberton, 'he understands human suffering. But how did you know his name?'

'Mrs Watt told me.'

'I wonder what else she tells you.' But the speculation did not seem to need a reply and after a few steps of silence she said: 'Did you move up again this term?'

'Yes, Miss Pemberton.' This time the monosyllable with the formally added name was not at all like the conventional replies he had made to her at first, which on his part were meant merely to confirm for her his supposed character of schoolboy addressing authority, but instead was the surrendering to her will of the simple key to his confidence.

She took it in the easiest way. 'So you're still with Mr Percy.'

'Yes, I'm still with Mr Percy.' He did not know how he divined that it would give her pleasure to hear the name repeated.

'He teaches well, doesn't he?'

He had always had the conception that some masters could teach well and others could not but had never before applied it. 'Yes, he does,' he said and tried to find a sentence that would intelligibly convey to her the complicated passages, not all explicit, between himself and

Mr Percy about the meaning of Shelley, the hierarchy of literature and, above all, the relationships between master, boy and school. 'He's very subtle.' It was a word extremely popular this term.

'Subtle,' Miss Pemberton repeated, giving it amused but serious consideration. 'So you think the masculine character capable of subtlety?'

It seemed she had known he had not really been thinking of Mr Percy's teaching. 'Yes,' he said, turning her question over and conjuring up Mr Norfolk being pushed in his car. 'Of course, it's quite rare.'

'Quite rare,' she said.

It struck him that in her was stored up an enormous fund of information which he might spend months— years—in exhausting. 'I would have been in Mr Chaplin's form,' he remarked, 'if he hadn't left.'

But this time she failed to grasp the motive behind his words, which was to find out whether Charlie's vacant place was truly symptomatic of a wasting disease in the school. 'I used to teach once,' she said.

'Did you really, Miss Pemberton?'

'Before I took over boils and cascaras. When my aunt was still alive. She used to do them in those days.'

He realized that she meant the Grey Chap's wife. 'Are you a B.A.?' he asked, remembering once hearing a rumour of her learning.

'No. We had a baby form of day boys then and so my ignorance didn't matter. Do you think that if I were I should——' She left the sentence unfinished. They were now among the lights of the little town and she said: 'I'm going on to the Hippodrome.' It was a new concrete building by the pier head, containing a café, a cinema and a ballroom.

He understood that she was giving him an opportunity for him to leave her gracefully. Even so, he felt that they had gone too far beyond the relationship expected by convention for him merely to raise his cap and make his adieu. He stopped and said: 'Well, I have to go down Station Road.' His action held her captive for a few moments, looking at her feet, pulling up the collar of her raincoat, as though she, too, had forgotten his true status and had to behave with him as she might have with a stranger. At length she raised her head and said: 'Good night, Bracher.'

He said good night, crossed the square to the island of public lavatories and then looked back for her among the people round the entrance to the Hippodrome. He also tried to pick out Mr Percy, for though it was hard to imagine him standing by the garish cinema posters or with his money ready to pay the admission to the ballroom, Gerald saw clearly in this moment how love must, like a still-life painter, use for the working-out of its inspirations the most banal material until it has transformed or succumbed to it. Nor were such relations exalted by their personae: in spite of the oblique, brittle correspondence, the brilliant shifts of concealment and allusion in an unfavourable environment, they must come at last to the same crude climax as had been enacted by those terrible visitors to the playing field in the summer.

With youth's automatic hunger he made his way to the fish and chip shop. Though he had failed to see Mr Percy's figure in the crowd, he did not doubt that it was with him Miss Pemberton had her rendezvous. When he thought about the affair which it was no longer possible to doubt existed between them, he marvelled

at the impediments to it revealed by Miss Pemberton's
letter or the space that remained between the two when
they were left alone at the Westport match, for since
they had the opportunity for love it seemed to him mere
perversion that they did not fly freely and with over-
whelming feeling into each other's arms—that any bar
to happiness was as artificial as those invented by a play-
wright to keep his lovers separated until the drama shall
have run the course demanded by those requiring an
evening's entertainment. And by the same reasoning,
he was convinced that if there was in fact something in
their situation preventing the consummation of their
relationship there needed only an easily-made mental
effort on either of their parts to remove it—as a novelist
may in a stroke not merely contrive the spatial union of
his characters but also supply them with the mental
processes necessary to bring them, if they have been out
of love or jealous or have quarrelled, together again for
ever. If only, he thought, he had Mr Percy's opportunity, how tender and staunch he would be!

He ate his fish and chips, shopped and walked back to
the House. When he went up to the dormitory he saw
that Matley had already undressed and must be in the
bathroom. On his chair seat on top of his underclothes
he had negligently left the white paper bag containing
his illegal Saturday night pie and Gerald evilly hoped
that the duty master would come in and discover it. But
when Matley returned to the dormitory, walking with his
head down so that he could observe the satisfactory
length and fullness of his Franciscan friar's dressing-
gown, he ostentatiously took up the paper bag, opened
it and drew from it a small brass crucifix.

'What on earth have you got there?' Gerald asked,

with the embarrassment of one who detects in another's painstaking work some gross error of ignorance.

'What do you think it is, Bracher?' Matley wore the overweening manner associated with his worst moments.

'I think it's a crucifix.'

'It is a crucifix.'

'What are you going to do with it?'

'I'm going to put it here.' Matley placed it reverently on his bedside locker which Gerald now saw had been cleared of all articles except a spread clean handkerchief.

'Where did you get it from?'

'I bought it tonight.'

'Where?'

'Woolworth's.'

'Woolworth's,' repeated Gerald, trying derisively to attach to that useful and innocent establishment the odium from which the object, by its very nature, must be exculpated—as the English sometimes condemn the ideas of socialism by reference to their alleged foreign origin.

'Woolworth's have some very good things,' said Matley mildly.

Several replies sprang to Gerald's lips but none of them seemed capable of logically destroying the position in which Matley, through being granted some tacit and ill-defined premise, had entrenched himself so complacently and ludicrously. And even when the other two occupants of the dormitory had arrived and added their questions and objections, Matley was still able in comparative silence to kneel at his lengthy prayers, not, as heretofore, facing his bed but in front of the locker.

IV

A day boy, junior to Gerald, approached him during the morning break with a book, in a curiously soft padded binding, and asked him if he would write down his 'confession'. On the corner of the book was embossed 'My Confession' and, inside, each page contained a number of questions, with spaces beneath for the 'confessor's' answers. When Gerald turned over the leaves he found some of them already completed, at first by quite senior boys, such as Goff, and even by Mr Norfolk and the red-nosed art master, but later, as the owner had begun to exhaust his victims or lower his standards, the spelling and neatness of the entries degenerated—and even their originality, for the lesser minds, confronted by such a conundrum as 'What is your favourite flower?' were apt to fall back on the inspiration and knowledge of their predecessors, so that the answer 'Dahlia' appeared again and again, and, because of the perils inherent in the copying of a text by an indifferent or careless scribe, with increasingly obscure orthography, like a corrupt passage in a contemporaneously printed Elizabethan play.

In the lunch hour Gerald set about writing in his own answers, approaching the task with the same excitement at being able to display himself to advantage as at the start of an essay or the putting on of a new garment. On the opposite page there was a completed 'confession' at which he idly glanced while thinking of his own. 'What is your favourite colour?' he read, and the surprising answer 'White' led his eye compulsively down the page.

'Favourite flower?   *Taraxacum officinale.*
Favourite author?   P. G. Wodehouse.
Favourite composer?   J. S. Bach.
What quality do you most
    dislike in others?   Violence.
In yourself?   Timidity.'

At this point he looked down at the bottom of the page for the name of the individual who had written in these disturbing answers and who could scarcely be imagined as existing in the world of Seafolde House, and to his astonishment found the legend 'J. P. S. Slade.' There was a perceptible interval during which this name indicated for Gerald merely the remarkable author of the confession, before it merged eventually with the actual individual whose existence had been previously manifested by other activities, as an artist's initial and sudden fame will strike those friends of his who know him only as a bank clerk. And then it was almost impossible for Gerald, with the composite personality in mind, to retain or even fully to recall the attitude he had formerly had towards the old Slade, so that if the latter had, at that moment, walked into the class-room, Gerald would have been forced to adopt the uneasy respect which a ranker must show for an old companion recently commissioned.

As it happened, when he next had the opportunity to scrutinize Slade, which was at tea, he had for the time being forgotten the revelation of 'My Confession', and though the boy must several times have come within the orbit of his gaze he failed to attract the attention which was due to him, as when we visit a museum we may pass without paying it any regard the object for which the endowment is famous and which beforehand we had intended to examine with special care. But in the evening, towards the end of preparation, looking up with tired eyes from his books and wriggling the second finger of his right hand against which his pen had been pressing so hard that it hurt the more when the pressure was relieved, he saw a few desks away from and a little in front of him Slade's pale profile, the cheek still slightly freckled from the summer, a lock of lank hair hanging over the brow, and he thought that this was the mind and body that had supplied the answers that had so surprised him. He remembered last term the encounter in the middle of the night when Slade had been suffering from toothache for which the boy had proposed the remedy of brushing his teeth, and in retrospect this seemed not foolishness but a sardonic or whimsical response of the same nature as those in 'My Confession'. Indeed, whatever of the commonplace or banal resided in the incident now seemed to Gerald to be due to his own obtuseness in treating it as such and failing to draw from the other the involved secrets of his personality which even the vulgar probing of the confession book had done with such success.

The groups of boys started to be sent over to the House in ascending order of seniority. Gerald, feigning to read, waited for the duty master's signal to the group that included Slade, which was the one before the last of all, his own. When it came, he quickly excused himself and followed the boys out of the room. They went at once to their own class-rooms to put away their books and Gerald was left in the hall by the notice board whose papers shook in the autumnal wind blowing through the open doorway from the dark beyond. He hung about indecisively, willing the boys to appear again, but though only a minute or two had passed he began to feel dreadfully uneasy at his lack of occupation, at the absence of proper reasons for his presence there, and went slowly across the playground to the urinals where at least he need suffer no guilt. While he stood there, going needlessly through the motions of the purpose for which he had been able to leave preparation, several boys came in, including Slade.

Gerald lingered plausibly by the entrance, under the crude unshaded light, intending to say to Slade should he improbably pass alone: 'I saw your confession in Collinson's book.' And miraculously Slade was the last to come out. But though Gerald could plainly see that Slade wore for him a suitably deferential expression—that, in fact, as must be obvious, the boy had no occasion to behave otherwise than as a complete inferior, ready to listen, to smile, to obey—he was himself seized with a paralysing shyness, and in a moment Slade had passed him and broken into a run across the playground. So that far from indicating his changed attitude Gerald had by his silence and solemnity increased his distance from Slade who, of course, could not be expected to divine the events and feelings which had led to this encounter.

He walked back to the school block, the wind snatching out his tie, bending his hair. With the collapse of his plan the day seemed to have nothing more to offer—nor, as he looked ahead, could he discern anything of happiness to offset the menacing shadows that hung over his life. He thought of Cropper, as one thinks of a tyranny wallowing in its banners, mass meetings, military triumphs. He stopped automatically in front of the notice board. The sheet which contained the graph showing the progress of the Chapel Appeal Fund had become torn and grubby, and somewhat obscured by more recent notices. The graph itself had long since levelled off—indeed, had lately not been maintained—and Gerald marvelled at his former interest in its upward curve.

From the assembly hall there suddenly came the distant notes of the piano, and instead of summoning up, as Debussy had intended, the Delphic dancers, the music brought to Gerald's perception, with a far greater immediacy than words would have done (indeed, since he did not fully understand the situation there could scarcely be words for it), the gulfs that lay between Mr Percy and Miss Pemberton. That the master should voluntarily return to the lonely occupation he had followed before he was 'keen' on the girl, that he should not every night when he was free have the felicity of waiting for her by the Hippodrome, seemed such poignant conceptions that Gerald's eyes filled with tears, through which, as it were, he heard the music go on to further depths of meaning and emotion.

Thompson came into the hall with his books: preparation had evidently ended. 'That was a long pee, Bracher,' he said, insinuatingly.

'You have a filthy mind in a filthy body,' said Gerald. 'And you need a shave.' He rasped the back of his hand against Thompson's pimpled cheek.

'Did you finish the trig?' Thompson called, as Gerald went back to the class-room in which preparation was held.

Gerald sent back an indecipherable shout. It struck him as utterly incongruous that the school's function should be to inculcate the knowledge of such things and that the minds of others should be filled with concern about them.

V

The Headmaster's entry at prayers was signalled by a peculiarly swift and definite opening of the door that led into the hall, so that no sooner had his unmistakable touch on the handle been identified and caused its frisson of apprehension than his fearful figure was already in the hall, striding towards the dais, the gown bellying behind. Frequently his fertile mind was so full of topics on which he had to address the school that he embarked on some of them before prayers. One morning he mounted the dais and said: 'I have heard of one boy who has the school's welfare at heart. One boy at least.' He paused, and Gerald, convinced that he could not be that boy, felt a sense of guilt that was scarcely lessened by his knowing that the rest of the school must share it. Then Mr Pemberton, instead of fulfilling the dread expectancy that he had roused, announced the number of the hymn. When it was over and he had said prayers he uttered the command that was constantly on his lips as he moved through the school. 'Be seated, boys.' The creak of iron, the swish of bottoms on wood, the shuffling of feet, though to a stranger to the world of school would have seemed to be nerve-rackingly prolonged, in fact died down in the minimum of time. 'I have heard of one boy,' said Mr Pemberton, 'who realized that the Chapel Appeal Fund was his concern. Of course, it was the concern of every one of you. Perhaps some of you even felt that. But how many of you translated that feeling into action? Tried with all his might to make the Appeal a success? I have heard of one boy, who without any prompting either from me or from his parents, took practical steps to swell the Fund. He had no more money than any of you, but he succeeded in making regular contributions. Do you know what he did, boys? He collected silver paper—collected it most devotedly, ever since the Appeal was launched, all through the summer holidays. He is still collecting it—and selling it, of course, to bring in money for the Fund. I don't mind telling you his name, boys, though I daresay he would not wish me to, because he hasn't worked for his own glory. I heard of this boy's work quite by chance.' At last the Headmaster permitted his stern countenance to relax. 'His name is Brian Cole.'

There came from the listening boys a faint involuntary escape of breath, marking the end of their suspense, but each contributor had been unable to keep from his suspiration an emotional tone, so that the *tutti* emerged in a ghostly groan, the off-stage murder of some aged Shakespearian monarch. Like severe ladies of an old régime, Mr Pemberton had the faculty of ignoring, without condoning, breaches of propriety which it did not suit him to reprehend. Now he smiled an aperture-less smile before he said: 'Stand up, Brian.' After a suitable pause, Cole's stout figure was seen to emerge in the middle of the school. 'Well, done, Brian,' said Mr Pemberton. Even Cole was unable to assimilate this honour with complacence: indeed, a shifty look could be discerned behind his defiantly appropriate grin, as of one who half anticipates that his chair will have been withdrawn when he sits down but lacks the moral courage to look behind him to find out. 'Be seated, Brian,' said the Headmaster, and Cole sank back into the mass though, like some member of a savage race returned from a sojourn in a civilized country, he seemed incompletely absorbed by it and there came from the area where he sat a few grunts and movements which might have drawn Mr Pemberton's anger had he observed them but by now he had swept from the dais and was already out of the hall.

After school that morning Gerald—though conscious of the uselessness of his action, as one too soon returns to a kettle one has set to boil—looked at the notice board to see if Cole's silver paper deals had sent up the graph of the Chapel Appeal Fund. But the tattered sheet was no longer there. He went out into the playground with an unaccountable feeling of exultation and seeing the football game in progress, with the ball at Thompson's feet, called for a pass and shot first time, with unusual adroitness, at the goal marked in chalk on the school wall.

This lunch-time occupation, into which he had gradually insinuated himself this term less from enjoyment of it than from a desire to exercise his rights as a senior boarder, now seemed quite different from the time when he had watched Mountain dominate it with his skill, as might some religious rite to an officiating priest who had once acted as acolyte on its periphery. No longer did it serve to distinguish its players as great ones, nor was Gerald conscious, once his participation in it had been accepted, that there existed a class who wished to play but could not. Cropper, of course, was one of these who played but it did not seem at all strange to Gerald to receive a pass from him or even to put one at his feet, just as zebra, which at night whinny with terror at the prospect of the kill, by day see quite nonchalantly a lion roam among them. Cropper was not a skilful player but since, unlike Gerald, he never attempted any feat beyond the limits of his skill, his playing of the game seemed a part of his now unassailable character: he turned it into an occupation that was not really worth his attention, that since it was a solace of those weaker than himself he was prepared temporarily to indulge, as a warder plays draughts with a condemned prisoner.

Blakey, who always acted the unrewarding part of goalkeeper, failed to save Gerald's shot and the ball rebounded from the wall. It came back to Gerald at shin height and with foolish abandon he swung his foot at it again and sliced it high into the Headmaster's garden. He gazed after it with stupefaction and yearning, imagining that he had the opportunity again of making the shot and had wisely decided against it.

The other players stood like a mob baulked of its victim. 'You silly ass, Bracher,' said Blakey.

'Well, what are you waiting for?' asked Thompson. 'Hop over the wall.'

Cropper had taken out his penknife and was paring his nails, but said nothing. Like a treacherous police official he was prepared to accept the advantages of, but not initiate, illegal action: indeed, Gerald felt that as soon as he should have set foot on the Headmaster's hallowed ground, Cropper might call him back and report the heinous offence. While Gerald hesitated, Slade, who had been watching the game, suddenly pulled himself to the top of the wall, and straddling it said: 'I'll get it, Bracher.' He dropped down out of view on the other side. Gerald, full of shame and relief, ran to the wall, put his toe in a crack, looked over and saw, with the mingled anxiety and pleasure with which one views the feats of some performing animal, Slade's figure wandering among the rhododendrons in the forbidden milieu.

'I can't see it,' said Slade in a voice that seemed unnecessarily loud. Beyond him rose the windows behind which the Headmaster had his private being, and Gerald realized that this was the mirror image of the view one had from Mr Pemberton's study—a view that had hitherto impressed him as not forming part of the landscape of school at all. He was trying to distinguish which in fact was the study window when he heard a preternaturally loud rapping sound and turning towards its origin discerned the figure of the Headmaster, a pencil poised in his hand, glaring through the glass at Slade. He lowered his head until his eyes peered through the weeds growing sparsely on top of the wall, magnified into a great forest. Slade, too, looked up and when Mr Pemberton saw that he had the boy's attention he made some violent gestures with his hand, indicating that Slade was to remove himself utterly from the garden. Slade by this time had found the ball and he held it up to Mr Pemberton's gaze, as though it were some mythological talisman capable, say, of preventing him being turned to stone. But the object only changed the Headmaster's agitation to a more terrible calm: he put his hand close to the pane and beckoned to Slade with his forefinger.

Gerald slid back into the playground. 'The Grey Chap was there,' he announced.

'Where's the ball?' inquired Thompson.

'I'll buy another,' said Gerald.

'You bloody well will.'

'I didn't ask Slade to get it for me,' said Gerald, but his cross tone did not relieve him of the burden of guilt and concern Slade had laid on him.

'That kid deserves a beating anyway,' said Blakey.

Gerald could not find it in himself to contradict this remark which once he would have accepted as the truth but which now seemed merely a confirmation of the world's cruelty and injustice. At lunch-time he threw covert glances at Slade, who sat near the bottom of the main table, trying to divine from his colour and mood whether or not the Headmaster had in fact caned him. After lunch, Gerald thought, he would behave quite naturally and if he encountered Slade in the ordinary course would inquire what had happened and find suitable words to express his appreciation of the younger boy's action. But in the event he found himself lagging or hastening, speaking absorbedly to others—almost subconsciously arranging things so that the encounter would not take place. And during afternoon school he kept returning to the situation, planning approaches of gratitude and sympathy, though every moment that passed made these more difficult to achieve. At tea he caught Slade's eye and as he turned from it in embarrassment he smiled what he imagined to be a rueful smile, expressive of all that had passed between them that day, but concentrating furiously on wrapping a golden tentacle of syrup round his knife he realized that once more he had quite failed to impart to Slade an adequate account of his feelings.

The next day a message came to report to Mr Norfolk's class-room at the end of afternoon school and when he got there he found himself one of a dozen or so boys who were, Mr Norfolk announced, to form the cast of the school play to be given at the end of term. A negligent atmosphere prevailed. Mr Norfolk himself was perched on the back of his chair, leaning against the cracked oilcloth of a wall map of the British Isles. 'If you chaps will kindly make a little less noise,' he said, 'I'll read the cast list.' The play was to be the familiar *Twelfth Night*. Mr Norfolk looked at the sheet of exercise paper in his hand. 'Orsino,' he read, 'Bracher.'

Trying to recall every detail of Orsino's role in the action, the moods of his speeches, excited yet daunted at the prospect of appearing on the stage in public, Gerald heard nothing more until a howl of laughter made him ask Dover, who was standing next to him, what the joke was. 'Blakey's got Sir Toby,' said Dover.

Mr Norfolk was continuing reading. When he came to the name 'Viola' he followed it with 'Slade'. Gerald looked round the room and sure enough saw Slade sitting in a desk at the back. 'Those of you who haven't already got copies of the play, take one of these,' said Mr Norfolk, indicating a pile on the table in front of him. 'First rehearsal in here this time on Thursday.'

There were some asinine questions from the smaller fry. 'Shall we hire costumes like we did other years, sir?' 'What if we don't know our parts on Thursday, sir?' In this atmosphere Gerald found it quite possible to walk over to Slade and say: 'I'm awfully sorry about this morning. Did the Grey Chap beat you?'

Slade looked up and Gerald found himself waiting for his answer with an inexplicable sense of anticipation, as though it were to usher in some time of continuous pleasures. 'Yes, he did, Bracher.'

'I'm sorry.'

'The Grey Chap doesn't like me,' said Slade, announcing it as it were a fact of no importance.

'You should have let me go for the thing,' said Gerald.

Mr Norfolk had dismissed the questioners and everyone was drifting from the room: it seemed to Gerald at once natural and extraordinary to go out with Slade. All but a few of the day boys had gone home and in the deserted playground a few crumpled leaves were rasping across the concrete.

'Why doesn't the Grey Chap like you?' asked Gerald, taking up one of the multitudinous points—perversely, perhaps the least important—that made urgent and absorbing these few minutes before the bell went for tea.

'My collars are attached to my shirts,' said Slade.

Gerald looked, and even in the fading light saw that this was so—that it was a species of cricket shirt that Slade wore, the collar fitting very low, so that the emerging stalk of neck seemed phenomenally long and slender.

'And because my overcoat isn't double-breasted,' added Slade, 'and my pyjamas are white.'

'I see.'

'My mother can't bear shirts with separate collars.'

But for Gerald further explanation was otiose: he said quickly: 'I saw your confession in Collinson's book.'

'Did you?'

'Yes. I wanted to ask you what *Taraxacum officinale* was.'

Slade hesitated, then said: 'Dandelion.'

'Dandelion?'

'That's another reason why the Grey Chap doesn't

like me. He beat me at the beginning of term for peeing my bed. It was very curious. I dreamt I was peeing and when I woke up I *was* peeing. Of course, no use telling the Grey Chap that.'

'No.'

'Now he thinks of me as a pissabed.'

'So you put *Taraxacum officinale* as your favourite flower.'

'Irony.'

'Did you go for the ball because the Grey Chap doesn't like you?'

'I hadn't thought of that.'

'How did you know *Taraxacum officinale* was the dandelion?'

'Looked it up in the dictionary,' said Slade. 'There's the bell for tea.' They started to walk over to the House. Gerald thought, seeing the top of Slade's head not very far below, how much the other had changed since that day on the football field only the term before last when he had seemed separated by a great gulf of age and physique. Even now some gulf remained, for, observing Thompson in the distance, Gerald dropped a pace or two behind Slade to exculpate himself from any criticism of his hobnobbing with a smaller boy.

VI

By an arrangement with the girls' school whose pupils were so fascinating a feature of church, weekly visits were paid throughout the year to the swimming bath in the girls' school grounds. It was an abiding hope that such a visit would someday coincide with the use of the bath by the girls themselves, but this had never been realized. Previously the school had gone in four separate sets on different days but this term there were only three. During a visit by the senior set, when everyone was out of the water and it was settling back into immobility, the reflected light from the roof windows rocking on the tiled walls, the muffled cries from the cabins echoing hollowly, Mr Squires, the instructor (who in summer was employed by the municipality as a life-guard on the beach), poked his head over the stable door of the cabin Gerald was sharing with Thompson and commented on this symptom of the decline in the school's numbers.

'If it goes on at this rate,' said Mr Squires, 'I shall be out of a job so far as Seafolde House is concerned.'

'Do you get paid so much a head, sir?' asked Thompson facetiously. He opened the cabin door and walked the few steps to the water's edge to wring out his costume.

'Of course, it doesn't worry me,' said Mr Squires, executing a slow knees-bend by the cabin door. 'It's the Reverend Pemberton who has to worry.'

The conception that the Headmaster was susceptible to worry was at first ludicrous and then deeply disturbing, as it might be setting out in a motor-car with a totally incompetent driver. Gerald said: 'Oh, Mr Pemberton knows what he's doing.'

'These are bad times for private schools,' said Mr Squires.

Gerald felt the embarrassment and shame that afflicts one at the criticism of some organization—one's family, say—with whose fate one is inextricably bound but which one cannot whole-heartedly defend. 'Seafolde House is all right,' he said.

'I suppose so,' said Mr Squires. 'As long as Alderman Cole is behind it.'

Thompson looked up from rolling his costume in his towel. 'What's Alderman Cole to do with it, sir?'

'Don't you chaps keep your ears open?' said Mr Squires. 'Well, I'm not giving away any secrets by telling you that Alderman Cole has a mortgage on Seafolde House. It's common knowledge.'

'What's a mortgage, sir?' asked Thompson.

'See? You're ignorant about everything. Tell him, Bracher.'

'A mortgage?' said Gerald. 'It's a loan of money.'

'And if the borrower doesn't pay it back, the lender sells up the property,' said Mr Squires.

'Well, well,' said Thompson.

Though the precise mechanics of the school's relationship to Cole's father no doubt constituted a startling revelation, it seemed to Gerald that in a sense he had always inchoately possessed the information, just as no fact about sex comes to one with full pristine force.

Mr Squires took a sniffing inhalation through his powerful breathing apparatus. 'Now I don't want you chaps repeating this and saying I told you.'

'Mum's the word,' said Thompson with the bogus sincerity which Mr Squires apparently accepted for the genuine article.

'And stand up, Thompson,' added Mr Squires, whose concern about posture was equal to Mr Pemberton's. 'You hold yourself like a paralysed nun. That's better. But keep your bottom in, man. Your back should be straight. If you go on the beach here in the summer you see all these girls standing with their bottoms sticking out and their backs as hollow as old race-horses and you hear people say what good figures they have. It's a mistaken conception. The back must be straight, bottom tucked in. Now, you chaps, fall in along the side of the bath when you're ready.'

Marching back to school, Gerald thought only of those girls on the beach—to Mr Squires's healthy extroversion mere examples of bad posture, but for Gerald infinitely alluring and remote, all the more capable of calling forth his tender yearning because they were ignorant of arranging their young bodies to the best advantage. And as his imagination conjured them up he was conscious of his eyes still slightly smarting from the chlorine in the water and of the damp, sausage-like arrangement of towel and costume in his chilled grasp, so that later when he recalled Mr Squires's suggestive words they came to him saturated with the physical sensation of that windy late October walk over the downs between the two schools and so in time (when he had at last forgotten the circumstances when he had first brooded over them) came to carry associations inexplicably charged with discomfort.

But behind the hollow backs and protruding bottoms the knowledge of the essential mechanics of Seafolde House existed like the news of a death which for a while cannot be assimilated because it involves a rearrangement of one's whole life. Mr Pemberton elevated Alderman and Mrs Cole and praised and excused Brian Cole because the Alderman had financial power over the school. Gerald came in a day or so to think of this proposition as too simple to be true—neglecting, for instance, the complicated richness of the Headmaster's character—as one finds it difficult to believe in the crude misdeeds of a political leader when his downfall has led to their revelation. He thought how natural it was that Alderman Cole's civic eminence should have prompted the Headmaster to ask him to distribute the prizes at Speech Day—an eminence which Mrs Cole, of course, shared and qualified her for her role at the Annual Sports. He could even think it plausible that, as Mr Pemberton had asserted, virtue resided in Cole's hiding of the weights; and certainly there was nothing sinister in the boy being praised for helping the Chapel Fund by collecting silver paper.

It was at this stage of his assessment of the matter that, as he stood idly reading the school notice board after school, Mr Pemberton came into the lobby, his gown chalky and low on his shoulders, the auburn fringe of hair infinitesimally disarranged—marks of a hard afternoon's teaching. He said: 'Ah, Bracher. Go to the post office and get me some stamps.'

Gerald immediately felt a great burden of anxiety: about the remembering of the exact proportions of two-penny and threehalfpenny stamps which the Headmaster had uttered only once and about the mechanics of going into the town, of buying the stamps and delivering them to Mr Pemberton who by that time would have withdrawn into some inaccessible region of his house. But when he had committed the details of his errand irrevocably to his memory and had worked out the precise phraseology of the request he would put to the clerk behind the counter, his mood changed to one of satisfaction and pride. This sort of task was, he knew, normally entrusted by the Headmaster to a Prefect: his being asked to go was a measure of his seniority and of the Headmaster's conception of him as a person of *savoir faire*—perhaps as a House Prefect in the making.

He was honoured, too, at being given this part to play in that mysterious activity of the school which manifested itself in bills, the Prospectus, the stockroom, the disappearance of masters.

As he got back he heard the bell go for tea: that he had a perfect excuse for being late increased his sense of importance, of being removed from the petty sphere of routine that applied to others. He made his way—and this solution of the problem that had so bothered him earlier seemed to come without his volition—to Mr Pemberton's study where his knock, as he divined it would be, was answered by the Headmaster's voice. Mr Pemberton was sitting at his desk: the lamp made a strong mark of the cleft between his brows and lit the papers, the much-repaired china pen-tray, the several pens, the coloured pencils, the inkstand, blazoned with some college crest, in front of him. Into this impressive theatre of work Gerald gently put the sheets of stamps.

The Headmaster ignored the gesture, not, as Gerald soon realized, because he was ungrateful or forgetful, but because his mind was on other things. 'Have you ever thought what it would be like to be blind, Gerald?' he asked.

'No, sir.'

Mr Pemberton closed his eyes and began groping delicately about among the impedimenta on the desk. 'You see,' he said, 'I could not even find my pen. Not that I should be able to use it anyway.' He opened his eyes. 'We don't appreciate our gifts enough. We ought to try to imagine every day that we have lost one of our senses so as to try to bring ourselves to a proper evaluation of our good fortune. Because even though we may be troubled in other ways, we still have our senses to enjoy the world with. Don't you agree, Gerald?'

'Yes, sir.'

'During the last months of her life,' said the Headmaster, 'Mrs Pemberton was blind. She had a tumour on the brain.' He paused and Gerald choked on some comment that had been incoherent from its conception. 'And you know what she was often saying in that dreadful illness?'

'No, sir.'

'*Lead kindly light*,' said Mr Pemberton. 'What a remarkable thing for a desperately sick blind lady to say! *Lead kindly light*. You know how that hymn goes on?'

'Yes, sir.'

'Then you see what a profound quotation it was. We must all wish to be so composed, so full of faith, at the end. You never think about that, I suppose? Health is like eyesight, Gerald: it can never be properly appreciated by its possessor. Terrible thoughts these, terrible thoughts.' The Headmaster, this time without handicapping himself, reached for one of the pens. 'Do you know how long I have had this pen-holder?'

'No, sir.'

'Eighteen years.' Mr Pemberton's horny-nailed fingers ran caressingly along the pen's length. 'I like it better than any of my pen-holders. You don't use a fountain-pen, Gerald, I hope?' Gerald shook his head mendaciously. 'Never use one. They ruin the handwriting.' The Headmaster drew towards himself a sheet of writing paper and held the pen poised over it, his forefinger (out of whose segments the red hairs sprouted in an almost regular pattern) curved gently along the holder in sharp contradistinction to the ugly bent first joint which appeared when Gerald took up his own pen. 'You may go,' said the Headmaster.

Happiness at the completed errand and the prospect of tea, rose in Gerald as he turned with conscious quiet and discretion towards the door. He had not reached it when Mr Pemberton said: 'Where is the change, boy?'

The grave and adult confidences which the Headmaster had imparted had driven from Gerald's mind a problem that had somewhat exercised it on his journey back from the post office. It had so happened that the payment for the stamps Mr Pemberton had requested had left over twopence halfpenny from the money Gerald had been given. Coming away from the counter Gerald had had more than half a mind to use up this surplus in the purchase of more stamps but the mathematical impossibility of employing it precisely all to add to the stock of twopenny and threehalfpenny stamps he had been instructed to buy, and also the sense that he must obey the Headmaster to the letter, decided him in the end against this course. Then he had imagined that on his return, when he handed over the stamps and the twopence halfpenny, Mr Pemberton would give him the coppers for himself, a reward for the service, and the prospect of this action—forced, he thought, on the Headmaster by the smallness of the change, and of great embarrassment to himself—had so bedevilled (as he saw now) his judgement that he had determined to save both their faces by silently keeping the money. And having made this decision and become familiar with it, walking alone along the sea-road in the dusk it had seemed to him that the Headmaster would know of it, too, without being explicitly told of it, and would approve of its tact and commonsense.

'It's here, sir,' said Gerald, blushing and sweating and fumbling in his pocket.

'Did you forget it?' asked Mr Pemberton.

'Yes, sir,' Gerald said, grasping gratefully at the excuse but recognizing, immediately he had answered, the irony in the Headmaster's question. He added quickly: 'No, sir. I thought . . .' His voice tailed away as he realized how impossible it was for him to explain the processes by which he had come to withhold the twopence halfpenny—indeed, unable now to follow them himself.

The Headmaster put down his ancient pen-holder and held out his hand into which Gerald placed the three coppers as one might pay the fee of a fortune teller who had just prophesied one's death. In Mr Pemberton's calm air and lack of expression Gerald delineated the long-held and unshakeable conception that theft and deceit were all that could be expected from a boy—even a boy with whom one has just discussed one's blind, dead wife.

VII

As one day an initially outrageous condition—a set of false teeth or a state of war—is found to be an unremarked and unremarkable part of existence, so Gerald found himself after the first rehearsal of the play in a condition of friendship with Slade.

'I've got to go over to the music-room to do my piano practice,' said Slade, one lunch-time. 'Will you come?'

'Yes,' said Gerald. 'I didn't know you took the piano.'

'Fancy Jacket choosing Stink-Bomb Billy for Sebastian.'

'Your twin brother.'

'Is he really anything like me?'

'The spitting image,' said Gerald. It seemed the height of self-indulgence to be able to tease Slade.

The music-room was cold and empty: Slade put his music case on top of the piano and opened it. Gerald said: ' "Now, good Cesario, but that piece of song, That old and antique song we heard last night: Methought it did relieve my passion much." '

'Balls,' said Slade. He began to play and Gerald saw with astonishment that his hands were deft beyond anything he had imagined. And they played the soft chords that Mr Percy had made familiar to him, bringing back the bitter-sweet atmosphere of the empty assembly hall and the ill-understood intimacies and absences of the master's affair with Eve Pemberton.

Slade suddenly stopped playing and said: 'Can't manage any more of that.'

'It's a Debussy prelude, isn't it?' said Gerald. 'Percy plays it.'

'Yes,' said Slade. 'Poor old Percy.'

'What do you mean by that?'

'His abortive love for Miss Pemberton,' said Slade. There was such a calm assumption of knowledge in his tone and so clear an indication that the topic failed to have his present interest that Gerald dared not go on to satisfy his curiosity. 'I don't feel like practising,' Slade went on. 'Shall I play you the three best melodies in the world?'

'Play what you like,' said Gerald, propping his elbows on the piano and holding his head in his hands.

'Well, obviously the slow movement from the *Pathétique* comes first.' He played the tune. 'And then the *Prize Song*.' He played that. 'And this week I've got a new one in third place. The *Veau d'Or* from *Faust*. Do you know it? Very vulgar. It has a perfectly marvellous introduction.' He played it. 'And then the voice comes in like this.' He sang a few bars. 'My voice is no good for it.'

' "Thy small pipe Is as the maiden's organ, shrill of sound",' said Gerald.

'Can't *you* sing it, Bracher?' asked Slade, playing the melody.

'No, but I can dance it,' said Gerald, springing up and cavorting round the room. His feet seemed seized with a preternatural nimbleness and invention and he heard Slade laughing. Then the music changed to a grave, slow theme. Gerald came gliding past the piano in the new tempo. 'Entry of the Grey Chap into Valhalla,' he said. Slade increased the speed and Gerald at last leaned across the piano panting like a dog. When he had got back his breath, he said: 'Do you know what song the Grey Chap's poor old wife sang on her deathbed?'

'No,' said Slade, tilting back the bentwood chair, his knees under the keyboard saving him from falling.

' "Lead kindly light amidst th'encircling gloom." '

'How on earth do you know that?'

'The Grey Chap told me himself the other night.' Immediately Gerald felt slip from his conscience the weight of guilt about his expedition to the post office.

'It's too good,' said Slade. 'You've made it up.' He began to play the hymn very slowly at arm's length.

'But you don't know *why* she sang it.'

'No, I don't know that.'

'Because she was blind, boy.'

Though this conception was terribly funny, as Slade's renewed laughter confirmed, Gerald felt when he uttered the words a pang of uneasiness at his cruelty, but it was a pang no deeper than if he had killed an insect and which was as quickly relieved by remembering the scientific fact of his victim's incapacity for pain. Nor, he told himself, was his maliciousness primarily or even at all the result of his own resentment, but because he knew that the Headmaster did not like Slade. All the same, he forbore from adding to his picture of Mrs Pemberton's demise. 'Who plays all this stuff?' he asked, looking through the pile of music on top of the piano.

'God knows,' said Slade. 'It's always there.'

'Here you are,' Gerald said. 'What about this?' He put on the stand a piece of music on the cover of which a negro in a straw hat was depicted playing the banjo while a negress sang at his side, her arm round his white-suited shoulder. In the background was a lagoon and palm trees.

'*The Coon's Honeymoon*,' read Slade and giggled. He opened the music and began to play.

'Rather good,' said Gerald.

Slade turned the page. ' "Trio",' he read. ' "Coon's evening song." ' Gerald suffered a fearful loss of breath occasioned by the too-sudden onset of laughter. 'Wait a minute,' said Slade. 'Wait a minute. Here's the next section. It's called "Coons dancing in the moonlight".'

Weakly, Gerald shambled into the middle of the room and staggered about. 'A coon dancing in the moonlight,' he said several times.

The door opened and admitted the visiting music master, Mr Hubble, who said: 'Come along, stop fooling about. I've got a lesson in five minutes. Oh, it's you, Slade. What on earth were you playing?'

'*The Coon's Honeymoon.*'

'Really, Slade.'

'Isn't it one of the pieces you teach your junior pupils, sir?'

'Of course it isn't. Now do clear out of here, you two.'

Slade stood up and fastened his music-case. 'I see Dunstan has left his violin here,' he said. 'Can you play the violin, sir?'

'No,' said Mr Hubble. 'But I once learnt the fingering.'

'Did you, sir?' said Slade in an awed voice. He was already removing the instrument from its case.

'Now I shouldn't mess about with that if I were you, Slade.'

'I was getting it out for you to show us how to finger it, sir.'

'But it's years since I touched a violin.' Mr Hubble took the instrument and tucked it below his Punch-like jaw: under his hooked nose his sunken mouth parted in a slight smile to reveal even little false teeth. 'You see your left hand comes round underneath the thingamyjig and then the fingers rest on the strings like this and move up and down for the various stops like this. Slade, just pass me the bow.'

Mr Hubble tentatively rested the bow on the bridge

and began cautiously moving it up and down. A loud moaning, edged with shrieks, reverberated in the small room: it was not, however, the noise merely that Gerald found so suddenly and alarmingly comic but the fact that within its cacophonous irrelevancies could be dimly discerned a funereal though familiar tune. Gerald, standing behind the master, could see Slade's grave face fixed on Mr Hubble's, and he pressed his nails ruthlessly into the palms of his hands and thought of death to relieve the seizure of laughter that was trying to burst through his body.

'Mendelssohn's *Spring Song*,' said Slade admiringly. 'You *can* play, sir.'

In the distance the bell went for afternoon school: Gerald muttered incoherently, and, without waiting for Slade, hurried with relief from the room. As he sat at his desk during the first period his thoughts went back to Mr Hubble's rendition and he could not help grinning behind his hand, but though the incident had lost nothing of its comic qualities it now seemed like some theatrical performance crowning a day quite outside the usual sequence of days, with very little to do with the normal existence that had to learn the causes of the Reformation and endure the oppressive presence of Cropper whose questing profile could be seen in a tilted listening attitude across the aisle between the desks. So it was on the ensuing Saturday when he found that Slade was not committed to going out with anyone else in the evening and that they could visit the town together. That this could be a permanent arrangement was a notion quite removed from Gerald's conception of life, which held pleasure to be exceptional, rare and usually guilty.

With Slade, the Wednesday or Saturday evening in the town took on a totally different character—though Slade seemed less to impose his own desires and knowledge on their activities than bring out of Gerald a life he had long wished to pursue but which had previously lain beyond some psychological barrier. Instead of eating fish and chips they had hot pies and cups of tea in a café which although proletarian in general character contained several ambiguous individuals, fragments of whose conversation came over the marble-topped tables, through the steam from the urn, as a curious mixture of scandal and philosophy. In particular, there was a thin young woman with an Eton crop who smoked cigarettes, and to Gerald it seemed that since Slade had brought him to this place, the younger boy had the entrée to its society and that it was only a matter of time or opportunity before he should get to know the thin girl and hear *tête-à-tête* her absorbing opinions.

But before going to the café, Slade had taken him to a covered market where, among stalls of toys, dress material and cheap jewellery, was a barrow stacked with secondhand books. Its appearance in the town Gerald thought he knew so well was to him like the translation into astonishing reality of one of his familiar wish-fulfilment dreams—the dream, say, in which in the grass of the playing fields coin after coin could be found and picked up, or where by an easy movement of the bent elbows the body is raised from the ground in flight. He felt under the luxurious compulsion not to omit reading a single one of the titles.

At first, the image he carried in his mind and which he vainly sought to match from the barrow was of a previously unread book by Oppenheim or Edgar

Wallace, for just as a youth faced by the freedom of a restaurant menu will choose the cabbage or rice pudding he has long despised and disliked at home, so Gerald found it needed a conscious effort to prevent his once habitual tastes, which in reality he had grown out of, from asserting their old power. But soon he saw that the barrow was loaded with an embarrassing richness. In these circumstances, when the books offered themselves to him like fabulously complaisant girls, he realized that any attribute of tedium which he had imagined they might have owned was due merely to their previous surroundings or associations, and that in themselves still burned the ardour and revelation implanted by their once-breathing authors. So that the *Essays of Elia*, which he had heard of because one of them was included in a collection used at school, appeared on the barrow not in its former dull and meaningless character but as a noble entertainment provided especially for him, to be tasted in calm and masterful excitement. Nor, it seemed to him, could any book be too difficult, since he was prepared, even eager, to bite slowly into it, going back whenever he lost the thread, savouring, memorizing, rejoicing in the inevitable progress marked by the imperceptible thickening of the pages to the left of his place.

When, for the price of half a pound of wine gums, he had two or three books under his arm, he joined Slade who was looking through a cardboard carton at the corner of the barrow. 'Two a penny,' said Slade. 'You can't go wrong. Or can you? *Our Mission to Uganda. De Bello Gallico. Theosophical Manuals*: *No. 2.*'

Among the pamphlets that Gerald fished idly out was

a thickish one on bad paper called *Merrie England*, which for a moment he imagined to be some historical romance and then saw was of that genus of publications whose character he had already dimly discerned through the *Fabian Essays* he had found in the Reference Library. On the fly-leaf was an advertisement for another work by the same author whose title, *Not Guilty: A Defence of the Bottom Dog*, more explicitly portrayed its character, and when he turned through some of the ensuing pages the mysterious amalgam of sordid fact and astonishing idea brought to him once again the notion that the perfect understanding of existence lay within his grasp. 'But this is not the worst. Besides the fact that the upper and middle classes take nearly two-thirds of the wealth the masses earn, there is the fact that those classes, and probably less than a tenth of those classes, actually own all the land and all the instruments by which wealth can be produced. Political orators and newspaper editors are very fond of talking to you about "your country". Now, Mr Smith, it is a hard practical fact that you have not got any country. The British Islands do not belong to the British people; they belong to a few thousands—certainly not half a million—of rich men . . .'

'Find another one to go with this and I'll treat you to it,' Gerald said.

'What reckless generosity!' said Slade. 'I'll have *Our Mission to Uganda.*'

In the café Gerald asked Slade what else he had got. Slade held up a battered little fat book.

'*Baedeker's Switzerland,*' Gerald read. 'What on earth did you buy that for?'

Slade turned over the pages. ' "Mont Blanc," ' he

recited, ' "15,782 feet, the monarch of the Alps (Monte Rosa 15,215, blah, blah, blah, Mount Everest 29,000), which since 1860 has formed the boundary between France and Italy, is composed chiefly of granite, and is shrouded with a stupendous mantle of perpetual snow. It was ascended for the first time in 1786 by so-and-so. The ascent, though very fatiguing, offers no great difficulties to experienced mountaineers, but travellers are cautioned, etc., etc. The view from the summit is extremely grand, though unsatisfactory in the ordinary sense." And so on. You see, boy, you can always rely on Herr Baedeker. A bit of comparative geography and political history, a reference to the changes in taste and habits of gentlemen on holiday, some knowing topography, and everything suffused, as Mr Percy would say, in poetry.'

Gerald was stunned not merely at Slade's cleverness but at his capability—which had been so striking a feature of his contribution to Collinson's Confession Book—to be interested in many things that were neither part of the school curriculum nor obviously the pursuits of one's leisure. It was as though Slade were equipped with some extra organ that enabled him to draw from the world—from the masters, his music lessons, his weekly visit to the town—some sustenance unavailable to the ordinarily endowed. So, on their way back to school that night, Slade suggested that instead of using the coast road they went along the sands.

They walked out to the water's edge and kept to the sand left hard by the veils of the ebbing tide, whose lightly foamed edges were distinguishable under the moon. Slade picked up a pebble and, running ahead, threw it far into the still sea.

'Why is your raincoat so long?' called Gerald, with fond mockery.

Slade stopped and turned. 'Mother doesn't like short coats. Just as she doesn't like shirts with unattached collars. As I think I've told you.'

'Why doesn't your father exert his influence and make you dress like a Christian?'

'My father's dead,' said Slade. 'Ages ago.'

'Oh.' Gerald himself took a pebble and bowled an elaborate leg-break. It occurred to him that when his father was divorced (as he must eventually be) he might marry Mrs Slade. As reading a tragic fiction our foolish wish is that the hero and heroine shall conquer the iron spirit of their circumstances and come together for ever, so Gerald immediately recognized the law of reality that the lives of his father and Mrs Slade should always pursue separate orbits, but was nevertheless touched and made happy by his concept of their conjunction. And it was not merely for himself that he desired it—that his relationship with Slade (which at the moment had no name or tradition) would thereby be given the permanence, the universal recognition, of the family tie—but also that he wanted his father to share in his own felicity, which he did not doubt would be conferred equally by the mother as by the son.

In his turn Gerald stopped and waited, looking up at the far black Zeppelin clouds that barred the lighter sky. When Slade drew level he took him by the arm and, shuffling grotesquely in the sand, drew him rapidly along the edge of the water. 'Coons dancing in the moonlight,' he cried.

VIII

Every year to the theatre of the large town across the estuary came a company with a repertoire of Shakespeare's plays to which visits were paid by parties from the school. On the night of a performance of *King Lear*, as the boarders waited in the drive for the charabanc that was to take them to the theatre, the solitary figure of Mr Percy came out of the House.

'Percy's in charge tonight,' said Gerald to Slade. 'Shall we sit with him?'

'If you like.'

'No one else will.'

But when they were getting into the charabanc Miss Pemberton came up. She attached herself to Mr Percy and Gerald on reflection realized that there was no significance in that, for she would naturally have attached herself to whatever master had been in charge. In the lighted charabanc it could be seen that she was wearing an unfamiliar dark coat and, round her throat, a narrow black velvet ribbon. It was the ribbon—giving to its wearer an air at once vulnerable and strange—that brought back to Gerald the memory of a dance he had been to during the holidays, a dance given for the birthday of the son of one of his father's business colleagues to which he had gone reluctantly, only for his father's sake, who had seemed to regard as important this widening of their social horizon. And then he had found himself engrossed in the affair with simple enjoyment, disappointed when it came at last to an end. Only afterwards did it pierce his heart, as he recalled specific and pretty girls he had danced with, the feel of their dresses at their waists, the simple harmonies of saxophone and piano in the small band—all gone beyond his power, never to be possessed again, never, indeed, possessed in the first place.

In the theatre Miss Pemberton and Mr Percy sat in front of Gerald and Slade. Enviously, Gerald observed the order of things which enabled the master to turn his head and speak to his companion, to help her ease her arms out of her coat. The footlights suddenly lit the proscenium curtain and the overture began—the same music, Gerald realized, that had been played at his visits earlier in the week: heroic and haunting. Gerald asked Slade what it was.

'I don't know,' said Slade. 'Ask Percy.'

'Shall I?' Gerald leaned forward in his seat but the pair in front of him were lost in their conversation with each other and he had to wait for a few moments before he could interpose his question.

'. . . stay in Winchester for the night,' he heard Mr Percy say.

'And then what?' said Miss Pemberton.

'Well, I shall have to get back, Tail,' said Mr Percy.

His nostrils assaulted by a faint scent from the silk lining of Miss Pemberton's coat thrown back on his seat, Gerald marvelled at the banality of what these two were saying to each other in the intimate dark and excitement of the theatre. 'Do you know what it is they're playing, sir?' he asked.

Mr Percy's head moved on its double chin. '*Finlandia*,' he said. 'A hackneyed piece by Sibelius.'

'Well, it's not hackneyed to me,' whispered Gerald to Slade when he had sat back and reported the information.

During the interval Gerald and Slade went out into the chill street. While they had been watching the play it had rained and ceased raining, and the wet pavements seemed like some suddenly manifested secret process of history. In the town's main square over which the theatre looked people were moving against the lighted windows of shops, and Gerald experienced a sense of freedom, as though he were not bound to the routine of school, as though, even, he were not himself but a creature capable of ignoring the demands of conscience and duty and pursuing the real ends of life. The illusion was at once heightened and punctured by Slade saying: 'Of course, we needn't go back for the rest of the play. We could nip off and find a congenial café and then go straight to the charabanc. Percy would never miss us while he has Evie's hand to hold.'

'I want to see the rest of the play,' said Gerald with priggish alarm.

'So do I,' said Slade. His voice was gentle and reassuring.

'Do you think Percy has fallen seriously for Evie?'

'Yes,' said Slade, leaning his fair head against the glass case of photographs on one of the entrance pillars and looking at Gerald with calm, clear eyes.

'And she for him?'

'Yes.'

'Well, why don't they get married?'

'Percy is married.'

'Married to Evie?' said Gerald incredulously.

'Of course not. Married to someone else.'

'How do you know?'

'My mother told me terms ago.'

'How did she know?'

'Percy told her.'

'Why should Percy tell her?'

'Why not? It was soon after he first came. Probably before he fell for Evie. Mother was talking to him at a Sports Day or something. She always talks to people about their private lives.'

'So he can't marry Evie,' said Gerald.

'Not unless he is prepared to be a bigamist,' said Slade. 'Come to think of it, he looks like a bigamist. Perhaps his present marriage is bigamous.'

'How on earth can anyone look like a bigamist?' Gerald seized crossly on the most trivial and obvious contradiction of the affair.

'That hair. That corpulence,' said Slade. 'That piano-playing.'

The bell rang, signalling the imminent raising of the curtain. Gerald left unspoken the question which at once had formulated itself in response to Slade's revelation: Why did not Miss Pemberton simply go to live with Mr Percy? But back in his seat, watching the play through the proscenium formed by the heads and shoulders of the two protagonists of his thoughts, he answered the question himself, for the powerful, wild, aged and ranting figure of the widower Lear, ostensibly strong and careless about his daughters but secretly possessive, changed in his imagination to that of the Headmaster, and he understood the ties that bound Miss Pemberton to minister for ever to Mr Pemberton's loneliness and fear of death, his sense of economy, his burden of the failing school, his need to rule.

In the charabanc going back to school, stimulated by the lateness of the hour and the strange circumstances, the boys started singing. Gerald glanced across the aisle to the pair of seats occupied by Mr Percy and Miss Pemberton. The master, sitting nearer, had put one plump leg over the other, revealing a gap between sock and trouser turn-up. It was almost with surprise that Gerald observed that the gap was occupied by a leg of white and indubitable flesh, as though only at this particular moment, to the strains of *Green Grow the Rushes* while the little lighted world flew through the dark fields, had he realized that Mr Percy was human, capable of suffering the excruciating pleasures and pains of the body.

IX

As Matley's devotions reached their climax, it so happened that Gerald's scepticism, fed by his reading, began confidently to try to impose itself on anyone he thought worthy of argument. One Saturday night Matley, in his Franciscan dressing-gown, over which he had arranged his bath towel in the semblance of a surplice, laid out his altar as usual on his locker and then from the paper bags containing his toffees and meat pie he drew out a brown paper parcel which when unwrapped proved to be a half bottle of invalid port. He poured some of it into an enamel mug, filched from one of the school washrooms, and then reverently unfolded from a handkerchief a piece of bread and butter evidently saved from tea.

'What the hell are you doing, Matley?' asked Gerald.

'I suppose I can take Communion, can't I?'

'Take Communion?' repeated Gerald, witheringly.

'Matley, you're a madman—a religious maniac.' He sprang from his bed and seized the Woolworth crucifix from the locker.

'Put my crucifix down at once, Bracher,' cried Matley. In his priestly role he always took off his glasses so as to improve his appearance, but he now hastily put them on in order to see what was happening to his cherished symbol, and went in dignified pursuit of Gerald who bent down and popped the crucifix into Dover's chamber pot.

'You filthy beast, Bracher,' said Matley, aghast.

'I say, Bracher, that's a bit thick,' said Dover, peering under his bed.

Gerald concealed a sudden terror that he had gone too far—not only in mocking Matley's beliefs but in sacrilege—by saying outrageously: 'That's the proper place for God.'

'You'll be punished, Bracher, you'll be punished for that,' Matley quavered.

'Who by?'

'Almighty God,' replied Matley, even in these amazing circumstances not forgetting to pronounce the words in the manner he had caught from the Vicar so that they sounded like the outlandish name of an American bootlegger—Al Mightah Gard.

'I call on him to punish me now,' said Gerald sardonically. 'I call on him to strike me dead.'

There was a silence which Gerald himself half expected to be broken by some supernatural cataclysm. But when a time had elapsed felt by everyone to be sufficient for a Supreme Being to exercise his power of interference in the natural order, conversational exchanges were resumed, in a very commonplace manner.

'I must say,' remarked Thorp, the other boy in the dormitory, 'I wouldn't have said that.'

'God scorns such puerile challenges,' said Matley.

Dover sank back on his pillow. 'Matley,' he called, 'do you mind coming and taking your thingummy out of my po?'

For Gerald the moment marked an epoch—a moment when his tongue had outrun his mind or, rather, when his tongue had blurted out what his mind had failed to formulate in simple terms—and afterwards he could scarcely recall a time when he had not thought the belief in God's existence absurd and the ceremonies of religion mere primitive superstition. So it was, too, when the passions of the General Election reached the school through the imperfect channels of an occasionally-seen newspaper and the reports by day boys of their parents' opinions, and Gerald declared himself to be 'Labour', thus in one word giving practical expression of his vague belief that the world was unjust and ill-managed, yet capable, through an intellectual effort of comprehension, of being totally transformed. Nor was it any surprise to him that the expression of his allegiance provoked derision or fear, for he saw that the necessary change in existence must be brought about by a race quite other than those people one encountered every day—that at Seafolde House, for example, only Slade and perhaps Mr Percy and Miss Pemberton, had the cerebral endowment to enable them to discover the truth behind life's immense façade of deceit.

Though when he was with Slade he rarely brought up these exciting political and religious discoveries, taking for granted that Slade had long ago freed himself from the bonds of superstition. The universe which he and

Slade created—with their growing list of habitual occupations together, their extending private empire over the creations of literature and music, the increasing esotericism of the language they used with each other, their fantasies about the figures of school, the code for the exchange of notes—was one in which private conduct was supreme and in which everything was measured against the values they had quickly and almost tacitly agreed between themselves and often represented by an invented word into which was compressed weeks of experience and rich ambiguities of allusion. Sometimes Gerald would think of the past and find it inconceivable that he had once, say, believed Slade's timidity at football to be morally reprehensible (for it was an axiom with them that games bred unwholesome passions, wasted time and stultified the intellect), or worried about Slade's untidiness and nonconformity with the rules of school.

But Gerald had by no means exhausted the revolutionary possibilities of his understanding. Once, after a Saturday afternoon match played under an incessant cold drizzle, he had rushed back to the house and been one of the first in the senior bathroom. It was a rule that each drawing of bath water on these occasions was to be used by at least three boys. Gerald had succeeded to a merely moderately soupy bath and was lying in it when Cropper, clad in his repulsively small and ginger dressing gown, his towel over his arm, entered the bathroom with slow dignified stride. He peered down and said: 'Get out of that bath, Bracher.'

'I've only just got in it.'

'Don't argue, Bracher. Get out.'

Beyond Cropper's motionless, menacing shape, other

figures were busily engaged in their various occupations, but a few of the nearer turned to watch the unfolding catastrophe by the bath. From his low, dramatic viewpoint Gerald saw the scene like one of those paintings of the German school which invests some supernatural or allegorical subject with a harsh and detailed naturalism, so that while in the foreground the Fiend Cropper and a few of his attendant smaller Devils were concentrating reasonably upon their nude and prone quarry, many others in remoter planes were cutting their toe nails, squeezing pimples and indulging in horseplay. These half-clothed manikins revealed, too, an adolescent anatomy utterly appropriate to the *genre*—immature and emaciated arms and legs or shapeless hulks of torsos rugeous with acne, with occasionally glimpsed genitals sometimes of exaggerated, sometimes of merely conventional, representation. And, displaying the painter's virtuosity, steam issued from the washbasins and the bath, images were doubled in the various mirrors, and towels, slippers, check sponge bags, open tins of green solid brilliantine, and muddied shorts formed several complicated groups of still life.

'When I've finished washing,' said Gerald, suddenly officious with the loofah. He felt the dreamlike vulnerability of the naked in the presence of the clothed, the stupendous embarrassment of the surgeon's patient or the torturer's victim.

'No one is to use the bath until the House Prefects have used it,' said Cropper, his nostrils clenched.

'I've never heard of that rule before.'

'I'm making the rule,' said Cropper. 'Now get out of there before I drag you out.' But prudently avoiding a scuffle in the water, in which the other's nudity would be at an advantage, Cropper stood motionless while Gerald feigned the normal motions of one at the end of an enjoyable tub and put all the time his fear would allow before the moment when he would have to yield possession. When eventually Gerald rose Cropper dipped the end of his towel in the bath water, took a firm grasp of the other, and began flicking the heavy water-laden part at Gerald's thighs and buttocks. At first the towel cracked harmlessly in the air between them but Cropper soon found the range and had raised three crimson weals before Gerald, trying desperately not to hurry, had seized his things and forced himself past Cropper's unsmiling, pertinacious, but almost indifferent presence, and out of the bathroom. He was amazed at the pain Cropper's trivial and childish action had caused him, amazed even more to find veritable blisters forming along the lines of the weals, and he quickly slipped into the lavatory to lock away his misery from detection.

The atmosphere of despair that flowed from the incident, choking the possibility of any future felicity, he felt even with Slade later in the evening, and when he cautiously sat down in the squalid café, Slade's sharp observation saw him wince, and the younger boy said: 'What's the matter? Got a boil on the arse?'

'No,' Gerald said, and was about to practise his usual tactic of secrecy and evasion by quickly introducing some other topic of conversation, when he realized that there was no part of his character or predicament he need conceal from Slade whose feelings and opinions were precisely his own, and with a joy he physically felt welling up in his chest he added: 'I had to suffer some torture from the ineffable Cropper after games. He's belatedly discovered the art of towel-flicking.'

Slade took a bite of the almost jamless and hugely equilateral jam puff he made an affectation of invariably ordering, and said: 'Does he often bully you?'

Yes, of course, it was bullying, Gerald thought, gaining the comfort of one who finds that his alarming fever and swellings can be subsumed under the familiar name 'mumps', and going on to reveal the origins and history of Cropper's animus. When he had finished, Slade said: 'It shows how hopeless the Grey Chap is that he lets bullying go on.'

It had no more occurred to Gerald to place the responsibility of Cropper's violence and hatred at the school's door than a primitive will attribute his sickness to a mosquito, for it had hitherto seemed to him a wholly natural incident of life, like sleep. But now, as it had previously been made possible for him to conceive a world in which the two-thirds of the wealth filched from the masses would be returned to them, he saw that his unhappiness was caused by a fault in the system upheld by the Headmaster. The same night, some little time after the light had been turned out in the dormitory, it was switched on again and the rather humpbacked figure of Dyce was seen standing in the doorway. Everyone took out the meat pies and crisps that had been plunged under the bedclothes at the noise of Dyce's entry.

'Thorp, you've left your towel on the floor in the bathroom and the lid of your dentifrice off,' Dyce said, in a voice of oleaginous reasonableness. 'Come and tidy them up.'

'All right, Dyce,' said Thorp, and jumped out of bed.

When the light had been put out again and the two had departed, Gerald surprised himself by saying: 'Well,

we know what those two are going to do.' As he spoke
he remembered Howarth telling him long ago of Blakey
being called out of his dormitory by Mountain, and that
almost inconceivable event was now by its historical
repetition made comprehensible and shown to be
practicable, as the death of a poisoner's second wife
explains the sudden demise of his first.

'I like not ye man with ye suspicious mind,' said
Dover.

After the food had been eaten and the talking had
ended, Gerald heard Thorp come back, and realized
that it was not, as he would once have thought, the
defective moral characters of Mountain and Blakey or
Dyce and Thorp that had bred this state of affairs, but
the system for which, equally with those who ruled the
greater system of society, Mr Pemberton was responsible
—for though he might have inherited it, or administered
it ignorant of its evils, he could not be separated from
its iniquities, nor his downfall from its inevitable over-
throw.

It was in this frame of mind that a few days later he
said to Slade: 'What do you think happened to the money
for the Chapel Appeal?'

'You obviously know,' said Slade.

'I think the Grey Chap put it in his pocket.' The fact
that this must be untrue and that he knew it must be
untrue, no more detracted from the malicious pleasure
of saying it than a conviction of the forgery of the
Protocols of Zion lessens the animus of an antisemite.

'Fatty Cole's silver paper money as well?'

'The whole shooting match,' said Gerald.

'Certainly there is no chapel.'

'Not a brick.'

'Did your father subscribe?' asked Slade.

'Yes. Did your mother?'

'No. She doesn't believe in organized religion.'

'Very wise,' said Gerald, admiringly.

They were on their way back to the House after a rehearsal of the play. As in *The Princess Cassamassima* the vital existence of the proletarian characters is carried on only on Sundays when they are free from work, so for Gerald only those times and events which bridged the gap his additional year made between him and Slade in the ordinary routine of school seemed to constitute his true life. Similarly, when the rumour percolated through the school that the Headmaster was out for the day, or when Cropper as a member of the First XI travelled to an away match, an eager flame burned through his body, he felt the potentialities of his mind, of his destiny, begin to stir, and he imagined that legendary epoch when he would be the fearless master of his environment.

'He's no doubt used the fund to stop the wicked mortgagee from turning him out into the snow,' said Gerald.

'Expound,' said Slade.

Gerald told him of Mr Squires's revelation of the financial structure of Seafolde House. Slade stopped on the steps of the House to assimilate the scandal, the light from the vestibule accentuating his smooth pallor and blondness, his head thrown slightly back on its graceful neck. 'Do you think,' he said, 'the Grey Chap has also made away with Alderman Cole's contribution to the Fund—which you will not fail to remember was to be equal to the sum of the other contributions?'

But Gerald did not hear the question, for at his mention of Mr Squires he began to think once again of the girls in summer on the beach, standing with their hollow backs and offered behinds.

X

It was, Slade revealed, possible to join the public library in the town: all you did was to get your form master to sign your application card. One day, when afternoon school was over, Gerald approached Mr Percy for this purpose. As the master signed his name, Gerald was struck by the contrast between the short, podgy fingers and the delicate handwriting, as though imprisoned in Mr Percy's gross frame was some tiny, sensitive being sending in this way its desperate calls to be released.

'A far cry from Dr Fu-Manchu, eh?' Mr Percy remarked, handing back the card.

'Yes,' said Gerald. It was indicative, too, of the long way he had come that he forbore to add 'sir' because in the state of unuttered intimacy between them it could only have a sardonic connotation. He noticed for the first time that Mr Percy's eyes were the light grey of a worn silver coin. Where the straight, boyish hair nestled above his ears—and he needed a hair cut as badly as he needed a new jacket—were a few coarse and unruly white strands among the brown. Poor, ageing, unhappy the master seemed to Gerald in that moment, though he had not changed an iota his icy, contained manner.

As Mr Percy was about to speak again some not un-substantial object crashed against the door leading to the adjoining and junior room, and from beyond came loud scuffling and cheering noises. Mr Percy got down from his chair with the automatism of weary authority and threw open the door. In the next room a few lingering boys were unseasonably playing cricket with a ball of string-bound paper and a real bat. 'Go home,' said Mr Percy into the sudden silence. And then he said: 'Where did that cricket bat come from?'

Cross-examination revealed that a boarder called Stoneham had extracted it illegally from one of the cricket bags stored in the cellars of the House. 'Give it to me,' Mr Percy commanded, and then, observing Gerald still standing in the doorway, he added: 'Perhaps you will see that it is returned to its rightful place, Bracher.'

With one of those fatal actions which seem quite foreign to our characters but which are perhaps expressive of a deeper truth, Mr Percy, before he passed on the implement to Gerald, idly made as though to face an invisible bowler and swung the bat in a powerful straight drive. What was behind the master was hidden from Gerald by the door, and he could not divine the nature of the alarming sound which seemed to accompany Mr Percy's motion and derived from that quarter. He stepped into the room, and saw—as incongruous a consequence as the fall of a great house through the insignificant appetite of the woodworm—the plump form of Brian Cole recumbent on the floor. Mr Percy, still holding the bat, was gazing down at this spectacle with an expression as fixed, livid and expressive as a mask for a tragic play. Following Gerald's example he knelt at Cole's side.

'Cole,' he said, 'I didn't know you were behind me. I didn't mean to hit you, of course.'

Blood badged Cole's face. 'Shall I get Miss Pemberton?' Gerald asked and even through his agitation he realized immediately that his question was ambiguous, for though he had meant to refer to Miss Pemberton in her role of Matron, for Mr Percy she was the very one who must be summoned to sustain him in this critical moment.

'Yes, Bracher,' replied Mr Percy, adding the name as though to demonstrate that he still had control over life, for his words and actions—and now he was slowly pulling a handkerchief out of his breast pocket—seemed to be from another, remoter order of existence, like those of a hypnotist's subject; or no doubt it was that the events of the last few minutes belonged to a stark, pre-civilized world Mr Percy had never conceived to be his.

Miss Pemberton was miraculously in her room, darning socks and sharing the sofa with Marcel. On Gerald's entry she took off a pair of horn-rimmed spectacles, as though making visible the change from her secret to her public self. Gerald told her of the catastrophe and without a word she seized the first aid box and flew from the room. Gerald followed, and as they crossed the playground she turned her head and said: 'Why was it Cole?'

Bewildered by the question, Gerald said: 'He just happened to be there.'

In the class-room he was surprised to see Cole, certainly not at death's door, sitting in one of the desks holding a bloody handkerchief over his eyes. The other boys had gone. Mr Percy stood by the master's desk as though he were taking a lesson. Miss Pemberton scarcely gave him a glance. She went straight to Cole and gently removed the handkerchief, revealing the expression of one who in the dark has omitted to take account of the last stair. 'Well,' she said, picking a roll of lint from the first aid box, 'it's not all that bad, Cole. But it looks as if it will need a stitch or two. Can you manage to walk down the road to the doctor's?' Cole nodded bravely. 'Will you tell the Headmaster, Mr Percy?' Miss Pemberton added, busy with the cutting of the lint, her throwing away of the words only making their import all the more terrible, and the formal mode of address, though no doubt only for the benefit of the two boys, seeming to mark the collapse of her intimacy with the master.

'It was a pure accident,' said Mr Percy.

Miss Pemberton substituted lint for handkerchief and said: 'Come along, then, Cole.' The pair left the room.

Some word, some gesture, from Gerald was undoubtedly called for, but twisting uneasily, avoiding Mr Percy's eye, he could do nothing but leave the master to his destiny. 'Well, thank you for signing the card,' he said as he escaped, but he was not sure that Mr Percy had heard him.

Serious as the episode was, it went completely out of his mind after he had satisfied Thompson's curiosity about it at tea-time, and he quite failed to connect it with the summons he received during preparation, to go to the Headmaster's study, imagining instead some culpable affair of his own. He knocked and entered and looked hastily at Mr Pemberton's face, which he saw with a sinking of the heart was very grave.

'Sit down, Bracher.' The command was almost unprecedented in this place. Gerald took the chair at the side of the desk, touching it only with his bottom. The Headmaster looked searchingly at Gerald's countenance and then said: 'Human malice is boundless, especially that malice which is exercised surreptitiously. Do you understand, Bracher?'

'No, sir. Not quite.'

'I've always regarded you as a fairly truthful boy, Bracher. Now I want you to tell me the truth about what happened in 4A class-room this afternoon.'

'About Cole, sir?'

'Yes, about Cole—and about any other individual who happened to be concerned.'

Gerald related the whole incident, omitting only the purpose for which he had approached Mr Percy in case the Headmaster would think it cast an aspersion on the resources of the school libraries. Mr Pemberton's reaction was quiet but startling: 'Why didn't you warn Brian to keep out of range of the bat?'

'I didn't see him, sir,' said Gerald warmly, alarmed at the insinuation of his responsibility.

'Mr Percy saw him, of course.'

'I expect so, sir.'

'And didn't intend to hit him quite so hard, no doubt.'

Gerald's face began to get hot. 'No, sir. I didn't mean Mr Percy saw him when he was swinging the bat but when he first went in 4A to stop the noise.'

'But having seen him once surely that was sufficient? Brian's figure is not one to be easily lost sight of.'

'I expect Cole moved round the back and Mr Percy didn't notice it.'

'Did you see him move?' demanded Mr Pemberton.

'No, sir. I was only suggesting——'

'If you invent portions of your narrative I shall find it difficult to believe that you were not criminally involved in this sad affair.' Then the Headmaster's voice changed. 'And it is a sad affair. Do you know that five stitches have had to be put in that unfortunate boy's forehead? He will be disfigured for life.'

'I'm sorry, sir.'

'It is easy for us to say we are sorry.' Mr Pemberton bowed his head slightly so that the lamplight gleamed on his nude skull. 'But what can his parents say? And what can we say to his parents—we who have been entrusted with the son they love above anything else? How can we explain it? Prove that we have exercised proper care of our trust?'

Again Gerald felt disquiet: how convincingly the use of the first person plural implied his guilt! But once more Mr Pemberton changed his tone. He lifted his head. 'I am going to confide in you, Gerald,' he said. 'I ask myself: why was it that this had to happen to Cole out of the hundred boys in this school? Why had the arc of that cricket bat to intersect with a boy's brow out of all the space in the school? Can you answer?'

Gerald wondered if Miss Pemberton had planted these questions in the Headmaster's mind. 'No, sir,' he said. 'Cole just happened to be there.' But as soon as he had spoken he understood what the questions meant, and how both uncle and niece could arrive at them independently.

'Ah, Gerald, Gerald,' said Mr Pemberton vibrantly, 'when you grow up you will come to realize that rarely in this world does the victim just happen to be there to take the fatal blow. Suppose, Gerald, you planned to inflict a great injury on the school and on its Head-master——'

'I'm sure it was a pure accident,' interrupted Gerald, in an agony to communicate the truth. 'Mr Percy said so himself.'

'Mr Percy said so,' Mr Pemberton repeated, with bitter irony.

'I say so as well, sir.'

'Your loyalty will commend itself to Mr Percy.'

'Really, sir,' said Gerald, despairingly, 'it was an accident. I know it was.'

The Headmaster rose abruptly and for a sickly moment Gerald thought that he was going into the corner for the cane. But he merely paced restlessly out of the orbit of the desk-lamp and then stood against the mantelpiece, lit by the flames from the fire like some slumped tragic figure from the great days of the German cinema.

'Chains,' he said, 'chains forged by those we love, and those who hate us, bind us in our life. I hope you say your prayers, Gerald. We need to pray as much as we can, manacled and helpless as we are. Do you know what Mrs Pemberton's dying prayer was in her last illness, Gerald?'

'No, sir,' lied Gerald.

'*Lead kindly light*. The point of it was that she was blind. She had a tumour on the brain. *Lead kindly light*. I wish all our prayers could be so profound and composed, and that our chains were only those of physical darkness.'

XI

On a day when, for the first time that winter, snow appeared—a few crumbs whirled about in the wind, reluctant to descend—it was all at once the Saturday of the school play. In the morning Mr Norfolk, like some foreman of the Pyramids, had supervised the erection of the stage, brought up in sections from the cellars under the House to the Assembly Hall. The curtains were found and their abstruse mathematics mastered. Instead of football, the cast had a dress rehearsal. The contents of the great skips from the costumiers pleased many and disappointed some. The colour of Dunstan's doublet and hose was felt to be particularly unfortunate. 'He looks as though he's fallen in a tub of shit,' said Blakey.

'How unlikely!' said Slade, striding about in his Cesario clothes.

'*You* look all right,' said Gerald to him covertly.

'So do you.'

'Do I? The tights fit quite well, don't they? I shall carry the hat: it's rather too *outré* to wear.'

'Very wise,' said Slade. 'It reminds me of nothing so much as a blancmange. Perhaps it really belongs to the costumes for one of those children's plays where the characters are things to eat.'

'Is your mother coming tonight?' It was a question Gerald had long been trying to find the right moment for.

'No, she's in Nice.'

'My father is coming,' said Gerald. 'Most embarrassing.'

'Don't be so neurotic.'

'Luckily he's driving back home after the play.'

The cast had an early tea and went back to the school block. Now the curtains were drawn across the stage, separating its exciting intimacies from the rows of chairs in the lighted Hall. In one of the class-rooms at the rear Mr Norfolk appeared with a large cardboard box full of greasepaint, eyebrow pencils and pots of cream— apparatus, like the bunting of Sports Day and the

234

sections of the stage itself, at once strange and yet quint-essentially part of the school. Each member of the cast sat in turn in front of him to be made-up. Since Gerald opened the play he was one of the first to be done. He went through to the class-room on the other side of the stage, which had served as a dressing-room, and looked at himself in one of the mirrors that had been brought down from the dormitories. The black eyebrows, the enlarged lips, the crude wrinkles at the corner of the eyes, had superimposed upon his own face the mask of sensual middle-age, still recognizable as the blank in-herited clay but indicating unmistakeably how the years are to mark it. Over his shoulder appeared Blakey's visage, reddened recklessly by Mr Norfolk and sur-mounted by a wig whose bald patch looked as dead and incongruous as the buttocks of a sunburned torso. Gerald grinned and observed that against the brown greasepaint his teeth were preternaturally white, and that the expression was not that which he had often seen grinning to himself in a glass, but the subtle, vulpine expression of pleasure of one who has long ceased to be satisfied by tepid and ordinary joys.

He turned: across the desks which, piled with clothes and huddled into a corner of the room, had ceased to have their normal and commonplace likeness, just as Blakey's ruffed and brocaded figure, at that moment striking a dramatic attitude, made the distempered and be-charted wall a pallid anachronism, he saw coming through the doorway a slim girl who nevertheless moved with boyish freedom and whose long gown he recog-nized from the afternoon's dressing-up. As this andro-gynous shape moved nearer it made itself no less ambi-guous, for Slade's fair hair was covered by a wig of greater fairness and length which did not by its exaggeration destroy the reality of the transformation but rather elevated it to a plane on which its reality was incapable of question, and the flesh of his face glowed through the smooth surface of its disguising powder with indubitable and ardent life. The gown revealed the length and slenderness of his neck far more even than his offending shirts, and its cut suggested that not far below rose a small pair of breasts—or perhaps it was that Mr Norfolk had planted them there in his pursuit of verisimilitude.

Shy and dumb in the face of the apparition, Gerald bent down and smoothed his tights over his calf: he was astonished when it said, apparently unconscious of its beauty: 'Bracher, I think I'm coming undone. Will you have a look at these hooks and eyes at the back?' The voice was Slade's voice, but emerging from that creamy face it took on the tones of familiar music heard in the open air, and Gerald felt a complex pang of pride and jealousy at this public dissemination of what had once been solely for him but only now—only by that —revealing fully its emotional effect.

He had time, among the breathless mechanical business of the play's performance and the stimulating yet oppressive commerce with the dimly discerned audience (among whom, illuminated by the footlights in a privileged row was the bust, as unreal and distinct as royalty, of the Headmaster) to be conscious of and to try to resolve the complications of Slade's disguises. For the play's main plot, which he thought he knew so well, now took on a further irony: the girl who played the part of a boy to win his love was herself played by a boy, whose every soliloquy was deeply ambiguous. And when the drama drew to a close and the errors had ostensibly been dissipated, the most startling dénouement remained unexposed. 'Give me thy hand; And let me see thee in thy woman's weeds'—as Gerald spoke these words and took the sinewy, brown and indubitably masculine fingers, he gazed as it were for the last time at the flushed and lovely face, and knew that after all it belonged to another sphere of desire.

When the curtains were finally drawn Gerald rushed back to the class-room to change, eager to spare his father a long wait in solitary embarrassment among the coats in the lobby even at the cost of accelerating the moment when he would have to receive the words of congratulation, the looks of love, whose restrained furtiveness only drew attention to their intensity of feeling. More and more it appeared to him that his father was the younger of them and that the years which had grizzled and moustached him had taught him nothing of *savoir faire*.

But at length he saw the tail-light of his father's car fade down the blackness of the drive, and he ran with relief and exultation to the House. In the Common Room sandwiches had been left out for the boarders among the cast because of their early tea: Gerald seized a couple and moved through the chattering groups towards Slade. The grey-flannelled figure had, Gerald thought, quite lost the disturbing enchantment of half an hour ago and now seemed merely to hold, as it always did, the warm promise of immediate accommodation to Gerald's mood, of an intellectual response incalculable not only in itself but in its reciprocal power of stimulating Gerald's own intellect; though as the younger boy turned his face in greeting Gerald saw that it was

still the countenance of Viola–Cesario whose brilliant
youthfulness made not quite supererogatory its lavish
fard. So, too, for a while longer, he must himself bear
the Duke's fickle haggard features.

'All right?' questioned Slade.

'All right,' Gerald said, and, to draw his friend apart,
added in a low voice:

> 'Cesario, come;
> For so you shall be, while you are a man;
> But when in other habits you are seen,
> Orsino's mistress and his fancy's queen.'

XII

The optimistic atmosphere of the Saturday of the play
persisted through the following Sunday, for the few
days that the term still had to run were felt by the boys
to be so short a span as not to make it worth while for
them to do any serious work or for the masters to exert
any serious discipline. Duties that were accepted at
other times as part of the boring and arduous natural
order, on this day called forth rebellious groans, as
while a monarch lies on his death bed his nobles suddenly discover the iniquities of taxation. After lunch
Slade said to Gerald: 'Let's cut the walk.' This was the
compulsory Sunday afternoon reconnaissance of the
coast road and the town's promenade.

'How, pray?' asked Gerald.

'We'll start off first, hurry on ahead, leave the drive
where it bends, and go to the Shed.'

'It's too cold for the Shed.'

'I'll get one of the maids to fill my thermos with tea.'

They had several times used the Shed as a means of escape into the privacy so hard to find in the House, and it had thereby taken on for Gerald a character far different from that it had owned in the summer when its mild notoriety as a hide-out for illegal smokers had been swollen by its association with the libidinous visitors to the playing fields. Like the music-room, the proletarian café, the book-barrow in the market, it was now a place whose familiarity no more destroyed its atmosphere of potential discovery, than knowing the décor and architecture of a theatre detracts from the exaltation given by its productions.

So as they sat with their feet stretched out on the forms that were now the Shed's only furniture, their overcoat collars turned up, books on their laps, cups of tea in their hands, Gerald thought only of the power of his mind, his growing mastery of the circumstances of life, his at present ill-defined but certain future fame.

'I can't think why we ever bother to go on Sunday walks,' he said.

'It's our good nature,' said Slade. 'Have a fag.' He tossed over a packet of Woodbines and a folder of book matches.

'I didn't know there were any left.' Gerald lit a cigarette and smelt immediately the rich aroma that brought back to him an indistinguishable sequence of such quiet, sequestered and unlawful moments. He threw the packet and matches back, and said: 'I really prefer Woodbines to anything.'

'That's through reading too much Robert Blatchford,' said Slade. 'Give me State Express.'

The shutter hung loose and left a view through the

unglazed window of a slate sky crossed occasionally by a gull's white side-slipping shape.

'Ten days to Christmas,' said Gerald.

'What will you do?' Slade asked.

'I don't know.' Perhaps, Gerald thought, the feeling of pleasure that the anticipation of Christmas gave was a mere hangover from childhood, and now happiness could only come from inside oneself. 'Get away from Cropper and the Grey Chap, anyway. What about you?' But he did not really want an answer, for he had suddenly realized that during the month in which they would be parted Slade would have encounters and interests destined to remain secret and uncontrollable.

It was through the window that later on they watched the school for signs that the boys had returned from the walk. When these were apparent they strolled with elaborate casualness into the class-room block. Almost the first person they saw was Blakey who said: 'Where the hell have you two been? Marshie's reported you missing to the Grey Chap.' A terrible gnawing attacked Gerald's solar plexus.

Gerald said to Slade: 'I'd better go and see Marshie.'

'Where shall we say we've been?' Slade's voice, beneath a mask of unconcern, had taken on the nervousness that Gerald recalled from the distant past. 'Got lost? Taken short? Those prunes at lunch were very dubious.'

'My God,' said Gerald, 'don't let's make it more complicated than it is.'

'Well, we'll just say we stayed behind in school. The Shed's out of bounds, you know: there's no sense in confessing to arson when they've got us for murder anyway.'

Mr Marsh, a pile of School Reports in front of him in the Masters' Common Room, expressed uninterest in Gerald's visit. 'After all, Bracher, you and Slade were out of circulation for nearly two hours. For all I knew you might have been drowned. The Headmaster knows about it and you'll have to go and make your peace with him.'

When Gerald reported this, Slade said: 'Shall I go to the Grey Chap? I will.'

'No, I'll go.'

'Wait till he sends for you.'

'No.'

'Wait until after tea, anyway.'

'Perhaps I will.'

'He'll be mellower. I don't suppose he'll say much. The end of term, the Christmas spirit, and all that.'

'I don't know,' said Gerald. 'He's never got over Percy smiting Cole with that cricket bat.'

'Cheer up. He can only beat us.'

It was true that in theory the Headmaster's ultimate sanction was merely a power of inflicting a temporary physical hurt and—on the sensitive—a rather more lasting sense of degradation. But this did not exhaust the sources of his power, no more than a demonstration of the absurdity of magic will revive a cursed primitive rigid in his hut. Nor was it relevant to tell oneself that the Headmaster's character was eccentric, his ideas unsound, his kingdom rotten, for simply because his rule existed made futile—inconceivable—any opposing party. Or, rather, the opposing party must by definition exist only to be ruled, only ceasing to be so when it achieved adulthood and thereby, paradoxically, shedding its ideology of revolt.

Tea lay uneasily inside Gerald as he trod the insubstantial ground to the Headmaster's house. But there was no reply to his knock on the study door, and finding Miss Pemberton in her room he learned that her uncle was out and would return too late for Gerald to see him.

So he had to live through Monday, the joviality of the day before breaking-up, with the prospect of the interview on his mind and stomach, sometimes hoping that it might even be possible to last out the few hours left of term without suffering Mr Pemberton's reproof, as one in an aerial bombardment reassuringly applies to himself the statistics of casualties. But at the end of afternoon school he waited about in the playground, keeping his eye on the school block for the Headmaster to emerge on his way over to the house, firmly intending to end his suspense. At last Mr Pemberton appeared in the lighted entrance, his hat already on his massive head, and started to walk across the playground disdaining to wrap his gown about him in the cold wind. Gerald followed.

As he stood by the door of the study, he saw on the hallstand the same gown and hat which lost for him no more of their *mana* by being divorced from their owner than would a headsman's axe and mask hanging there. When he entered Mr Pemberton looked up and said without the slightest hesitation: 'I was waiting for you to come, Bracher.'

'You were out last night, sir. And I thought it best not to disturb you earlier today.'

The Headmaster leaned slightly back in his chair and clasped his white hands, but said nothing.

'It's about the walk yesterday, sir,' Gerald went desperately on. 'Slade and I were missing.'

242

'Yes, boy. I know.'

'It was the last Sunday of term and rather foolishly we decided to cut the walk. We've no excuse, sir.'

Mr Pemberton said: 'I am disappointed in you, Bracher.'

'I'm very sorry, sir.'

'I wonder if you understand what I mean, boy. I am disappointed in you. I had formed the opinion that you were a good influence in the School. Now I have completely lost that opinion.'

Gerald was dumbfounded. 'It was just because it was the last Sunday.' he mumbled.

'You still don't understand me,' said the Headmaster. 'I thought you were a moral boy. Now I see otherwise— that you are susceptible to weakness and folly. I would like you to tell me why you have formed this association with Slade, a boy very much your junior.'

It was not quite true that they had the same interests. 'We get on very well together, sir,' Gerald said, rather foolishly.

'I'm surprised,' said Mr Pemberton. 'Quite frankly, I do not regard Slade as a very admirable boy.'

'Perhaps if you knew him better, sir . . .'

'Do you imagine that I don't know my boys inside out? Slade is untidy and unco-operative. He has some very strange ideas, which I'm distressed to find you've picked up from him. Mrs Matley spoke to me with great concern after the performance on Saturday. I need not tell you what about.'

The abrupt play of the Headmaster's mind was quite bewildering. 'Mrs Matley, sir?'

'Naturally. Matley had told his mother about your blasphemous behaviour. He is a devout and serious boy.

I understand that you have made a practice of uttering these outrageous views of yours—or of Slade's—often at the very time of Matley's bedside prayers. I cannot forgive that, Bracher. It affects the school's good name. I shall send a report of the whole matter to your father.'

For a moment it seemed to Gerald that his atheism was outrageous and he could, he felt, quite easily have broken down, confessed his sin, pleaded with Mr Pemberton to keep his father ignorant, and promised to reform. But the moment had passed when the Headmaster said: 'What have you got to say, Bracher?'

'They weren't Slade's views, sir, they were mine.'

Mr Pemberton ignored this remark: he seemed sunk in thought. Gerald was suddenly conscious that his every muscle was tense and he cautiously eased his neck so that his eyes were no longer fixed on the Headmaster's face but looked beyond it to the familiar engraving of the Death of Nelson on the study wall. He saw as it were for the first time that the Admiral's legs muscularly filled out a pair of white tights and were posed, as he lay supported by his officers, in the shape of a wishbone, and this image, so incongruous in the presence of death, reminded him, for some reason he had no time to analyse, of the departed Mountain.

The Headmaster's voice broke the silence. 'Where were you with Slade yesterday afternoon?'

'In the Shed,' replied Gerald automatically, only after he had spoken remembering that he had arranged with Slade to say that they had stayed in school.

'Ah,' said Mr Pemberton, 'Did you know that that place was out of bounds?'

'Yes, sir.'

'What were you doing in the Shed?'

'Nothing, sir.'

'Were you behaving improperly?'

Gerald remembered the Woodbines. 'Yes, sir.' And then, as one on his way to the radiologist who breaks the seal of the note sent by his physician and reading 'suspected carcinoma' takes some moments to apply the words to himself, Gerald leaned forward and said vehemently: 'No, no. Not improperly.'

'You know what I mean, I see.'

'We were smoking.' But the word had ceased to have its normal connotation.

'You were smoking,' repeated the Headmaster, the tones of his voice too complicated for them to be characterized as either ironic or sceptical. 'The infantile Slade was smoking, too, was he?'

Gerald did not reply. 'Don't be surly and stupid, boy,' cried Mr Pemberton, rising so abruptly that Gerald thought he was going to be struck. But the Headmaster remained by the desk, gazing oppressively down on him. 'I shall report this "smoking" to your father, too.'

Gerald looked up, seeing the hair growing out of the Headmaster's nostrils. 'We were not behaving improperly,' he said, and his anger was such that the words seemed to him not the weak and unconvincing asseveration that they were, but an outrageously bold challenge to the Headmaster's power and ideas.

'I don't want to hear any more about it,' said Mr Pemberton, scornfully. 'I am completely disgusted and disillusioned. You may leave the room.'

Gerald rose and, since Mr Pemberton was standing so near, his eyes swept up the buttons of the waistcoat, past the watch-chain and the peeping spectacle-case, beyond the strange piece of cloth that filled the space between the v of the waistcoat and the clerical collar, to the big feline face and the bald skull. And then he found himself looking down into the blue eyes, the diluted blue from a rinsed fountain pen, and with the revelatory sense of shock that might accompany one's first sight of a piece of sculpture one has previously only seen in photographic reproduction, lacking any comparative scale, he realized that the Headmaster was a small man.

Gerald walked out of the House into the playground, dark under a glittering sky. As he went into the urinals the tang of disinfectant and the cold air brought back to him the days when he had first arrived at school—a time historically remote, as though the earth had been moving this year on some grossly extended orbit. His emotions, his eyes and lips, tender with the outrageous injustice dealt out to him, he said aloud: 'I won't give Slade up. I won't give him up.' And brooding on the imminent holiday which he would have to bear under the constant agonizing expectation of his father getting Mr Pemberton's report, his mother's image came into his mind and, as though he had never held any contrary opinion, he thought immediately that she too had stuck out for love as he must, and his whole body yearned to embrace her across the hemisphere of their separation, to tell her of his sympathy and understanding.

When he came into the playground again he saw Mr Percy walking away from the entrance to the school block. Longing to talk, to make contact, to re-establish his normal personality, Gerald intercepted the master, and said: 'I've done a very silly thing, sir—packed that book you lent me in my trunk with my other books. And now all the trunks have gone off luggage in advance. Will it be all right if I return the book next term?'

'What book was it, Bracher?'

'Keats's *Letters*.'

'Keep it,' said Mr Percy. 'I shan't be coming back next term.'

Like the superficially inappropriate but deeply significant reply of a neurotic to a word in a psycho-analyst's association test, Mr Percy's disclosure called up for Gerald the vision, as he had seen it in school earlier in the day, of Cole's forehead, from which the dressing had been removed for the first time to the public view—a forehead which superimposed the frowning expression of some great thinker on Cole's face, whatever emotion he might really be experiencing.

'Not at all? Not ever?'

'No,' said Mr Percy, moving off.

Stupefiedly, inadequately, Gerald called after him: 'Thank you very much for the book.' The stout figure did not turn.

Too agitated to face even Slade's questioning, Gerald moved back towards the House and crossed over to the edge of the playing fields—the same fields that Mr Squires, during the visit to the baths last week, had asserted would be split up into building plots when Alderman Cole exercised his rights as mortgagee. The noise of the sea came like a symptom of a cerebral disease.

Gerald turned and looked at the isolated mass of the school buildings, the turreted, many-chimneyed mansion and the more regular shapes of the school block, their darkness against the just less-dark sky printed with rectangles of yellow that would, had he not instantly visualized the persons and activities they illuminated, have conveyed a sense of comfort and happiness. He remembered in his first term that one day in class the Headmaster had called for the definition of a symbol, which proved to be 'the representation of a moral thing'. It seemed to Gerald that the school was a symbol, but he could not imagine clearly the moral thing of which it was a representation.

When his trembling died away and the ordinary matters of life—the bitter wind, the imminence of tea—impinged on his consciousness, he began to walk towards the school. As in those drawings by Stubbs a horse is depicted in the verisimilitudinous action of trotting but the representation is actually of a horse's skeleton, so it seemed to Gerald that the school and the Headmaster, though going through the plausible motions of ordinary existence, were in fact demonstrating a truth about the nature of being which they possessed without knowing and which it had taken their death to reveal.